LAST GIRL MISSING

LAST GIRL MISSING

A
DETECTIVE
CALLIE FORDE
MYSTERY

K.L. MURPHY

LEVEL
BEST BOOKS

For those who are missing—never to be forgotten

Praise for Last Girl Missing

"K.L. Murphy kicks her thriller game into high gear with this new novel: *Last Girl Missing* has everything readers want from a good thriller—a perplexing mystery, a ticking clock, plenty of secrets, and characters who pop off the page. You won't be able to put it down."—LynDee Walker, Amazon Charts bestselling author of *Fear No Truth*

"Clear your calendar, because once you start *Last Girl Missing*, you won't want to put it down. With deft plotting and high emotional stakes, Murphy's latest outing brims with immersive detail and edge-of-your-seat suspense. This is a writer who has mastered the art of making suburbia sinister."—Mindy Quigley, award-winning author of the Deep Dish Mysteries

"K.L. Murphy is a master of suspense..."—Heather Weidner, author of the Delanie Fitzgerald Mysteries and Jules Keene Glamping Mysteries

Chapter One

Erin Hamill tightened the belt of her robe with one hand and juggled her coffee cup with the other. She padded up the stairs, slowing outside the door to her daughter's room. Swallowing a slug of coffee, she banged on the door with her fist.

"Get up, Nat." Hearing nothing, she banged again and raised her voice. "Now." With a sigh, she crossed the hall to her son's room.

"Jeremy. Leaving for church in half an hour." This time, she was rewarded with a groan.

In her own room, she sat down at the thrift store table she'd set up in the corner. Makeup, brushes, and a large magnifying mirror crowded the surface. Her ex-husband wouldn't have liked the addition or the clutter, but his opinion didn't matter anymore. She gave her cheeks a final swipe of blush and slipped into a grey shift dress and black flats. A glance at her watch told her she was close to being late. She hurried out of her room and down the stairs. Jeremy stood hunched over the sink, spooning cereal into his mouth from a bowl.

"Why don't you ever sit down to eat?" she asked her son. "We do still have a table."

He slurped another bite, and milk dripped from the spoon. "Would you rather I spill on my khakis?"

She pressed her lips together. What she wanted was for them to sit down to breakfast together like a normal family, but normal had stopped being possible a long time ago. And he was right about the pants. They were so threadbare that another washing might put a hole in them, and she couldn't afford a new pair until her next paycheck.

"Where's your sister?"

His narrow shoulders rose and fell. "How should I know?"

"Not again," she muttered under her breath. Things were hard enough without Natalie thumbing her nose at everything Erin wanted her to do. Going to church was something she wanted for all of them. It wasn't that she was the religious sort, but since the divorce, she'd known she needed something that counted as support, and therapy was expensive. A couple of hours each Sunday wasn't. So, she dragged her children with her. She enrolled them in the youth group and joined a bible study. Jeremy seemed to understand her need to cling to something solid, but Natalie had fought her from the beginning. Erin could still remember her daughter's attitude, the way it had radiated off of her, teenaged scorn oozing from every pore.

"It's boring," Natalie had said, her glossy lips pushed out in a pout. "And you know I teach swimming on Saturday mornings. Sundays are my only day to sleep."

"Three months, Nat. Let's try it for three months. And then, if you don't like it, you don't have to go."

"I don't have to go now."

"You do if you want to use my car."

"That's not fair."

Shaking off the memory, Erin grabbed her phone and her purse. "Nat," she called up the stairs, "you'd better be dressed and in the car in two minutes." Jeremy followed her out the front door as she searched her purse for her set of keys. Finding them, she looked up and stopped short. The car wasn't in the driveway or on the street. Her son came to stand next to her.

"Where's the car?"

She whirled around. "That's what we're about to find out." Erin marched up the stairs, hot anger bubbling with each step. She didn't bother knocking this time.

"Natalie, where the hell—" Her words fell away as she took in the empty room. A pink comforter, the fuzz worn down to knubs, hung halfway off the bed. A pile of shoes and dirty clothes spilled out of the closet. "Oh, for

2

Chrissakes." Erin swung around toward the bathroom. "Natalie, we're going to be late."

The bathroom, though, was empty, too. "Christ," Erin muttered. She called down to Jeremy. "Is Natalie down there?"

"Haven't seen her, Mom."

Erin's hands landed on her waist, and she tipped her head back, trying to calm her breathing. She went back to Natalie's room and her unmade bed. Blinking in the shadowy morning light, she reached out and laid her hand on the sheets. Cool. She checked the pillow. The same. "Goddammit."

Downstairs again, she pulled out her phone to check her messages. Nothing about spending the night out.

"What's the deal, Mom?" Jeremy watched from the doorway.

Erin waved her hand to shush him, finding Natalie's name, and placing the call. When it went straight to voicemail, she wanted to curse again but Jeremy was there. She faced her son now. "You call her," she said. "Maybe she'll pick up for you."

"No answer," he said a moment later.

Erin threw her purse back on the counter. "I can't believe she'd pull this. Not right now." She sat down and scrolled through her phone until she found the names she was looking for. She made call after call, her pulse racing faster with each conversation.

She got Sarah first. "No, Ms. Hamill. I haven't talked to Nat since yesterday. She was babysitting last night, wasn't she?"

And Beth Anne. "I texted her a couple of times when I got off work, but she didn't answer."

Then Lara. "I haven't talked to her."

Three more friends and every answer the same. No one had spoken to her since she'd gone to her babysitting job. No one had heard from her but Erin. She went back to her own texts. Natalie had texted at eight forty-five.

Finally got the kids to bed. The parents said they might be out late. Don't wait up. See you in the morning.

She read the text a second time. A third. Her hands shook and the phone slipped through her fingers, landing on the table with a thud.

3

"What's wrong, Mom?" Jeremy hovered over her.

Her breath came faster, and she leaned over. "Get me the bag."

Jeremy handed her the crumpled bag she'd taken to leaving on the counter. She took it from him, placing it over her face. Breathe in. Breathe out. Minutes passed. She kept breathing, the weight on her chest lighter with each inhale and exhale. Calmer, she sat up straighter and picked up her phone again. Nat had texted when she'd arrived at her job. It had been sent at a minute after seven. One word.

Here

The one before that had been sent when she was at the mall.

Leaving

All short. No punctuation. Not like the last one. Using manners and good grammar and being more solicitous usually meant Natalie wanted something, but no request followed. She stared hard at the words and took another long breath. She told herself she was overreacting. She had to be. But no amount of reason could explain where Natalie was right now. She racked her brain. She'd called every friend she could think of, hadn't she? She brought up her contacts again, going slower.

"What about Tina?" she asked.

"Mom, they haven't been friends since they were ten. Tina's a weirdo."

"Carolyn Hunter?"

"Didn't she move to Texas?"

Erin fell back against the chair. Natalie wasn't in her room. Not with a friend. That left only two options. Neither was good.

"Can you call your dad?"

Jeremy's face brightened. "You think she's there?"

Erin didn't know, but things had been difficult between mother and daughter lately, and Natalie had threatened more than once to go live with her dad.

"He doesn't treat me like I'm five," Natalie had argued. "Nag me about homework or cleaning my room." She'd lifted her eyebrows. "Or make me go to church."

It had taken every ounce of Erin's self-control not to speak her mind about that one. "He lives in a one-bedroom, Nat."

"I'll sleep on the couch. And he'll get a two-bedroom if I ask him."

The confidence in Natalie's voice had nearly broken Erin's heart. Dan wasn't the man—or the father—he once was. If his girlfriend didn't want Natalie living there, she'd be back on Erin's doorstep within a day, maybe two. She could hear her friend Ellen in her mind.

"Let her go. Let her find out what an ass her father is now. At the beck and call of someone barely out of school herself."

This wasn't entirely true. Dana, a former student of Dan's at the college, had her master's degree now. So, not a child, exactly. Dan and Dana. The cuteness wasn't lost on Erin. Presumably, the affair hadn't begun until a year ago, but Erin wasn't sure she believed that. Late nights, distracted conversations, secret calls. All the telltale signs had been there for a long time. The only real truth was that Dan had a new life, one that Dana ran with an iron fist. It would be easy to encourage Natalie, to let her discover the truth about her dad, but Erin couldn't do it. It wasn't as selfless as it sounded. The truth was, she wasn't sure she could handle the fallout with Natalie. Or Dan.

Jeremy stood waiting, his phone in his hand. "Should I call him?"

"Yes," she said, even as she rose from the chair, her own phone in her hand. She left him in the kitchen. Her own calls were not for his ears. Ten minutes later, she was no closer to finding Natalie. There had been no young girls admitted to Hampstead General overnight. No reported accidents. Her head hung low, her mind pinging back and forth between relief and a growing sense of dread.

"Mom? Did you find her?"

Erin lifted her head slowly, tears stinging. "No. Is she with your dad?"

Jeremy paled, his adolescent skin suddenly sapped of color. "No. He wants to know what's going on."

Her jaw tightened. "If he were here, he'd know, wouldn't he?"

Jeremy flinched, and she wanted to take back the words as soon as she'd said them. Erin wasn't angry at her son. She wasn't even angry at Dan. She was scared. "I'm sorry. I didn't mean that."

He nodded once, his chin quivering the way it had when he was five, when he'd fallen and skinned his knee, doing his best to hold back the tears.

"It's okay," he said, even as his voice, already going through the change, cracked. "Where's Nat?"

She didn't answer right away. She could lie, but he would know. And there'd already been enough lying to last them a lifetime.

"I'm not sure," she said. "All I know right now is she isn't here." She forced a lightness into her voice she didn't feel. "Guess we won't make it to church after all."

Jeremy stared at her. If she thought she might be rewarded with a smile, she was mistaken. His shoulders sank, and he seemed older somehow. Sadness washed over her, and then he said the words she hadn't wanted to speak out loud, the ones that pierced her heart.

"Natalie's gone, isn't she?"

Chapter Two

Detective Callie Forde watched as the woman's son leaned in close to his mother. The ex-husband, Dan Hamill, stood in the corner, his arms folded over his chest.

"Okay," Callie said, "let's start again." She flipped to a clean page in her notebook. "What time was your daughter babysitting last night."

"Seven."

"And where was that?"

"I'm not sure exactly. Over on Montrose, maybe. It was a new family. The Randolphs." The woman's words came out in fits and starts. "She'd been referred to them by another family she babysits for sometimes."

"And who was that?"

Her body rocked as she thought. "The Holts, maybe." The rocking slowed. "Yes, the Holts." With fumbling fingers, she pulled up their number.

Callie glanced at her partner, Detective Todd Zeleniak, who nodded. "We can get the address from them." She focused on the mother again. "What time did she leave the house?"

"Six forty-five."

"And she texted you when she arrived?"

"Yes. And again later."

"Fine. We'll need to take a look at your phone." The woman nodded. "Can you make a list of all her friends for us?"

"I called them already."

"Yes, ma'am. But we may need to speak to them on our own." Callie kept her tone neutral. She didn't want to upset the woman any further, but she knew friends weren't always forthcoming when questioned by parents. Not that they were inclined to spill all to the police, but that kind of questioning brought a different level of urgency.

Zel sat forward, his bony elbows on his knees. "Is there a boyfriend?"

"No."

Her response was quick. Too quick for Callie's taste.

Zel seemed to agree. "Don't mean to be rude, ma'am, but are you sure?"

The mother got to her feet. "No, Detective, I'm not sure." The gray dress she wore was creased and fraying at the hem. Wisps of sandy brown hair curled at her temples, escaping from the ponytail held in place by a large silver barrette. She twisted her hands around a wadded-up tissue. "I don't know where my daughter is, so I'm not sure about anything, am I?"

The man in the corner stepped forward, the first move he'd made since they'd arrived. "Erin, calm down. This isn't helping."

Erin's head whipped around. "Why do you care? You don't live here anymore. What would you know anyway?"

"I know Natalie likes a boy in her chemistry class."

The woman gasped, falling back into her chair. Erin's face broke then, crumbling as her ex-husband's accusation hit the mark. Her body sank lower, and she buried her face in her hands.

The boy put his hand on his mother's back. "It's not true, Mom. She doesn't like Garrett anymore."

Callie wrote the name down and made a mental note to pursue that line of questioning later. If the girl didn't turn up first.

"I'm sorry, Ms. Hamill, but there's something I need to ask about your daughter." A slight motion of Erin's head told Callie to go on. "Does Natalie have a history of disappearing? Or running away?"

Erin's chin dropped to her chest, and she took several long breaths. "She did run away. One time."

"When was that?"

"Last year. After her father and I separated." She swiped at a stray hair, pushing it off her forehead. "She was angry at both of us. I think she wanted to punish us somehow."

"What happened?"

Erin shrugged. "She took an old tent and sleeping bag from the garage and went over to the campgrounds off Route 74. Do you know that one?"

"That's about thirty miles outside of town, isn't it?"

"Yeah, that's the one. She called an Uber to drop her off. On my credit card. Can you believe that?" She shook her head at her daughter's nerve. "Anyway, when she wasn't here for dinner, I tracked her with that app, the location one, and I knew exactly where she was. I called Dan, and he went and got her. I figured if she was mad about the separation, she could take it up with him."

Callie's gaze went to Dan. His face hardened, but he said nothing.

"And since then?"

"You mean, has she run away again? No."

"Were you able to track her phone this morning?"

"I tried. It's not working."

This didn't surprise Callie. If Natalie didn't want to be found, she'd know to turn off any tracking capability this time. She decided to take a different tack.

"Why don't you take me through what you know about your daughter's habits," she said now. "Who her friends are. How she spends her time. What she did yesterday before she left to babysit."

"Sure. Okay."

Erin shredded the tissue as she told them what she knew, her voice sometimes sure, other times more reticent. Callie, taking notes, couldn't help but notice the way she occasionally turned to her son for answers or the way she ignored her ex-husband during the exchange.

Confirming what she'd heard, Callie asked, "So, after she taught swimming lessons, she went to the mall and hung out with her friend Sarah, then came home?"

"Yes."

"And what time was that?"

"Maybe close to five. I asked her what she wanted for dinner, but she said she wasn't hungry."

Callie smiled. "That's unusual for a teenager, isn't it?"

"Boys, yes, but girls can be finicky. Worried about their weight, you know. I tried to tell her she was beautiful, but she told me I wasn't the best judge."

Mothers and daughters, Callie thought. Best friends and enemies. She guessed Natalie and her mother were no different.

"Anyway," Erin said, "she went up to her room until it was time for her to leave to babysit."

Zel leaned in. "Does she do that a lot? Spend time alone in her room?"

Pink blotches appeared on Erin's cheeks. "Not too much."

Callie didn't say anything, but she hadn't missed the way the boy ducked his head at his mother's answer. Neither had Zel.

"Does your daughter have a computer in her room?" he asked.

Before Erin could answer, the father spoke up. "She has a laptop. I gave it to her a few months ago. To help with school."

Zel nodded. "Cellphone and laptop. Tablet?"

"No."

"Do you monitor her social media accounts?"

Erin's face went pink again. "Y-yes. Some. I mean, I'm on some of the same accounts, so I can see her posts. There was nothing inappropriate, if that's what you mean."

Callie caught the look Zel sent her and gave a small shake of her head. No real monitoring. It wasn't the first time they'd encountered parents who didn't understand what their kids were doing, weren't aware of the fake accounts or who their online "friends" were. Still, now was not the time to give them an education. If Natalie didn't turn up soon, they'd learn fast enough.

"What was she wearing when she left?"

"Um, a long-sleeve blue t-shirt and shorts."

"Okay. We're going to need a recent picture of your daughter and a description of your car."

"Right." She got up, went into the hall, and came back with a framed picture. She handed it to Callie. It was one of those posed school portraits, the kind with the artificially blue background. Natalie was a pretty girl with a nose that turned up slightly at the tip and swinging, white-blond hair. In the picture, she wore a slouchy sweater that highlighted her swimmer's shoulders.

"This is recent?"

"From the winter. She didn't want me to buy it, but I've bought them every year."

Callie stood up, and Zel followed. "Thank you, Ms. Hamill." She nodded briefly at Dan. "Mr. Hamill. We'll take these and get started."

Erin's hand shot out, grabbing Callie by the arm. "Shouldn't I be doing something? Be out searching for her?"

Callie tried to pull her arm away, but the woman's fingers held on.

"The most important thing you can do," she told Erin, "is be here for your daughter when she comes home."

"You think she will? Come home, I mean?"

Callie's breath caught in her throat. She had no way of knowing whether or not anything bad had happened, if the girl had decided to run away again, or if she was simply holed up with a friend. What she did know was that there hadn't been a missing child in Hampstead in five years. Sure, kids got lost in the woods or snuck off or ran away for some reason they couldn't quite explain later, but they came back. Not like the one all those years ago. She shook away the memory. This wasn't then, and Natalie wasn't Emma.

"Don't worry." She pried Erin's fingers from her arm. "We'll bring her home, Ms. Hamill. I promise."

Chapter Three

C allie slid behind the wheel. "Don't say it."

Zel threw up his hands. "I didn't say anything."

"You were thinking it."

"Damn right, I was thinking it," he said, his voice rising an octave. "Why in the hell would you promise that lady you'd bring her daughter home? Christ, Cal, you know better than that."

Zel was right. She did know better. Making promises was a bad idea. No matter the reason. She tried to brush away her own misgivings.

"Chances are, she'll be home in a few hours anyway. She probably went out to a party after babysitting, got drunk, and passed out with a friend. Remember that happened last year with the Gordon girl."

"Yeah, I remember," Zel said as he took the photo from her. "Pretty girl. You're probably right. The frat boys would love a girl like her to come around."

The thought had already crossed Callie's mind. Natalie wouldn't be the first high school girl to draw the attention of older boys. "Exactly. Now she's trying to figure out a story to tell her mother before she goes home."

"Or she ran away, but yeah, that sounds about right." He set the picture aside. "Any problems at the campus you heard about? Citations? Drunk in public?"

"No. Nothing."

"How do you want to play this?"

Callie stared down at the picture and sighed. "She'll probably be home by lunch, but I'll call it in anyway, just in case."

He gave her a sideways glance and shrugged. Getting the dispatcher, she gave him the information on the car and a description of Natalie.

"Okay, Cal," Zel said. "Now, we've got a missing person. Where do you want to start?"

"The Randolphs, that family she babysat for. Let's find out what time she left their house."

"I'm on it." Zel made a call. "Can I get an address for a family called the Holts? I've got a phone number."

Callie followed his directions to an adjacent neighborhood, pulling up to a gray split level with a neat yard, a smattering of flowers in the front beds, and a pair of bikes abandoned in the driveway. The Holts invited the pair in, leading them to the backyard where the kids were playing on a wooden swing set. More flowers peeked out of clay pots.

"Natalie is one of the kids' favorite babysitters," Anna Holt said when they sat down. "She taught them both how to swim and she works up at the pool in the summers." She tipped her head as though something had just occurred to her. "I think she lets them stay up later than our other sitter, but I figure it doesn't really hurt them, you know." Her earlier smile faded then. "But you don't care about that. Why do you need to know about Natalie? Is she in some kind of trouble?"

"The reason we're here," Callie said, "is to ask if you could give us the address for the Randolphs. I believe she babysat for them last night."

The couple exchanged a glance. "The Randolphs?"

"Yes," Zel said. "Her mother said you gave them a referral, recommended Natalie?"

Tiny frown lines appeared between Anna's brows. "I'm always happy to refer Natalie, but I don't know anyone by that name."

Callie shifted, the warm sun baking her skin. "Have you recommended Natalie to anyone new recently? Anyone at all?"

Both Holts shook their heads. "No. Most everyone already knows Natalie from the pool," Anne told them.

Ned spoke up. "I'm on the board, and no one with the name Randolph has joined recently. I'm pretty sure about that."

"How many neighborhoods use the community pool?" Zel asked.

"Three. Hartwood, Hartfield, and Hartland."

"I'm sensing a theme."

"Yeah," Ned said with a laugh. "But Hartwood is the big one the pool is named after. Hartwood Community, it's called."

Zel nodded. "Is it required to join the pool if you live in one of the neighborhoods?"

"Not at all. A lot of families wait to join until Memorial Day weekend." He lifted his palms. "That's when the pool officially opens. But swim team practice and lessons started two weeks ago."

"Why do you want to talk to this family?" Anne asked.

"We just want to ask them a few questions," Callie said. "Is there anyone else Natalie babysits for on a regular basis?"

Anne's head cocked to one side. "The Thompkins. I mean, I know she's always looking for more jobs, but our two families are her regulars. She's usually sitting for one or the other of us each week."

Callie kept her voice as light as possible. "But not this weekend?"

"Well, no. Actually, we went over to the Thompkins last night for a cookout. There were two other families there, and all the kids played together. We didn't need a sitter."

"Okay. Well, if you hear anything about this new family, would you let us know?" Callie slid her card across the patio table. The Holts agreed, and they all stood in unison. At the door, Callie paused. "By the way, when was the last time you heard from Natalie?"

Anne frowned, fresh worry creeping across her face. "Is something wrong?"

"We don't know that anything is wrong, Mrs. Holt. We have a few questions. That's all."

The woman gave a short nod, but Callie could see she wasn't convinced. "The last time I talked to Natalie was a week ago Saturday. Ned and I went out to dinner and a movie. It was quite the splurge night. You know how expensive movies are these days, and with a sitter…" her voice faded. Callie waited. "Anyway, we got home around midnight. She told us they played a board game and then a video game before the kids went to bed." Anne licked her lips. "I think I asked her if she'd started thinking about colleges, but I could see she didn't want to talk about it."

"Was that odd?"

"Not really. I think college feels unattainable ever since her parents got divorced. I've had the impression money has gotten tight. Well, tighter. Two households will do that, I guess. And Dan took a sabbatical after the separation, so no tuition break if she stayed local. Anyway, I didn't want to press her on it, but Natalie's a smart girl. Honor Roll."

Zel piped up. "Natalie told you about her grades?"

"She didn't have to. I'm a counselor up at the high school. That's why I want to make sure she applies. Maybe get a scholarship. And there's always community college. It's a great way to start with less cost, you know."

Callie did know. She'd started that way herself before transferring to Tech. "Well, thank you both. You know how to reach us."

Back in the car, she rested her hands on the steering wheel and stared out the window, unseeing. Anne Holt cared about Natalie. Her mother cared about her. And her brother. Presumably, her father, too, although the jury was still out on him as far as Callie was concerned. Families trusted her. She had a strong student record. Still, she hadn't come home after a babysitting job. There were no accident reports or other incidents. She could be at a friend's house. She could be with a boy. She could have run away again. There were any number of explanations, but Callie had a bad feeling in the pit of her stomach.

Zel interrupted her thoughts. "Hey, we going anytime soon?"

She shifted toward him. "How many hours since Natalie sent her mother that last text?"

"I don't know. Fourteen? Fifteen?"

She sat back against the seat. Natalie should be home soon—if she was coming home. But what if she wasn't? What if she didn't decide to stay out all night because she was drunk or run away to teach her mother some kind of lesson? What if she'd been taken or gotten lost and was hurt somewhere? What if she was, in fact, missing? A hard knot lodged in her throat. If Natalie was missing, then time would be their enemy. It already was.

"We need to follow up with every one of her friends right now," Callie said. "Figure out if this is some kind of stunt like last time or..."

She felt Zel's eyes on her then, and she didn't finish. She didn't have to.

Chapter Four

Beth Anne Peters and her parents sat on a sofa opposite the detectives, their shoulders touching as though conjoined into one linked being.

"Where do you think she went?" Beth Anne asked. "Have you talked to Sarah? They went to the mall yesterday."

"We did." Callie balanced her notebook on her knee. "Did Natalie say anything unusual yesterday or this week?"

The teenager shook her head, her light blue hair swinging softly across her cheeks. Callie did her best to hold the girl's gaze, but it wasn't easy. Beth Anne's eyes, the same shade of blue as her hair, were dusted in bright pink shadow. More pink dusted her cheekbones and glistened on her lips. She reminded Callie of cotton candy spun from sugar. The detective pushed the image from her mind.

"Was Natalie seeing anyone? Did she have a boyfriend?"

"No."

"Was there a boy she liked?"

The girl giggled a little. "Natalie liked everyone."

Callie lifted one eyebrow.

"I don't mean it like that," Beth Anne said, her laughter gone. "I meant she was always changing her mind. Every month, she had a crush on a different guy, but nothing ever happened. She was never really serious."

"What about…" Callie paused to check her notes. "Garrett from chemistry?"

"See, that's what I mean. She liked him for, like, two weeks, but then he wore a t-shirt from some band she hates. They got in an argument, and she didn't like him anymore. Said he was an idiot. She's kinda dramatic like that."

"Uh-huh. Is there an ex-boyfriend?"

"Well, there's Mick from freshman year, but they only dated for like two months. She got tired of him so…"

"Does Mick have a last name?"

"Carlton. But he has a new girlfriend. They've been together for more than a year."

"Okay. Anyone else?"

"Not really. She went to Homecoming with Jimmy Bartlett, but they're just friends. None of the guys in our school are that cute, really. They're all so immature."

Zel cleared his throat. Callie took the hint.

"What about at the college?" she asked. "Surely, you've seen cute boys there."

"Well, sure, but," Beth Anne hesitated, aware that both her mother and father were listening to every word. Her cheeks grew pinker, although Callie wasn't entirely sure how that was possible under the layer of blush the girl was wearing. "But we don't know most of them 'cause we're still in high school."

Callie ignored the parents to focus solely on the girl. "Beth Anne, I wouldn't want to get Natalie in any trouble, but her mother is worried about her. I'm sure she's fine, but the sooner we locate her, the better her mother will feel." The girl's blue eyes widened. "So, I was wondering, is it possible that Natalie met a boy from the college? Maybe she went over there after she babysat last night, lost track of time, and fell asleep."

Beth Anne rocked forward a little, breaking the chain with her parents. "We-ell. She might have met someone, but I'm not sure."

Callie sat forward. "You're not sure?"

"She started snapchatting with a group of kids that were older."

"Did she ever meet any of them in person?"

"Not that I know of."

"Okay. Anyone else she was chatting with? On another site, maybe?"

The girl stared at the floor. "I don't know."

"If you did know," Callie said, "it could be important." The girl didn't move. "You wouldn't be in any trouble, I promise."

Beth Anne's parents moved in on each side of her. "Honey, is there something that would help the police? Was Natalie doing something her parents wouldn't approve of?" The mother grabbed at Beth Anne's hands. "Was it a boy? Or drugs?"

The girl's head jerked up. "No, Mom. Nothing like what you're thinking. There's nothing." She glared at Callie then. "There's nothing."

The faces of Beth Anne's parents cleared, and Zel let out an audible sigh. The girl's eyes shifted, and Callie swallowed her own disappointment. Beth Anne had lied. Was that to protect Natalie or herself? Either way, if Natalie didn't turn up soon, she'd have to talk to Beth Anne again. Possibly without her parents.

Neither Callie nor Zel spoke as they walked into the police station that sat on the corner of Hampstead Drive and Main. More than a hundred years old, the small three-story brick structure was fronted by large white columns. Callie often thought the building was far grander on the outside than on the inside. The detectives climbed to the third floor.

At the coffee machine, Callie filled her cup and added a heavy dose of powdered creamer. She didn't like the powdered stuff, but it didn't do any good to bring in real cream. She'd tried it, and every time, the cream would be gone before she could pour a second cup, lapped up the way she imagined people who went to black tie parties lapped up caviar and champagne—not that she had much experience in that department. Still, the sludge they called coffee in the Hampstead Police Station wasn't drinkable without some major doctoring, so powdered creamer it was.

With her cup in hand, she made her way back to her desk, slowing at the oversized bulletin board. Her gaze wandered over the sketches and photos of wanted criminals that were tacked side by side next to missing persons posters.

"Again, Forde?" Henderson hovered behind her.

Callie liked Hendo. He'd been around the department for more than two decades and had a halo of thinning salt and pepper hair to prove it. The little hair he did have left on top, he combed over, fooling no one.

"It's not like it changes every day," he said, gesturing with his own coffee mug. "What is it you're always looking at anyway?"

It was a good question, and one she wasn't sure she could answer. The faces that stared back at her were strangers. Or at least no one she'd ever met. And yet, she felt like she knew them. "I don't know, really. I think I just don't want them to be forgotten or something."

Hendo laughed and pointed at the image of a man with a heavy mustache and beard. "Yeah? You don't want him to be forgotten?"

She studied the face of Frankie Wilson. Large block letters were printed over his head. WANTED. At the bottom of the flyer was a description and more detail. She knew the facts by heart. Wilson had been suspected of armed robbery and murder in a convenience store over in Richmond and another one in Roanoke—five people killed in all, two more injured. All for less than a couple grand. But as luck would have it, a North Carolina man called to complain about suspicious activity at a trailer park, a shampoo theft at the adjacent campground showers. Good thing it was a slow day in North Carolina. After six months on the run, Wilson was picked up with less than two hundred dollars in his pocket and lavender-smelling hair.

"Probably be a better world without that one, if you ask me." Hendo reached up and ripped the poster down. Balling it up, he tossed the sheet basketball-style in the trash.

Before she could respond, another voice rang out.

"Henderson, Zeleniak, Forde, and Chang. Conference room. Five minutes."

A chorus of groans echoed, followed by the sound of shuffling feet and squeaking chairs. Callie, still clutching her coffee cup, grabbed her notebook and pen and joined the other detectives. When everyone was seated, the captain entered, taking the chair at the end of the table.

"Okay," he said. "You've all heard about the missing girl." He held up a stack of printouts with Natalie's picture and physical description. "These will be distributed within the hour. Forde, can you give us an update?"

Callie walked to the front of the room. "Natalie's mother last heard from her daughter at eight forty-five last night. We don't know officially how long she's been missing as we haven't been able to locate the address of the family she babysat yet." Callie gave a brief rundown on their conversations with Natalie's family and her friends.

Hendo lifted his hand. "How likely is it that she's run away? You said she's done it before."

The other detectives grunted, shifting in their chairs. While Hampstead wasn't a hotbed of crime, no one wanted to spend a lot of man hours on a runaway. Five or six kids a year left town on their own. Sometimes, it was family issues. Other times, the reasons were drug-related. Even their small college town had been hit by the opioid wave. Two kids and a handful of adults had overdosed in the last ten years alone. The possibilities weighed on everyone. But the kids who'd left Hampstead to follow their dreams or get the hell away from small-town life and overbearing parents were accounted for.

"It's possible," Callie said. "The divorce seems sticky. No love lost between the parents. Could be Natalie wanted out. But no obvious signs of drug use or anything else. And most of her friends said she seemed okay." She paused. "Except one who mentioned some friction between the mother and daughter. We're going to follow up with that."

Chang then. "Do we have phone records yet? Any suspicious texts?"

"We're trying to get them from the phone company, but it's Sunday, so probably not until tomorrow morning. The phone is in the father's name, so we have access to some of the information. He'll sign anything if we need it."

"Good." The Captain spoke up. "Forde and Zeleniak, I want you to take another run at the parents."

Callie understood this plan. Situations like a missing child sometimes turned out to be one of the parents. In this case, she didn't think the mother was that good an actress, and as for the father, something told her he wasn't looking to have his oldest child around more than he already did. Still, standard procedure dictated that the parents get a second, and possibly third, look.

"By tomorrow," Jackson was saying, "we should have the paperwork for bank accounts and any other records to give us a better handle on what's been going on in the household. The rest of you, focus on getting the girl's picture out and locating the car. Any questions?" With none, a chorus of chairs scraped the floor.

"Forde. Zeleniak. A word in my office."

The pair followed Jackson down the hall. Seated, Callie held her notebook in her hand, her foot tapping. She knew the captain wanted a more detailed update, but every minute that passed could be crucial.

"Where are we on the girl's social media?"

"She had a couple of public accounts. Nothing stands out there," Zel said. "The usual selfies. Pictures with friends or school stuff. But without passwords, I can't get in. Callie got the names of a couple of accounts her parents didn't know about from one of her friends. She had a Finsta and—"

"A what?"

"Finsta. Fake Instagram. That's where they post the real stuff. Same kind of thing on Snapchat. Give your parents the name of one account. Share a few happy posts in case they check and put everything else where they won't. Kids can run circles around their parents with this stuff."

"But the mother found her once. Didn't she use an app?" Jackson asked.

Zel snorted. "Sure. But I'd lay money on it that Natalie turned that off pretty quick. I'm not saying parents can't get lucky, but it won't happen twice."

"Fine." Jackson directed his attention to Callie, his expression grim. "What's the likelihood the girl ran away?"

She took a deep breath. "On paper, fifty-fifty. She's done it before. Parents have a nasty divorce. Maybe the daughter doesn't get along with mom. Money might be tight. Possibly an older boy or someone else."

Callie knew Zel watched her, knew which direction he leaned. Not that it made him happy. His own daughter had disappeared two days after her eighteenth birthday, two months shy of her high school graduation. They found her in D.C., waiting tables, living with four other young people in a two-bedroom with a leaky roof and a broken toilet. Said she was sick of being told what to do and how to do it, and she'd be damned if she'd spend the rest of her life in Hampstead the way her mother did. Anyplace was better. Even sleeping on the floor. She'd been gone two years now, still in D.C., and still living a life that counted more as squalor than anything else. Zel kept tabs, but it didn't bring him comfort. "She's eighteen," he'd told his wife. "What do you want me to do?" But Callie knew it ate at him just the same.

"A college boy?" Jackson asked now.

Callie shrugged. "We don't know yet. It will help when we see her texts, who she called."

The captain folded his hands together on his desk. "Give me the other version, the one where she didn't run away."

"Some of the same. Could have met a boy after her babysitting job. Things could have gone south. She got hurt."

"Running away sounds better," Jackson said. "What about the family she babysat for?"

"Still gathering info on them, but based on the text she sent the mother," Zel said, "seemed like any other babysitting job."

"Well, keep me up to date on that. What else?"

Zel again. "Didn't appear anything was missing from her room. All her clothes were there. Her backpack. Toothbrush. If she ran away, either it was sudden, or she would have to buy all new stuff."

"That happens."

"Sure. Her friends all seem surprised that she didn't go home, though." Callie flipped open her notebook. "One friend said, 'Natalie had been super happy lately. She wasn't as upset about her parents anymore. She was doing good in school. This doesn't make sense.'"

"Super happy, huh?"

"That's what she said."

"But that could be because she was running off with someone."

"Who? There's no boyfriend."

"That we know of," Zel said.

Callie started to argue, but the Captain raised his hand. "I want you to keep your head clear on this, Forde. Don't go off half-cocked thinking the worst. History isn't repeating itself here."

Her face flamed, the reprimand stinging. She opened her mouth to tell him she hadn't been thinking about the past at all, but the words stuck in her throat. She had been thinking about that other case, hadn't she? Not that history was repeating itself, but how much she was reminded of Emma and her disappearance. Closing her mouth, she stood, forcing her shoulders back. "I understand, Sir. My job is to find Natalie Hamill. That's all."

"Good," he said with a curt nod. "As long as we understand each other."

Callie got out before he could say anything further, but back at her desk, his words rang in her ears.

Her desk faced Zel's, a matching set with the long edges lined up back to back. Papers and a stapler lay across the middle, making the two metal desks appear as one large tabletop. Zel rolled his chair forward, his long legs jutting underneath. His jaw moved up and down the way it did when he had something he wanted to say.

"Spit it out," she said.

He leaned forward, his lanky body halfway across the desk. "Captain didn't mean anything by it, Cal." She shrugged but said nothing. His jaw kept moving. "How is he anyway?"

Callie looked away. Zel hadn't needed to say her father's name. They both knew who he meant. It was a loaded question, one with no simple answer. She chose to be honest. Sort of. "Good. Thinking about going back to work."

"Really? Has something happened to change his mind?"

She shook her head at that. Her father still couldn't walk, still spent too much time in front of the TV, sitting silent more than she or her mother would like. Mostly, he still blamed himself. Yet, she couldn't help noticing the way he perked up when she talked about a case. He missed the job. She knew it. Five years had passed since the shooting. Five years where her father would only wheel himself from the bedroom to the den, erecting a shell no one had been able to crack. Callie had watched her mother's hair turn grey, the sparkle in her eyes dim, her energy and spirit wane. It was as though her father's injury was contagious, each of them frozen in some way, each of them unable to fully heal. Callie, though, had her work.

"Not really," she said now. "But we're talking about it." Another half-truth. Callie talked. Her father stared at the TV.

"That's good," he said.

The hope she heard in his voice broke her heart. It was a reminder that the shooting had affected them all. Zel had been first on the scene. He'd spent hours in the hospital, come around the house day after day. But her father had shut Zel out, too. They were glad he was alive, but her father didn't see it that way. She'd seen him once, through the open door to his room—weeping, banging on his legs with his fists, over and over, muttering, "Useless. Useless." At the time, she'd escaped to Ben, falling into his arms, her own tears spilling over her cheeks. But even that was gone now. Another casualty.

Sweeping away the maudlin thoughts, she pushed her notebook aside and slapped at her keyboard. Finding the page she wanted, she pored over statistics and data. None of it gave her comfort. "You'd think it would get better," she said.

"What's that?"

"Missing kids." Her finger kept the pages scrolling. Numbers and statistics filled the screen. She read them out loud. "Does it seem like the number of abductions is rising?" Zel didn't comment, his features still. She rattled off a few more numbers. "Social media is making it worse. It's so much easier now. You can be anyone online. I could be a twenty-five-year-old male model or a rich lawyer or a sumo wrestler." She pointed a finger at her partner. "You could be a..." a grin spread across her face. "A Kardashian."

His laughter rang out then, and he made a hair-flipping motion. When he'd stopped laughing, he said, "A Kardashian, huh? I wouldn't mind the money that came with that."

"Who wouldn't? Except you'd have to live on camera."

"Well, I'm out then. I can't think of anything worse. I guess the Kardashians will have to go on without me."

"Poor Kim." Her smile faded as her attention returned to the screen in front of her. "We need to get into Natalie's social media accounts."

"We will."

She closed the page and stood up. "We'd better follow up with the family. And the Randolphs? Do we have an address yet?"

"Waiting to hear back to see if any homes were bought in the area with that name. I've got Miller on it."

Callie knew better than to expect fast results there. "What about the utilities? They'd have to have lights and water."

"I've been promised the information by tomorrow morning."

"Dammit," she said with a groan. "We need to know what time she left that job." She checked her phone, mentally calculating the hours since Erin had last heard from her daughter. Nearly eighteen.

Zel pushed back from his desk. "Ready to go back to the Hamill house?"

"Might as well." She reached for her notebook. "We can talk to the neighbors again while we're there, see if they noticed anything."

"Forde." Callie spun around to see Hendo waving his phone in the air. "We've got the mother's car."

Callie jumped to her feet. "Natalie?"

"'Fraid not."

She exhaled. "Where?"

"Charlottesville. The car is parked on the street, not far from the bus station. The weekend meters are nine to five, and it wasn't paid. Parking Enforcement Officer keyed in the license plate and got a hit."

It wasn't as good as finding the girl, but it was a solid stroke of luck. The APB on the car wasn't even two hours old.

"Who's there now?"

"An officer is on the street; another is headed over. Should be there in about five minutes."

"Good. Have them watch any shops or restaurants and get someone in the bus station." She pulled on her jacket as Zel got to his feet. The Hamills would have to wait.

26

Chapter Five

C allie glanced at the clock on the dash and back at the car parked down the street. The hours had dragged since they'd taken up position at the far end of the block, one that allowed them a view of the Hamill vehicle and the entrance to the bus station. Her eyes burned, and her stomach grumbled, but she ignored both. The streetlights popped on ahead of the sunset.

"What are the chances Natalie came back before we got here, saw the car was being watched, and got nervous?" Callie asked, her fingers drumming against the armrest.

"Possible, I guess, but why? If she overslept somewhere, she's in trouble anyway. More likely, she boarded a bus and is long gone—"

"No one answering her description bought a ticket. They showed her picture around the station. No one saw her."

He nodded. "Okay, let's go with your theory. She came here to meet someone and left her car parked. Maybe she came for a party? She lost track of time. She stayed overnight with a friend. If any of that were true and she came back to her car to go home, she wouldn't be looking for us." There was truth in his words. Callie shifted toward him, never taking her eyes off the beat-up car parked down the street. "What I think is, she came here after her babysitting job, ditched the car, and is in the wind."

"You think she ran away?"

He lifted his shoulders. "Or sending her mom a message."

She understood his reasoning. They'd canvassed the shop owners, the waitresses at the diner. No one had seen Natalie. And Beth Anne had been hiding something. Was it a plan to run away? Her mind went back to Natalie's room at the Hamill house. Normal. No signs of drugs. No recent behavior to indicate running away. But there was the divorce, the spats. Still, Callie wasn't sold. Snatching up her phone, she texted Chang.

Are you still at the mother's house?

After a minute, the response came back.

Yep.

Has she heard anything from her daughter?

Nothing.

"Damn. Nothing new at the house," she said. "How old do you think that car is?"

They both stared at the Honda Pilot with its balding tires and broad dent in the rear bumper.

"Twenty years, give or take a couple."

Callie looked at the clock again. They were closing in on twenty-four hours since anyone had heard from Natalie Hamill. Zel was right. Waiting was getting them nowhere.

"Damn," she said again and threw the car door wide. "Call Angie. Let's see what forensics can find."

Two hours later, the lights set up on the street still blazed. A pair of uniforms stood near the corner. A second pair of officers—forensic specialists—worked the car from end to end, inside and outside. Callie and Zel watched from the perimeter. She held her phone to her ear.

"I ordered some food like you said, Cal, but she hasn't touched it. All I've gotten in her is some green tea."

"How's the son?" Callie asked Hendo. He'd relieved Chang for the evening.

"Anxious. Worried. Bored. About what you'd expect from a kid his age. He ate, but not much. Every time one of their cell phones rings or buzzes, they practically jump out of their skin."

She rubbed her temples. "Okay. I should be there in an hour."

Zel waved at her from near the Honda. "They're about done. They have some preliminary findings for us."

The taller of the two forensics specialists peeled off her gloves as she

28

approached. "Detectives."

"Good to see you, Angie," Callie said and meant it. Officer Angie Brown floated between Albemarle, Green, and Madison counties. She did good work.

Angie shoved the gloves in her pocket. "A couple of things that might interest you."

Callie held her breath, waiting.

"First, whoever drove this car wiped the driver's side clean. Not a print on the wheel or seat."

A chill crawled up Callie's spine. This was not the kind of thing done by a teenaged girl running away.

"What about other prints?" she asked.

"Plenty in the backseat and in the passenger seat. We've taken as many as we can. We'll move to identify as soon as possible."

"What else?"

She pointed at the tires. "Firestones. Not much tread left, but the rear right tire did have enough tread to show traces of red clay. The clay was still moist. Had to have been picked up in the last few days."

Zel frowned. "Doesn't exactly narrow it down."

"No, but after I analyze, there could be sediment or other markers within the clay."

"Okay," Callie said. "Is that all?"

"One more thing. There was an odor in the trunk. Not overpowering but there."

"What kind of odor?"

"In the acetone family would be my guess."

Callie's mouth opened and closed. "Chloroform?"

"Maybe. We'll run a test on the carpet of the trunk, but I'm not holding out a lot of hope there. The smell is already almost gone."

"Any sign of a purse or a phone?" Callie asked.

Angie shook her head and handed Callie a large plastic bag. "Here's everything that was in the car, which wasn't much."

Callie peered inside. A manual and registration were encased in plastic.

Empty food wrappers and a half-drunk bottle of Gatorade were in another. Coins, a pen, and a single sock were in a third.

Angie closed the bag again. "I'll take this back to the lab. See what I can find. My partner took pictures of where each item was found. We'll forward them before the end of the night." She hesitated. "The car's pretty dirty. Lots of crumbs and sticky spots. Probably been a while since it's been cleaned. The hairs we did find could have been there for weeks. Might make it hard to separate what's relevant here."

"Thanks, Angie." Around them, the lights were removed while a tow truck pulled away with the Honda. Other than the bus station and a coffee shop, the other businesses were closed.

Zel climbed back in the car, his hands rubbing his thighs. "Jesus. Chloroform? That's not good."

Callie switched on the ignition. Zel was right. Along with the news that the steering wheel had been wiped clean, it all added up to the one theory no one had wanted to believe. Natalie Hamill didn't run away or get drunk and lose track of time or shack up with a boy. She'd been taken. Kidnapped.

Chapter Six

"Y ou found my car?" Erin pushed past the detectives to the front walk, her hands clasped to her chest. "Where's Natalie?" She whirled back around, searching their faces.

Callie watched as realization sunk in. Erin wrapped her arms around her thin body, swaying on her feet.

"I'm afraid we haven't found her yet," Zel said. "Why don't we go inside and talk?"

Seated again in the small den, Erin chewed on her knuckles. Wearing the same grey dress as that morning, her hands shook the way Callie's did after too many cups of office coffee. Jeremy took one trembling hand in his and held tight.

Callie explained what she could. "Your car was parked near a bus station in Charlottesville."

Erin blinked. "Charlottesville?"

"Yes, ma'am. Does your daughter have any friends in Charlottesville? Any family?"

The woman pressed her free hand to her head. "A cousin on Dan's side, but we haven't seen her in ten years. I don't even know if Marla still lives there."

"That's okay. We'll check it out." Callie took down the cousin's name. "Anyone else? A friend?"

The boy spoke up then. "A girl she used to swim with moved there a couple of years ago. Tracy Temple. I don't know if they were still friends, though."

Erin nodded. "Yes, I remember her. She slept over a couple of times."

"Good," Callie said. "This is helpful." She leaned closer to Erin. "I want you to know we're doing everything we can. We have Natalie's picture posted. We canvassed the area around the car. We've put in a request to see if there's any activity on her phone or her debit card." Erin stared blankly, fighting tears. "We're going to need to keep your car for a couple of days while the lab runs prints and tests."

"Okay," Erin managed to croak.

"Other than you, your daughter, and your son, can you tell me anyone else who might have been in the car in the last week or so?"

Erin's already wavery voice grew shakier. "Why?"

"We need to determine if Natalie was alone. It's possible there was someone else in the car."

Her free hand flew to her mouth. Her son still squeezed the other. "What are you saying?"

Keeping her voice even, Callie said, "I'm not saying anything other than it's possible she wasn't in Charlottesville alone. We'll need to take your prints and your son's and get a list of those names."

Erin's lips trembled, but her son spoke up. "I can get that for you."

Callie's gaze slid to the boy. He had the narrow shoulders and hollow chest of a young man who hadn't yet hit his growth spurt. Dark brown hair hung over his forehead, and freckles dotted his nose and cheeks. If she'd initially thought he looked like every other teenage boy, she thought something different now. There was a watchfulness in his gaze, a protectiveness in the way he hovered around his mother, and she understood. The father was gone. Whatever the reason and whatever problem his sister had with the divorce, he'd taken a different path. He'd stepped into the role of man of the house.

"Thank you, Jeremy. Why don't we go in the kitchen and work on that list?" She shifted in Zel's direction, seizing the opportunity that had presented itself. "Maybe you could fill Ms. Hamill in on everything else, see if there's anything new she remembers that might be helpful."

"Sure." He scooted forward. "Is that okay with you?" Zel asked the woman.

Callie led Jeremy down the short hall to the kitchen. He slowed, fresh worry lines etched into the smooth skin of his forehead.

"Zel will take good care of her," Callie said.

"Yeah, okay," he mumbled.

The kitchen, like the rest of the house, was small but clean. A wooden table and chairs were crammed up against the wall in the corner. A bulletin board with a calendar and pictures of the kids hung over the table. If the furniture was a little worn and mismatched, the space was homey enough.

She pulled out a chair for the boy. He glanced once more down the hall, then sat.

Callie wrote down the handful of names and numbers Jeremy gave her. Other than family, he'd had a friend in the car, and he guessed Natalie's two best friends had also been in the car. When she closed her notebook, he jumped to his feet.

"Jeremy, wait." She kept her voice low. "I'd like to ask you a couple of questions while you and I have this time together."

He wavered, rocking toward the hall. "I don't know."

"You want to help me find your sister, don't you?"

"Yeah."

"Please. It might be important."

His teeth closed over his bottom lip, but he sat down.

Callie set her notebook on the table. "This is between us, okay?" The lines between his brows deepened. "I know you're worried about your mom. She's lucky to have you, you know." He stayed silent, mouth shut tight now. "But kids don't tell their parents everything, and I get the impression the divorce was pretty hard on your sister."

"Yeah," he said finally.

"And your mom. And you."

"A little."

"I'd like to get a handle on what might have been going on in your sister's head this weekend. Find out how you think she'd been doing or who she might have been involved with. Even the tiniest thing could be important. Do you understand?"

He nodded. She thought he was a serious boy, maybe too serious for someone his age, but she pushed away any sympathy. That wouldn't help her find Natalie.

"Good. Let's start with how your sister was after the divorce."

"Bad. Upset. Angry." He paused. "She and my dad were pretty close, I guess. They bonded over swimming. He was a swimmer in college, so...anyway, she kind of blamed my mom, I think."

"Did you blame your mom?"

"No." His skin darkened. "My dad was cheating on my mom. She didn't deserve that."

"Okay. I can understand you being angry," Callie said, choosing her words. "Did your sister know what your dad was doing?"

He chewed his lower lip. "Neither of us knew at first. We didn't find out until a few months after he moved out." Callie waited. "My dad was living with her then. The other woman. Dana, I mean. Natalie kind of flipped at first. Dana's a lot younger than my mom. But Natalie forgave him. I think my dad told her my mom didn't make him happy, which made Natalie think my mom didn't try. That wasn't true, though. My mom is the nicest person in the world. If anyone didn't try, it was him."

Callie's heart broke with each word the boy uttered, but she forced her feelings aside.

"Okay. That was then. How about in the last month or so? Did your sister still blame your mother?"

He seemed to think about it before answering. "I don't think so. Probably because my dad didn't have time for Natalie anymore. I mean, we had dinner with him every other weekend and sometimes during the week, but Dana takes up all his time. I think maybe Natalie was hurt at first, then mad."

"But not at your mom anymore?"

"Well, they still fought. I think she still blamed her, but mostly, Natalie liked to make Mom feel guilty. She wanted to go out more, have her own car, you know, stuff like that. Everything my mom does is stupid, too. The way she dresses. Our house. Everything." He took a breath. "Oh, and my mom was making us go to church. Natalie hated that, but Mom wouldn't let her use the car unless she went. That really made her mad."

34

Callie considered what the boy had said. There was nothing that rang any bells, but the mother-daughter relationship was fractured at best. Had that made Natalie an easy target? "Was going to church new?"

"Yeah. It was helping my mom." His gaze flickered past her to a crumpled paper bag on the counter. "She gets anxious sometimes, and church helps, I think. There's a bible study and a support group for divorced people or something. I don't really mind it so much, but Natalie didn't think it was cool."

"What does your sister think is cool?"

Jeremy shifted, bit his lip again.

"It's okay, Jeremy. I'm not going to tell your mom, but I really need a true picture of what Natalie might have been thinking, who she might have been spending time with."

"Yeah, okay." His gaze wandered up to the bulletin board, to the pictures, before dropping again. The words came tumbling out then, earnest in their defense of his sister. "Boys and parties. That's what she's into, I think. But all her friends are. It isn't just her. She's a junior."

He was protecting his sister like a good brother, and Callie found herself liking the boy more and more.

"That's fine. No judgment here," she said with a small smile. "But what I need to know is if she was seeing any boy or if she might have gone to any party last night after she babysat."

"I don't think so. She wasn't dressed for it."

Callie already had a description of the girl's clothes: a blue t-shirt, jean shorts, and gold sandals, but she pressed him anyway. "What do you mean by that?"

"Nothing really, but I can usually tell when she's going somewhere by how she's dressed or if she takes a bag with her that has extra clothes. Last night, she didn't. She looked normal."

This made some sense and while it was still possible the girl had stashed something in the car or at a friend's, she let it go.

"And the boy from chemistry?"

"She didn't like him anymore. I heard her talking to her friend Sarah about him. She thought he was a jerk."

"Did she like someone else then?"

Jeremy hesitated. "I don't think so, but I don't know for sure. She was in a group to meet guys, the kind where you swipe and DM. My mom didn't know about that."

Callie's fingers twitched. This was new. "A dating site?"

"Sort of. It's on Insta, but it's private. Someone in it has to invite you. My friend saw his sister's phone when she didn't know he was looking. That's how he saw it."

"Do you know anything else about this group?"

"I know it has a stupid name. Hooked. Gordon told me that. And some of the guys don't look like they're in high school. Not old like a dad, but in college or a little older, maybe."

"And your sister was on it?"

"Yeah. Gordon saw her picture. You could put up a profile. He said hers was okay. Normal." She read the guilt that crossed his face. "That's why I didn't tell my mom. She wasn't doing anything wrong, I don't think."

"Okay. Thank you for that, Jeremy. One last question. How did your sister seem yesterday?"

"Same as always. Yelled at me for eating the last of the bread. Called me a dork 'cause me and my friend were playing Fortnite. That's about it."

"So, you didn't notice anything else?"

"No."

Callie slid her chair back, getting to her feet. "Oh, wait, one more thing. Did she say anything to you about this new family she was babysitting for?"

"Not to me, but I heard her talking to my mom. She said the dad had called. He'd gotten her number from the Holts." Callie frowned. The Holts had denied knowing any family with the name Randolph. "She said they had two boys, six and eight maybe. I can't really remember. Anyway, she did say the guy said he'd pay her fifteen dollars an hour. She was pretty happy about that."

"Fifteen, huh? That's pretty high."

"That's what my mom said."

"And you're sure it was the dad that called? Not the mom?"

"I-I think so."

"Okay, thank you, Jeremy. You've been a big help."

"You're going to find her, aren't you?" His voice broke as it rose higher.

A lump formed in her throat as she appraised the boy. In another year, maybe two, he'd be taller than Callie. He'd fill out, and his voice would deepen. His sister should be here to see that, to see him finish growing up. Hell, Natalie deserved to grow up, too.

You're going to find her, aren't you? Erin had asked her the same question earlier, and she'd made a promise then. That was before they'd found the car with its clean steering wheel and odor of chloroform in the trunk. Something happened in that car. Maybe something ugly. Still, there'd been no obvious trace of blood, no sign of injury. More than a day had passed since anyone had heard from Natalie, but she had to believe the teenager was alive. Somewhere. She had to.

"Yes, Jeremy." She drew herself up, her hands balled into fists. "We're going to find her."

Chapter Seven

Callie drove through the streets of Hampstead on autopilot. She knew the smart thing would be to go home, but she couldn't remember when she'd ever been accused of doing the smart thing. Ben once told her it was both her superpower and her fatal flaw. She guessed he might be right.

When she reached her parents' neighborhood, she slowed. The houses loomed like shadows against the sky with their darkened windows and low-slung roofs. Turning onto Sycamore, she extinguished the headlights, coming to a stop in front of a rambling ranch. Unlike the other houses on the block, light flickered from the front window. Callie got out and crossed the street, her feet silent on the pavement. An owl hooted in the distance, and the wind rattled a nearby branch, but otherwise, the street was quiet.

The light coming through the front window brightened and faded again, the pulsating glow of a television. Pictures and videos played across the screen, slideshow-style. Callie watched herself at the age of six twirl across a stage. At eight, she stood with her older brother on the beach, shovels clutched in their sandy hands, a floppy hat on her head. There was her father at a cookout waving a metal spatula, her brother holding up a basketball trophy, her mother and father dancing, heads tilted back in laughter. The faces changed, got older, and the film rolled on. Her brother after he graduated from boot camp. Her mother's winning pie at one of the July Fourth contests. Callie, graduating from college and later, moving into her first apartment, wearing a hat again, this one wide-brimmed and trimmed in leather. She remembered the night her father gave it to her.

The box it came in had made her laugh out loud. He'd wrapped it himself, using so much tape it should have come with a child-proof warning. By the time she got it open, the ball of discarded tape was the size of a softball. Pushing aside the tissue paper, she held her breath, running a finger along the butter-soft edge.

"I had it made for you, Cal. I know how you've always loved hats."

It was true. She did love them. All kinds. Bowler hats, berets, baseball hats. They were different and fun to collect.

"It'll keep you from burning," he'd said.

She loved it already. "It's beautiful, Dad, but you know I can't wear this for work. It's not regulation."

"True, but maybe after you make detective."

Her eyes had widened, and he'd put an arm around her. "Because you will, Cal. I have faith in you. I always will."

Now, he sat in his chair, mesmerized night after night by the same home video. Her heart banged in her chest. It was nearing the end now. The grand finale. Her father, Detective John Forde, in full uniform.

He'd led the team back then, had been so sure of his place in the world. She couldn't see him now, but she knew he sat in his wheelchair, the remote in his hand, watching. He'd paused the home movie on that image, the same as every other time. She stared with him. She saw the gray that had crept into the hair at his temples, the laugh lines that bracketed his mouth, the way he held himself erect, wide shoulders filling the screen. He was physically smaller now, a fact that only added to his misery.

Callie leaned against the tree, rooted, watching until the home movie started over again. Grainy photos of her great-grandparents and grandparents played now. Eyes stinging, she forced herself to move, to get back in her car, to leave him with his memories. She'd lied to Zel, the same way she'd been lying to herself. He wasn't better. Not better at all.

Instead of heading home, she turned toward the western side of town, where the land was less populated, the crops grew tall, and cows and horses roamed the fields. A half-mile from the dairy farm, she pumped the brakes. What was she doing? Ben wouldn't be alone, and even if he were, why would he want to see her? They'd been over for a long time now. Her chin fell to her chest, and she took a deep breath, the memories rushing back.

Ben had inherited the dairy farm when he'd been in his second year of law school. Callie remembered hearing the news when she was an undergrad. His parents had been returning from a vacation in Florida, their first in a decade, and got caught in a fifteen-car pile-up on I-95. She'd stayed at school, but her parents had gone to the funeral, along with half the town. She hadn't known Ben all that well back then. He was older than her brother, more studious, quieter. It was only after she'd come home that she'd gotten to know him. Against her father's wishes.

"Godammit, Callie. He's playing for the other team, defending the same people we're working to get off the street." His face had darkened. "Did you hear about the Planton case from up in the northern part of the county? The guy shot his wife twelve times. Twelve. And your new boyfriend is trying to get him off."

"He's not my boyfriend," she'd said, even as she wondered if that was true. She'd been home only a few years by then and was eager to work her way from street duty to detective when she'd run into Ben at the Hampstead Tavern. She remembered the sound of his voice, low and silky, asking to buy her a drink. Even now, the memory sent a delicious shiver up her spine. His fingers had brushed across hers, unleashing a strange fluttering in her stomach. One drink had led to two, which had led to lunch the next day and then dinner, and then a few more dinners. But if she'd known the details of the Planton case, they were vague in her mind.

"Dad, he's county criminal defense. He was assigned the case. That's his job."

"That's my point, Cal. His job is to get people off. And I heard he's using the insanity defense with Planton." Her father's upper lip had curled at those words. "Is that what Mary Ellen Planton deserves?"

She'd hesitated. The insanity defense stuck in the craw of most cops. Her father was no exception. Still, she cocked her head to one side. "Is it possible the man really is unbalanced?"

"No." Her father's jaw had tightened. "I've known Planton for years. And

Mary Ellen. She was a friend of your mother's until she had too many bruises to hide, and she stopped seeing anyone. Planton may be a sick man, but not the way Ben is trying to paint him."

She'd nodded but said nothing. As time passed and she'd refused to give up her new boyfriend, they'd come to an uneasy truce on the subject. Ben and her father were cordial enough, and she'd learned not to discuss work with her boyfriend. But her father had been right after all. When things had gone down in that parking lot, and he ended up in a hospital bed, there was plenty of blame to go around. After the initial shock, sides were taken, and Ben asked questions she didn't like. She'd pushed him away when she had no answers and tired of fighting, he'd let her. In the end, they'd all paid the price. The silver wheelchair served as an unhappy reminder.

Silently chastising herself, she turned the car around. Did she really miss Ben or only the memory of him? Whatever had happened between them was a long time ago, and he'd moved on. Ben had a new life now, one that didn't include Callie Forde.

Chapter Eight

The man looked down at the girl, watching her as she slept. Thick ropes encircled her wrists and her feet. Another anchored her to the bed, but the mattress was soft, and the sheets were clean. He'd given her that. He wasn't a brute. He'd make her as comfortable as the situation allowed, and when it was safe and she'd learned her place, he'd take the restraints away. Her leg twitched, and he tensed, but she slept on, lost in a dark world. Satisfied that the sedative he'd injected would keep her quiet for hours, he reached out and trailed a finger over the length of her body. So beautiful. So pure. Her snow-white hair hung limp over her pale cheek, and her chest rose and fell in a slow rhythm. He leaned closer, breathing in the scent of her. The faint odor of chlorine clung to her skin, and he wrinkled his nose. He'd never liked the smell of pools. They always reminded him of his childhood and those years when he didn't know how to fight off the bullies. Even now, he could feel their hands pushing him under the water, over and over, laughing like hyenas while he sputtered and coughed, snot running from his nose.

He stood up then, backing away from the girl, his breath coming in short spurts. Closing the door and locking it behind him, he leaned against the wall, reminding himself he wasn't that boy anymore. He'd grown up. He could outsmart them all now. Hadn't he proved that more than once?

His heart rate returning to normal, he sat down at his computer. There was work to do. He'd have to move the girl soon to the place he'd prepared, but not until the time was right. The mother had called the police, and the girl's picture had been on the news and was already being taped up on store windows and telephone poles. Figured. Now, the mother paid attention. Too little too late, if you asked him.

Fingers tapping the keys, he went about his daily routine: updating his posts, scrolling through his social media, checking on his apps. He created order out of chaos. That's what people didn't understand. Structure and discipline. Those were the things that defined a man and his ability. The man who could walk through the storm was a man to be reckoned with. He was such a man.

Unable to stop himself, he rose, returning to her room. He pushed open the door, his movements silent. He didn't hear her snores until he stood over her. Her shirt had risen above her slender waist, exposing the soft skin that stretched across her taut belly. His nostrils flared and he reached out, pulling the shirt back down. She wouldn't wake, but if she did, no one would hear her. He'd soundproofed the room months earlier. Preparation. Patience. That's why his plan would work. And because he deserved this. In a few days, Natalie Hamill would cease to exist. She would start a new life, whether she wanted to or not.

Chapter Nine

Callie sat in the hard, plastic chair with her hands in her lap and her legs tucked under the seat. "Thanks for seeing us this morning," she said.

Zel, silent, shifted uncomfortably next to her.

Principal Carter, silver hair glinting under the fluorescent lighting, gave her a wan smile. "I wish I could say I was glad to see you, Callie." He lifted his palms. "But under these circumstances…"

She made the appropriate comments and explained what she needed.

"The idea that something could have happened to Natalie is terrible. Obviously, we want to help where we can, but…" He ducked his head. "Although she's still a minor, there are privacy issues. You understand."

Anticipating this, Callie had already paid an early morning visit to Erin Hamill. "Her mother gave us permission, and she's available by phone to verify." She handed over a signed letter.

The principal's face cleared. "Very good." He called in his secretary. "Polly, can you get Detective Forde a copy of Natalie's class schedule? And have counseling put a file together, please."

The woman nodded and disappeared.

The secretary returned with two copies of the schedule. She handed one to her boss and one to Callie. Natalie, if she were in school, would be in her second class now. Chemistry, followed by English before lunch.

"It looks like Natalie is taking a few advanced classes," she commented.

"Oh, yes. Natalie is a good student." His frown reappeared. "I can't understand where she could be."

"That's what we're trying to find out, Mr. Carter. Did anything unusual happen at school last week? Any incidents she might have been involved in?"

"Oh, no."

"Anything she might have witnessed?"

"Not that I'm aware of."

"I'm sure it will be in her files, but can you think of any time Natalie had to be called to the office or was given detention?" Again, he told her no. "Okay. We're going to need to speak to each of her teachers and her guidance counselor. Is there a room where we could set that up?"

"Of course. You can use my conference room." Carter led the way, his shiny shoes squeaking as he walked. He opened the door and waved them in.

Callie held up the schedule in her hand. "Why don't we go in order? Starting with her first-period teacher." The principal nodded and ducked out. Ten minutes later, there was a knock at the door, and he was back, followed by a short, stocky woman in black stretch pants and a pink paisley top.

"This is Audrey Dobbs. She's Natalie's history teacher."

Fifteen minutes later, the detectives had learned nothing more than that Natalie wasn't shy and seemed to enjoy group projects. The next several teachers had similar comments.

"She seemed to have a lot of friends. Was popular with the other students. I know she was a swimmer and was in the Spanish club."

"She turned her work in on time. Prepared for tests. No problems I can think of."

"Perhaps a little chatty but always respectful."

Zel leaned back and let out a long breath. "Not sure this is getting us anywhere, Cal."

Callie couldn't disagree, but this was how the job worked. They had to follow up on any leads they could, and like every teenager, Natalie spent a large portion of her day in school. When they finished with her teachers and counselor, they would check out her locker before heading out.

"Who's next?" she asked.

Zel consulted the sheet. "The Spanish teacher."

Callie read the name and smiled. Elena Quinton. Mrs. Quinton had been her teacher a decade and a half earlier. When the woman walked in the room, Callie's smile broadened.

"Mrs. Quinton, so good to see you."

Elena's eyes crinkled, and her own lips turned up. "Why, Callie, I didn't know you were here."

"Yes. You may have heard that Natalie Hamill is missing." The older woman's bright smile disappeared. Callie waved her hand toward her partner. "You know Detective Zeleniak, don't you?"

"Oh, yes. I had his sister for three years, although I believe you took Latin, didn't you?"

"Yes, ma'am."

Callie cleared her throat then. "Mrs. Quinton, we're trying to find out if you noticed anything unusual with Natalie lately. Did she seem preoccupied? Did she seem upset about anything or anything unusual happen in class?"

Elena raised a hand to her short, iron-gray hair. "Well, I can't say if she was upset about anything outside of school, but she may have been a bit annoyed with me."

The teacher's words made Callie sit up straighter. "What happened?"

"Oh, nothing alarming, really. A teenage girl and her phone." Elena's lips pursed. "They are both a godsend and a curse, aren't they?"

"You're preaching to the choir," Zel said. Callie knew that, like most parents, Zel and Marcie had battled with their own daughter over her phone. After she'd gone, he wished he'd tried harder and didn't mind sharing that message. As much as Callie loved Zel, this was not the time to go down that rabbit hole.

"What did Natalie do?" Callie asked quickly.

Elena folded her hands together. "It was very unlike Natalie. I want you to know that, but when it comes to boys, even girls like Natalie can behave in ways they wouldn't otherwise." Callie leaned forward. "It was last Thursday, I believe, and I'd scheduled a short quiz, one part written and the other

46

part oral. The written section was at the beginning of the class. When they finished, I began calling the students up one by one to test their oral skills. While I completed the oral part, the students were expected to finish the worksheets I'd passed out." She paused. "During one of the oral exams, I heard a giggle and a whisper. I let it go with a reminder that we need quiet, but a few minutes later, I heard it again. When I looked up, I saw Natalie turned around in her seat. I got up and put a finger to my lips for quiet from the rest of the class. Natalie didn't hear me walking toward her desk, nor did the other student."

"Who was that, Mrs. Quinton?"

"Beth Anne Peters. I saw that Natalie was scrolling through a series of pictures of a young man. Beth Anne must have noticed me then because she said my name. Before Natalie could react, I took her phone from her hand." Her mouth turned down then. "I have a very strict rule about phone use in class." Her face softened again. "Of course, I remember what it's like to be young, to have a crush, but still..."

Callie's mouth had gone dry, and she licked her lips. "Did you know who the boy was?"

"No, I didn't. He wasn't a student here. I know that." She paused again. "And I wouldn't say he was a boy. Rather, a young man. Early twenties if I had to guess. Perhaps older."

A young man. The words sounded eerily familiar to the young detective, and she considered Mrs. Quinton's information. "Were the pictures on a social media account? Or from her library?"

"Social media, I'd say. There were captions, though not very clever ones if you ask me."

"Did you see a name on the account?"

"Well, there was something, but I wouldn't call it a name. Normally, I would have put the phone in the drawer right away, but I had a funny feeling about those pictures. I looked at a couple, and that's when I saw the account name."

"What was it?"

"It was some kind of shorthand. You know kids can't write these days.

Everything is abbreviated."

"A handle?" Zel asked.

"I suppose. Anyway, I wrote it down." She pulled a slip of paper from her pocket.

Callie and Zel read the note before exchanging a look.

uluv2hot2handel

"As you can see, whoever wrote this can't spell." She clucked her tongue. "Anyway, the typical procedure is to turn the phone over to the front office, and the student gets it back at the end of the day, but since this was the last class, I didn't bother." She paused, her face softening. "And Natalie's a good girl. She promised it wouldn't happen again, and I believed her."

"Did she say anything else about it?"

The older woman's head sank lower then. "Not really. I warned her about the dangers of the internet, but I could tell she wasn't listening. She told me she knew what she was doing." The teacher's voice softened, and she seemed to age another decade in that moment. "Those were her words. 'You don't have to worry about me, Mrs. Quinton. It's just for fun. I know what I'm doing.'"

The hairs on Callie's neck rose. *I know what I'm doing.* Like five years ago, when the last girl went missing.

Chapter Ten

Zel tapped on his tablet. "According to what the brother told you, it's a private group, Cal. We'd need to create a profile and then find a way to get invited."

"We can reach out to Natalie's friends."

"Sure, but I'm not sure we need to. A guy like that is trolling, right? There's a good chance he's on other sites, the kind young girls hang out in."

Her hand rested on her hip. "And you know about these sites?"

"Marcie made me see if Julie was on any. She was worried."

"Was she?" Callie asked.

"Not that I could find, but I've got a feeling about this guy. That handle is a dead giveaway."

"Giveaway for sleazeball."

"Yeah. Give me a half hour to put together a profile and check out some sites."

Callie looked over Zel's shoulder as he worked. He mumbled to himself as his fingers tapped and swiped. Less than twenty-five minutes after he started, he found their man.

"Got him."

Callie stepped closer. The name was at the top of the screen. *uluv2hot2handel*. The man's page contained five pictures, three of which were shirtless, the better to show off rippling biceps and rock-hard abs. His stats read like a young girl's dream, too. Six feet one inch. One hundred and seventy-five pounds. He claimed to love romcoms and reading, and long walks on the beach. He also promised his date a night they'd never forget.

49

"A guy like that," Zel said. "Why's he need to be on a dating site? It's schmucks like me who need them. Hell, that's how I met my wife way back when."

She pulled back in surprise. "Really? I didn't know that."

"I never told you?" He twisted around in his seat to face her, a lopsided grin creeping across his face. "There was really only one site worth using then. My mom made me," he said.

"What? Your mother? She's the queen of propriety."

"I know, but she said if I didn't hurry up and give her some grandchildren, she'd sign me up herself. So, I did. Felt kind of creepy, to be honest, but then I started to get the hang of it. Marcie was my fifth date. We met for a beer and ended up talking for hours. Turns out my mother was right again," he said with a laugh. He poked her in the rib. "Maybe you should try it."

She wagged her finger at him. "Oh, no. That's not for me."

"Don't knock it 'til you try it," he said, still smiling. "Or I might sic my mother on you."

She slapped him lightly on the arm. "Don't you dare."

Their laughter faded as their attention was drawn back to the screen. Callie studied the sculpted face of the young man in the pictures and read the rest of his bio. Nineteen. Student. Adventurous. Old enough to appeal to young girls, but young enough to pass as a college student. Still, she agreed with Mrs. Quinton. She'd eat her shirt if this guy was nineteen. "How do we know this is really what the guy looks like?"

"We don't, but we're going to find out. I'll start the paperwork to get a warrant for the guy's information."

Callie nodded. "Have we gotten anything from the phone company yet?"

"Not yet. Might be a day or two longer. And I've got warrants in the works for all of Natalie's social media accounts. One or two are bound to come in soon."

It wasn't enough, but it was something. "Thanks, Zel." Her mind pinged back and forth between the little they knew and the larger amount they didn't. The trace of chloroform, now confirmed by Angie. The wiped prints. What it didn't tell them is if Natalie had met her kidnapper willingly—at least at first.

I know what I'm doing.

The more time passed, the more Natalie's disappearance made her think of Emma Nicholls, the last girl who'd disappeared from Hampstead. Maybe it wasn't exactly the same, but it was close. A young girl, possibly unhappy at home, searching for something to grab onto. She meets a guy online. He messages her, and they talk. They send pictures. Make a plan to meet. And she's never seen again. Under the best of circumstances, the police track the suspect down and locate the girl. She's brought home, albeit forever changed in ways no one wants to imagine. Other times, the girl is sold, lost to the underground industries of porn, prostitution, or slavery. Callie never failed to be astounded by the dehumanization of these young girls, at the horror and suffering. Kidnapping. Abuse. Sexual assault. Murder. None of these were new crimes. Only the methods were new and everchanging in a modern world.

In the worst cases, the girl is never found. No trail is ever discovered. She's gone, vanishing as though she'd never been there at all. Of course, that's never really true, but after enough time, the media forgets. The public forgets. Only the family keeps the girls' memory alive. And the cop who couldn't find her. The Emma Nicholls case had been the first of its kind in Hampstead, and Callie's father had taken more than a passing interest. It haunted him still. It haunted them all.

Callie glanced over at Chang who was working the tip line. He waved a hand and shook his head. She knew what that meant. Nothing they could work with. There were most likely calls out of curiosity, some calls from folks trying to help, and more than a few from crazies. Tip lines brought them out like flies to honey.

She dropped into her chair and flipped her notebook open. Her gut told her the car was important, that it still held a clue to the identity of whoever had taken Natalie—not that he'd made it easy. He'd wiped the car wherever he'd been. The steering wheel. The door. The seat. So, she could presume he hadn't worn gloves. Wiping the interior was smart, but not failsafe. He could have missed something. She sat up straighter and picked up her phone.

Angie Brown answered on the second ring.

"I was wondering," Callie said, "if there were any prints on the rearview mirror or the side mirror or any buttons on the dash."

"You must be telepathic, Detective. I was just about to call you. I got a partial thumbprint from the bottom of the rearview mirror. It's not enough to test against the database, but it's enough for me to say it doesn't match the mother or the girl."

"What about the kids' friends?"

"We're still collecting those prints. I'll let you know as soon as I've ruled them out."

"Anything on that red clay?"

"A dead end. There were traces of it on the road from a larger vehicle, probably a truck. Most likely picked it up from the street in town."

Disappointed, Callie thanked her and hung up. She tapped her pen against her notepad faster. If the print belonged to the person in the car with Natalie, he or she had made a mistake. What else could the car tell her? The trace of chloroform. This one wasn't as obvious as it might appear. Chloroform wasn't illegal to buy or even make. The ingredients could be bought easily from chemical supply stores, online, or at the local supercenter. Tracking down any recent purchases would take manpower and a lot of time, something Natalie might not have.

Her mind drifted back to the boy on the dating site, *uluv2hot2handel*. Everything about him screamed fake to her. She couldn't ask Natalie about him, but maybe it was time to find out more from someone else who'd seen that profile. Within minutes, she had the principal on the phone.

"Mr. Carter, is there any chance I could speak to Beth Anne Peters? I know she's in class, but it's important."

He agreed, and not long after, Beth Anne's nervous voice came over the line.

"Hello?"

"Beth Anne, it's Detective Forde. I have a quick question for you. It's about a dating site, Hooked."

"I wasn't on that."

"No one is suggesting you were, but Natalie was." In the silence that followed, Callie repeated what she knew of the incident in Spanish class. "You're not in trouble, Beth Anne. It's more about wanting to find out if Natalie messaged this guy *uluv2hot2handel*."

There was the sound of a sniffle. "Do you think this has something to do with Natalie being gone? I mean, he seemed so nice."

Callie's breath caught. Natalie *had* contacted this guy. "What do you mean he seemed nice?"

"He seemed normal, I guess. She showed me a couple of messages after she swiped on him. She only did it for fun, you know, because his profile is so stupid. But then, he talked about his life at home, how his dad is a jerk, and how he's really not like what his profile says. He admitted those weren't really his pictures and sent her a real one. She liked it better. He looked regular, you know, not like a model or something."

Callie wrote "real picture" in her notebook.

"Had they gotten close?"

"I don't think so. I mean, they could have, but it's only been a couple of weeks."

Beth Anne was right. Usually, these kinds of predators took their time. Still, maybe he had a reason for upping his timeline.

"Had she messaged any other guys from the group?"

"A couple, but she said they were losers and stopped talking to them."

"So, only this guy that you know of?"

"Yes, ma'am."

Callie's fingers closed tighter over her pen. "And no other boys from school or at the college? You're sure?"

There was only dead air.

"Beth Anne?"

"She did have a crush on this one guy. He worked at the college coffee shop, so I think he's a student."

"What's his name?"

"Harry."

"Harry what?"

"I don't know. We never talked to him except to order lattes. But I think he has a girlfriend who works there, too. I saw him kiss her once."

The tightness in Callie's fingers loosened. Most likely another dead end, but she'd check it out anyway. That brought them back to the boy on Hooked. "Is there anything else you can tell me about this guy she was chatting with on the app?"

"Not really. Except I think his real name was Ryan or Brian or something."

Callie jotted down the names. But it was Beth Anne's next words that solidified the feeling she could be onto something.

"And I don't know if he lives there, but I think he's from Charlottesville."

Chapter Eleven

Hampstead had long been referred to as Charlottesville's smaller, uglier stepsister, although Callie thought that description was harsher than necessary. Both were college towns, but where Charlottesville boasted a sprawling campus, a world-renowned hospital, and a thriving downtown, Hampstead's college was more contained, occupying less than three hundred acres. The school bordered what was loosely referred to as downtown but was actually nothing more than six square blocks of buildings, shops, feed supply stores, a diner, a pair of taverns, a hotel, and two restaurants, neither of which served seafood. The only chain restaurants were on the college campus or at the strip malls that bordered the outskirts of the town's limits. Callie knew no one would ever include Hampstead on a list of best party schools with offerings like that.

Houses and apartment buildings fanned out on the north and south sides of downtown, creating mini suburbs with strip malls anchored by grocery stores, pizza deliveries, and Chinese takeout. To the west, farms dominated the area, and twenty miles to the east was the only other real contributor to the town's economy outside of the college—a packaged materials processing plant, formerly a paper mill.

As far as metropolises went, Hampstead wasn't even on the map. Callie remembered when her college roommate had come for a visit.

"Tell me again why you want to move back here, Cal. This place makes Richmond look like L.A."

"Same reason you want to go back to Richmond," Callie had said. "It's home."

Her roommate had laughed at that. "You're wrong. As soon as I get a job in D.C., I'm outta there. We're supposed to spread our wings and all that, right? That's my plan."

A part of Callie had admired her friend's adventurous spirit, but the other part of her, the deepest part, loved Hampstead and its quiet ways. She loved the way people waved at each other, the way they looked out for each other, the way you could find a parking space without driving all over town. Life in Hampstead might not be as fast-paced as D.C., but it was the right pace for Callie. And for as long as she could remember, she'd wanted to be a cop, a detective like her dad.

"Callie," he'd said when she applied to training, "are you sure? You could go anywhere."

"I'm sure, Dad. This is what I want."

She'd caught a glimpse of worry, even a bit of fear, but she'd seen something else, too. Pride.

She stared down at her notebook now and drew a circle around the name she'd gotten from Beth Anne. Ryan or Brian—also known as *uluv2hot2handel*. Ryan or Brian, who might have lived in Charlottesville. Had she been messaging him the day she disappeared? Without the phone records, Callie couldn't know. She slapped the top of her desk with the palm of her hand, the sharp sound like a crack in the small squad room.

"You okay, Cal?" Zel asked.

"No, I'm not okay," she said, her voice louder than she'd intended. "Sorry, it's not your fault. But it's been almost two days now. Two days." Her voice broke on the words.

He cleared his throat before he spoke again. "I'm afraid my news isn't going to make you any happier."

The knot between her shoulder blades tightened. "Give it to me."

"Miller got back to me. I've got a list of house sales, but none for Randolph." He handed her a piece of paper. "Maybe they're renting."

"Possibly." Callie read through the shortlist. "This only covers three months. Let's go back six."

"Sure," he said and waved a second page. "Nothing with utilities either but could be the wife has a different last name, and she does the bills." He paused, his arm dropping. "Or maybe the name wasn't Randolph at all. Maybe the mother got it wrong. She hasn't exactly been the most reliable source of information."

Callie sat back, thinking about the idea. It was possible. The mother had been all over the place every time they'd spoken with her. She thought about the son saying his mom needed some support, remembered the crumpled paper bags she'd spied in the kitchen and in the living room. If Callie were asked, she'd guess that Erin Hamill was a woman barely keeping her head above water *before* her daughter went missing. She wasn't judging. That would be hypocritical, and she knew it.

"Are there any similar names?" she asked now.

His brows furrowed. "There's a Randle. Had power turned on at an apartment over on West Gibson. I can't see the girl driving across town for a job in that neighborhood."

"Fifteen dollars an hour could be a reason."

He looked doubtful. "Doesn't fit with the other family recommending her though."

"Well, let's think about that. We've been assuming all along that Natalie's mother had the name right. We've also been assuming that everything Natalie told her mother about that babysitting job was true. Maybe she got the job some other way, in a way her mom wouldn't have approved of."

"Like what?"

Callie waved a hand in the air. "I don't know. Maybe she met the guy at a convenience store, and he asked if she babysat kids. Could have met him at the mall or online. We'll have Hendo follow up." She let out a long breath. "It feels like we're getting nowhere."

Her partner didn't say anything for a moment. "We're doing everything we can, Cal. We've got warrants out. We've got the tip line. Bank records coming. Angie on the car. We can interview different friends, that other family she babysat for, the Thompkins."

"We need to find this Hooked guy. He's our best lead."

Zel sighed. "We'll get the reports soon."

"I'll believe it when I see it," she said. "Remember how long it took after the Williamson stabbing?"

"Yeah, stalling with these guys is practically their company motto."

Grunting, she tapped her pen against the side of her desk, the tinny sound lost in the noise of the chatter around her. Mind racing, Callie tapped faster. They needed to get information about the young man in that private dating group. "Wait," she said, dropping the pen. "What if there's another way to find out about this guy?"

He sat back, crossing his arms. "Okay. I'll bite. How?"

Callie hurried around to his side of the desk and pointed at his tablet. "That profile you created. What was her name? Jenna?" A plan formed in her head. "Okay, I'm Jenna, and I'd like to meet the man of my dreams, a guy who likes to walk on the beach, exactly like *uluv2hot2handel.*"

A slow grin spread over his face, and he leaned forward again. "Yeah." He opened the app and found the page again. "This is us. Like it?"

A picture of an attractive young woman stared back at her. "Perfect. How do we get in touch?"

"This is one of those sites where the girl is in control. She has to make the first move."

"How?"

"A swipe."

Callie dried her sweating palms on her slacks. "Do it. Swipe."

Chapter Twelve

"Any response?" Callie asked for what she was sure was the twentieth time since they'd enacted their plan.

After swiping, they'd typed a message: *Hi! I like ur pics. Hope u like mine.* Zel had uploaded a second picture of the same woman. The girl in the photo, a cop, was young enough to pass for sixteen with a fresh face, blue eyes, and shiny hair. She wore a tank top cut low to reveal cleavage and a pair of distressed jeans. Casual but sexy enough. *I'm looking for someone to hang & maybe talk to. DM me if u want.*

"It's only been an hour," Zel said. "But I'll check again." His face broke into a grin then. "Got him."

Callie was at his side in less than two seconds. "What did he say?"

Hey Jenna. U look good. What do u want to talk about?

It wasn't much, but it was a start. "How about this?" she said.

Zel typed and pushed send, then asked, "If he has Natalie, why would he care about Jenna?"

She gave the only answer she thought made sense. "Because guys like this never stop looking for their next target." He nodded. Neither said what they were both thinking. If the guy behind this profile was abducting girls, he wouldn't stop until he was caught or dead.

Five years earlier, when Emma Nicholls had vanished, the evidence had led police to a dating and messaging app her parents hadn't known about. Callie couldn't dismiss the similarities now. In the Nicholls case, they'd followed a string of messages from a Henry Jones but got nowhere. The name and profile were an alias: Henry Jones, a ghost. The FBI had gotten involved when Emma's picture showed up on a private website they were investigating. In the end, all law enforcement got was a dead FBI agent and a Hampstead detective confined to a wheelchair. The website vanished, and worst of all, Emma had never been found. Every year, on the anniversary of Emma's abduction, Callie's dad made a call to the girl's parents. After, he wept, his chin low against his chest.

Too much about Natalie's disappearance reminded her of the Nicholls case. A vulnerable teen. The use of social media. The messages. Every fiber of her being ached for Natalie now.

"Cal?" Zel was asking now. "You with me?"

Drawing herself up, she gave him a brief nod.

He leaned back in his chair. "You know, if he gets suspicious of us, of Jenna, I mean, he'll shut the account down."

That wasn't an option. "Then we'll have to make sure he doesn't, won't we?"

Too anxious to sit still, she spun around, finding the bulletin board. Natalie's picture was front and center now, the word "MISSING" stamped across the top in bold, capital letters. Her gaze found the other picture, the one in the far corner. Emma Nicholls. Sixteen. A student at the high school like Natalie. Blond. An athlete—like Natalie, although Emma played field hockey. Callie moved closer to the board. Her stomach twisted. The girls could have been sisters.

"Cal? You there?" Hendo waved his hand in front of her face.

"Yeah. Sorry." She brought her focus back to the present and Hendo. "Do you think they look alike?"

"Who?"

"Natalie and Emma?"

"The Nicholls girl?" He cocked his head as he studied the board. "Now that you mention it, yeah. But don't all teenage girls look alike? They all wear their hair the same way and wear the same kind of clothes? It's like a tribe. I swear, sometimes I can't even tell which one is my Lynnie when they're all together."

She studied the pictures again. He was right. They had similar looks, but there were differences, too. "I guess you're right," she said. "Hey, what did you need anyway?"

"I narrowed down that list of sexual offenders for you."

"A fifty-mile radius?"

"Yep." He waved three printed pages.

"How many are local?"

"Four in the area. I checked their records. Two are in their seventies now and in nursing homes. There's another guy, Joe Pearlman. Convicted of rape fifteen years ago up in Northern Virginia. Moved here last year after he got out. Works at the supercenter outside Charlottesville stocking shelves. Called up there and he pulled a shift Saturday night for the overtime."

"We should still check him out."

"Already asked to have someone go around and check him out."

"Thanks. You said there were four?"

"Yep. Last one is a guy named Brian O'Neill."

Her chin came up. "Brian?"

"Yeah. Know him?"

"No." She sipped her coffee and told him about the dating app. "What did he do?"

"Funny you should ask. He went on one of those sites where you sell stuff, posted a chair, and lured this woman to his house to pick it up. He offered her a spiked lemonade, and when she woke up, her skirt was up around her neck."

"How long ago was that?"

"Eleven years. He's been out five. An accountant of all things. He works at the packaging center. Got the job through one of those rehabilitation programs."

"How old was the woman?"

The detective checked his notes. "Thirty. Married with two kids."

Callie considered the information. The age of the woman was different, but he'd used the internet. And it wouldn't be the first time an offender was less than discriminating in his choice of victim. She took the papers from his hand and a half hour later, her car whizzed past the sign telling them to turn for the packaging plant.

Zel's phone dinged as they reached the gates. "It's the dating app. Jesus, it's like this guy can't shut up."

"What's it say?"

He squinted at the screen. "Jenna, I can't believe how fast this is going, but you're my dream girl. Does that sound stupid? When you said you saved a turtle in the road last week, all I could think of was we're the same. Both of us love animals." He looked up. "There are heart emojis and turtle emojis."

"Is that all?"

"Nope." He read on. "I can tell you're the kind of girl I can talk to, share my troubles with, and hold close." Zel snorted. "This guy is so full of it. I bet he sells the same load of bull to every girl that DMs him."

"That's what we're counting on," she said. "Send him another message."

"Shoot."

"If only I weren't grounded. My stupid parents don't let me do anything." She paused. "Add a frowny face."

"Done."

Callie slowed to find a parking space.

Zel held up his phone and waved it toward the plant. "You know what the odds are this guy O'Neill is the same punk on the dating app, right?"

Pulling into an open space, she didn't answer immediately. O'Neill's parole officer had given the guy a clean bill of health when they'd called. Said he showed up on time, completed his community service.

"The guy has a girlfriend," the parole officer had said as though that precluded bad behavior.

It was true that in the years since O'Neill's release, there'd been no additional problems. Not even a speeding ticket. But everyone thought Ted Bundy was a good citizen, too, before the world realized he'd been assaulting and murdering women all over the country. Zel was right that the odds were lottery-sized small, but she didn't have the same optimistic view on life and people that he had. Zel gave folks the benefit of the doubt as a rule. Callie leaned toward doubt.

"Yeah," she said now. Overhead, dark clouds moved across the open sky, matching Callie's mood as she strode across the parking lot. "I get it, but waste of time or not, someone has to check him out. Might as well be us."

"Sure. Just sayin'."

She slowed as they neared the door and forced out a long, slow breath. She wasn't mad at Zel. She wasn't even mad at O'Neill. She was mad at herself. She'd made promises she shouldn't have, promises she hadn't kept. But she didn't have time to worry about being nice. Not until she brought Natalie home.

She yanked the door open and waved her partner inside, mouth set in a hard line. "I think it's time to introduce ourselves to Brian O'Neill."

Chapter Thirteen

"I've followed all the rules," O'Neill said, pulling off a pair of reading glasses. He kept his voice low. "Ask my P.O. or my boss."

"We did," Callie said. "But we'd like to ask you a few questions anyway."

O'Neill swept his longish hair from his forehead, his eyes darting around the open work area. A dozen desks sat spaced around the room, each flanked by a guest chair and a fake potted plant. While most of the employees pretended to be absorbed by whatever was on their computer screens, a few stared openly.

The man got up from his chair. "Let's go somewhere a little quieter."

"Sure," Zel said without bothering to keep his own voice down. "We can do that."

The detectives followed the man to a small conference room. He shut the door behind them, then went to the window facing the interior of the building and pulled the blinds closed.

"Do I need a lawyer?" he asked.

"Not unless you've done something," Callie said.

"I didn't."

"Good." She placed her notebook on the table. "Can you tell us where you were Saturday night?"

His mouth dropped open.

"Mr. O'Neill?"

"I was home."

"Alone?"

"No. My girlfriend came over."

"What time was that?"

"Nine-thirty, maybe. I'm not sure."

Callie wrote it down. "How long was she there?"

"She spent the night." He lifted his shoulders in a half-shrug. "She's my girlfriend."

"Can we get a name?"

"Do you have to?"

Zel leaned in. "Is it a problem?" he asked, his tone sharp.

"No, but…" his voice drifted away.

"She doesn't know about your past? Is that it?"

The man licked his lips, his face growing pinker under Zel's glare. "I'm gonna tell her. But I want her to really know me first. I'm not that man, the one I was before."

Callie's eyebrows jumped. "Oh? And what kind of man were you before, Mr. O'Neill?"

He sat back with a thump, the air seeming to go out of him. He stared at a spot over her head, his mouth twisted downward. Seconds passed. A minute. Callie didn't move, waiting. When his gaze slid back to hers, he looked older, his cheeks sunken.

"I didn't like women back then. I hadn't had much luck with them. High school was bad. College worse." He looked from one partner to the other. "You don't know what it was like. The teasing. The jokes. They played pranks."

Callie stiffened. A sallow-faced man, O'Neill was small in stature but stout in build. Patchy stubble dotted his rounded cheeks but couldn't hide the deep scars that could only have come from acute teenaged acne. His skin might be clear now, but it wasn't hard to visualize the man being picked on as a boy. Still, no amount of abuse from mean girls justified what he'd done.

"Part of me wanted to hurt them back. All of them. I didn't care who it was, really." He swallowed, his voice quieter now. "After they arrested me, I told them everything. All of it. And in court, I pled guilty. Did you know that?" He didn't wait for their answer. "I deserved to be punished. I knew that, and more than that, I knew I didn't want to be that guy. I was ashamed. So ashamed." Tears spilled over his cheeks. "When I was in prison, I found an online therapist. They let you do that, you know. Anyway, that helped. When I got out, my parole officer gave me a name of someone local. Dr. Hammond. Do you know him?"

"I've heard his name," Callie said, her pen mid-air.

"He's helped me a lot. I was angry, but I'm not anymore." He waved a hand toward the door. "And I like my job. I'm good at it. My boss knows about my past, but that's all. No one else." He was pleading now. "I have co-workers. I don't want them to know. I don't. You're going to tell them, aren't you?" Snot dripped from his nose.

"That's not why we're here," Callie said. "We don't need to do that."

He sniffed. "I don't understand then. Why are you here?"

Zel spoke then. "A girl is missing."

O'Neill gasped out loud. "Oh, God," he breathed.

"Since Saturday night."

Callie looked down at her notebook, at the blank page in front of her. Coming here had most likely been a waste of time, but she would finish what she'd started. That was the job. "Where were you before nine-thirty, Mr. O'Neill?"

His face swung back toward her, his breath coming faster. "Home. Waiting for Frannie. She was supposed to come earlier, but she had to work late at the bookshop. It wasn't her night to close, but the other salesgirl went home sick."

"We're going to need to talk to her," Zel said. His tone was almost apologetic now, the sharp edges from earlier gone.

O'Neill paled. "Do you have to?"

"I'm sorry, but unless someone else can verify you were home from seven to nine-thirty, we do."

He covered his face with his hands, shaking his head. "There's no one. I live alone."

Callie ripped a piece of paper from her notebook and pushed it along with her pen toward the man. "Could you write down her name and number for me, please?"

Hand shaking, he wrote, then lifted his head. "Are we done? I have to get back to work now." He ran fat fingers through his hair. "I don't know what I'm going to say to them about why you're here."

"I'm sure you'll come up with something," Zel said, standing.

Callie watched Zel follow O'Neill to the door. The short man was barely more than half Zel's height, a penguin next to a giraffe. The image brought a small smile to her face. With a sigh, Callie reached into her blazer and pulled out a plastic bag. As carefully as she could, she slid the pen and paper across the table, dropping them into the bag. As she sealed it, she gave a shake of her head. O'Neill's prints would be in the system. He was an ex-con. But she bagged the pen out of habit anyway.

Neither detective spoke as they took the elevator back downstairs. She hadn't liked O'Neill's whiny tone or what he'd done eleven years earlier, but he had pled guilty and served his time. And if his alibi checked out, she'd have no choice but to let it go. Which meant she was no closer to finding Natalie. Another dead end.

Chapter Fourteen

The man walked around the oversized trunk, circling it the way a wolf circles its prey, his dark eyes focused, lips parted in a slight curl. He reached out to unlatch the trunk, sliding the key into the lock, but before he could turn it, a noise came from inside. He froze. A second sound, like a knock. His hand dropped the lock, and he sat down, waiting. The sound grew louder, faster, and steadier until it faded out, followed by muffled sobs.

Outside, the sky darkened, and the wind picked up, whistling as it blew through the trees. The man peered out, glad of the clouds and the plop plop of large raindrops hitting the window. It wouldn't be enough to make up for the dry weather in recent months, but it would make moving the girl easier. From the trunk, the sobs turned into a low moan. With a sigh, he sank to his knees and bent toward one of the holes he'd drilled in the case. He spoke just loud enough to be heard.

"I need you to be quiet now."

There was another sob and then silence.

"I'm going to unlock the trunk. You will be still and allow me to give you something to keep you calm." Another sob. He tried not to let it bother him. He'd known she'd be difficult, had expected as much. It's why he chose her, why he waited. "Don't fight me. If you do, I'll go to your house." He waited a beat, imagined her mind churning. He leaned in closer, his voice more of a whisper now. "Find your mother and your brother."

As he let the words sink in, the wind outside whipped up, and thunder boomed. He smiled. It seemed that even Mother Nature was on his side.

Taking a small bag from his pocket, the man's fingers brushed over the soft fabric pouch. From it, he pulled out a syringe and a small bottle of clear liquid. With practiced hands, he loaded the syringe and set it aside.

"Remember. I expect you to be still. Do. Not. Move."

Again, he slipped the key in the lock. This time, he turned it, releasing the brass hinges. The lid squeaked open. Drawing in a breath, he took in the sight of her. Her cheeks were stained with tears, and her upper lip glistened with snot. Her hair was matted now, and he sniffed the sour sweat that coated her skin. Lines creased his forehead, and he had to tamp down on his revulsion. Her appearance, her odor, wasn't her fault. He wouldn't blame her.

Taking the syringe, he injected the girl in the thigh. "Good girl," he said as he punctured her skin. To her credit, she remained curled up, her hands and feet bound, the rag in her mouth damp with drool, her wet lashes closed tight.

He sat back on his heels, watching until her body seemed to go slack, her limbs loosening.

"When you wake up," he said, "we'll talk about your new life. You need to forget about your mother and your brother. They're part of your past now. You will be reborn." The storm outside raged louder, nearly drowning out the sound of her whimper. "This is the first day of the rest of your life. Your new life."

Chapter Fifteen

Wishing she had her favorite wide-brimmed hat, Callie dodged the raindrops as she dashed toward the car and slid behind the wheel. It took her a moment to catch her breath.

"Now it rains?" Zel asked, wiping the moisture from his face and hands. "Just kidding," he said. "I know we need it, but I'm soaked."

She laughed. "Me, too. Hey, would you check that dating app again?"

"Already on it." A few seconds passed as they pulled out of the lot. "Nothing."

Her gaze found the rearview mirror and the receding vision of the packing plant. In the hour they'd been interviewing O'Neill, Zel's fake profile hadn't received a single message. It could be their target had gotten wise. Or it could be a coincidence, a dirty word to most cops worth their salt.

"Is Chang at the Hamills'?" she asked. The click of the wiper blades slowed, the rain already tapering off.

"Yep. Probably playing video games with the kid."

Callie hoped Chang, who wasn't exactly known for his winning personality, was helping to keep Jeremy's mind off his missing sister, but it was the mother she was most worried about. She told Zel about spotting the crumpled paper bags. "I think Natalie's mom has panic attacks."

"Yeah? Teenagers are hard, Cal, even when the parents aren't divorced. They don't think much beyond their own needs and whatever's right in front of them. Whatever they think or want is the most important thing in the world." His voice took on a sad, husky quality. "That's no one's fault, just how it is. It's science. They hit thirteen, and bit by bit, they turn into little aliens living in your house. They don't speak the same language. They don't want you around. They sleep like vampires, and when they're awake, God help you. They're impulsive and reckless and so sure they know what they're doing. They're right, and everything you do is stupid. It's a real thing." A grimace crossed his face. "My wife read every article out there, every bit of evidence about why teens act the way they do. Natalie's mother could have been mother of the year, and they still might have argued." He lifted his shoulders in a weary shrug. "I feel sorry for her."

His words still echoed in her brain long after dark, long after most of the others had gone home for the night.

Zel yawned, long arms stretching upward. "Think I'll call it a day, Cal. You gonna be much longer?"

"Almost done," she said, stifling a yawn of her own and holding up a stack of papers. "Just going over these statements one more time. See if we missed anything."

"It's after nine," he said, his voice soft. "You need to get some sleep."

"I will."

She lifted her hand in a wave, barely hearing the sound of his footsteps descending the old stairs. Finishing the statements, she shuffled through the notes on her desk, the pictures of the abandoned car, and the hastily written reports from the county forensics office. She had pieces and parts but nothing whole, nothing that made sense.

Callie picked up the printed screenshots of the messages Zel and Dating App Brian had exchanged. The last had been received at four fifty-eight that afternoon. Zel had sent two more since, but there'd been no response. One minute, the contact was hot to meet Jenna of the fake profile and the next, it was crickets. Something had spooked him, but what?

Pushing the pages aside, she found Hendo's report on the Randle rental, the one who'd recently signed up for power and water. Turned out that Taylor Randle was a nursing student who'd signed a lease but hadn't yet moved to Hampstead. Which meant they still hadn't located the Randolphs and couldn't verify what time Natalie had finished her babysitting job. It occurred to Callie that Natalie might have used the job as a cover to meet the boy from the app or one of the college kids, but without more, she had to assume Natalie was where her text said she was.

Without much more she could do for the night, she swept the files into her bag and switched off the desk lamp. Halfway home, her phone buzzed.

"Forde here."

"Is it true? About the girl?"

The voice on the other end vibrated with anger. She'd heard it before, though rarely directed at her. "Dad, are you—"

"Don't dad me. Is there a girl missing or not?"

She whipped her car around the corner, doubling back toward her parents' neighborhood. "I'm coming over."

"I didn't ask you to come over. I asked you a goddammed question." He was yelling now, his normally soft rasp hard as stone.

Her fingers locked over the wheel. "Yes, Dad. A girl is missing." Slowing at the last stoplight, she considered how to explain, but before she could get out three words, the line went dead.

Callie banged her hand against the wheel. "Shit. Shit. Shit." How had she let this happen? Why hadn't she told him before he saw it on the news or one of his old cronies dropped it in conversation? Pulling up to the house, she saw him through the large window, silhouetted in the light from the TV. From her car, she could see her mother creep into the room carrying a glass before disappearing again. That's how she thought of her mother now, as the great disappearing woman. The Maura Forde she used to know, the one with the too-loud laugh and louder clothes, was gone. The Maura she knew now was somber. She didn't laugh, and her clothes came in grey and black.

The detective watched as her father sat motionless, his once strong arms pressed against the hard metal of his chair. She leaned back against the headrest. Everything had changed since Emma Nicholls vanished. There'd been suffering and pain, the kind anyone would expect after a loss. But the rest of it, the ripples of blame, guilt, and sorrow that had torn through their own family and the town, that was something else. Five years later, Hampstead had healed as best it could. But Natalie's disappearance would change that. That kind of heartache never really went away. It only hid, sliding just far enough below the surface to fool a person into believing things were better, biding its time.

The front door swung open in Callie's hand, and she breathed in the stale, musty air. The windows stayed closed now, the house shut up most days like a mausoleum. He didn't look around, didn't acknowledge her. She crossed the room, flipping on the lamp. His hair, greying in the last photo, was now no more than a handful of silver threads. He wore a faded t-shirt stained with something that might have been pizza sauce and a pair of baggy sweatpants that hid his wasted legs.

"How did you find out?"

He didn't answer, his features frozen in what she'd come to recognize as his perpetual scowl.

"Don't tell me. It doesn't really matter anyway. I know you're mad, but I didn't tell you because—"

"Jeri Carter told your mother. I heard her say it when she brought over one of her godawful casseroles tonight. I don't know why your mother won't tell her we don't need any food. It's been five goddammed years, but your mother is too nice. Always has been."

"Maybe she likes having someone to talk to." She hadn't meant to say the words, but they'd slipped out before she could stop herself. His dark eyes flashed, and he wheeled his chair farther from her, showing her his back.

"I'm sorry," she said.

He grunted without looking at her. "Of course, you are. Everybody's sorry." He picked up the TV remote and turned up the volume. "You can go now. And turn out that lamp."

Callie didn't move. Behind her, on the TV, the game show host introduced the players. Everyone on the screen smiled and laughed. She wondered if her father actually saw what was on the screen or if he was only killing time, waiting—for what she had no idea. She looked back at her father, at the man they'd almost lost, remembering how grateful they'd been that he'd survived. What they didn't know was that the shooting had taken more than the use of his legs, it had taken his sense of humor, his patience, his identity. She understood his loss, mourned for him and with him, and yet, it had been five years. In all that time, he'd done nothing more than exist, than breathe. He'd not lived one single day.

"Actually, I'm not sorry." She snatched up the remote and hit the mute button. "What I'm sorry about is not telling you what an ass you've been to Mom, for a long time. Thank God for people like Jeri. At least mom knows someone still cares about her." His back stiffened, but he said nothing. "What I am sorry about is that I miss the father who taught me to believe in myself, to trust myself, to keep trying no matter what." Her voice shook with each word. She knew she should stop. It was cruel what she was saying, but she was like a hurricane now, whipped up, pounding at him. "What you've done to Mom is wrong, and I'm not going to let you do it anymore. She doesn't need to be cooped up in this house day after day because you refuse to leave. She needs to get out. To see people." She stepped closer. "I'm sorry that you can't see how many people love you, how much they want to see you again. I'm sorry for what happened to you. I am. But I can't keep crying. I can't keep tiptoeing around you, worried about everything I say and do, acting like it's okay that you live like a hermit. I can't do it anymore, Dad. I can't."

She saw his head sink lower and his shoulders roll forward then, his body shrinking in the chair. Callie stood, uncertain. Had it been too much? She couldn't be sure, but she did know that she'd had to say it even if it didn't make any difference. And she was going to make him go to counseling this time, make all of them go, whether he wanted to or not. They couldn't heal any other way.

She went to him. "I love you, Dad."

"I want you to go now," he said.

She fell to her knees, tears pricking her eyelids. "I'm sorry, Dad. I had to say it."

His hand came up and touched her cheek. He held it there for several seconds before letting it drop and rolling back.

"Goodnight, Callie."

He wheeled away from her and disappeared down the darkened hallway, leaving her alone in the empty living room, the only sound that of her own muffled sobs.

Chapter Sixteen

S oft sunlight crept across the floor, warming Callie's face and skin. She blinked, her swollen eyes crusty with dried tears. The light stung, and she pulled the covers over her face. Memories of her father and the hurtful words she'd flung at him played on repeat in her head. But another image, that of a desperate mother, made her push her own troubles to the back of her mind. She felt sorry for her father, for all of them, but she didn't have time for regret. That could come later.

Padding to the bathroom, she ripped off her oversized t-shirt and turned on the shower. If she hurried, she could be in the office by seven. Two large cups of coffee later, she sat at her desk, scrolling through the pages that had come in overnight. There were copies of Natalie's school records and medical records. Neither contained anything remarkable, so she set them aside. She clicked on her computer, scrolling through the emails that had piled up overnight. Halfway through the second page, she saw it. An email from the Hamill's cell phone service and a link to the texts they could recover.

The letter, while short, outlined several caveats. First, there were only fourteen days of texts. Apparently, the phone company only stored a thousand texts at one time before deleting and since teenagers averaged up to a hundred a day, that's all they had. Callie could live with that. Second, the phone company did not have the passwords to her social media accounts. They would have to keep waiting on the social media app companies for the girl's personal information, but none of that mattered now. The encrypted link would show her Natalie's most recent text messages. It was more than she had when she'd walked in the door that morning.

Zel's voice broke into her thoughts. "You look zoned in."

She quickly explained about the email, and he brought his chair around to sit next to her. Callie's skin tingled as she clicked on the link. The texts were organized by contact and appeared in alphabetical order, from oldest to newest. Callie scrolled through the As but found nothing that might be relevant with regard to Natalie's disappearance. She moved on to the letter B. Although there were twenty entries, only three of the names had conversations during the time period listed. The first was Beth Anne. There were dozens of older texts between the girls about music and TV and boys and parties, and dozens more since she disappeared, all asking where she was and filled with worry for her friend. The older conversations jumped from topic to topic with lightning speed, and Callie found herself marveling at the mind of a teenage girl. She sat up as she read the most recent texts before Natalie was reported missing. The first had been sent at twelve minutes after six.

Natalie: *Sitting for that new family tonight*

Beth Anne: *The 15$ one?*

Natalie: *Hope they like me*

Beth Anne: *Don't eat all the ice cream this time lol*

Natalie responded: *Text u when i'm done*

something to tell u

hang out after at HC?

Beth Anne had answered with a thumbs up. *Who is he?*

Lol better in person c u tonight

Another thumbs up. There were two more incoming texts from Beth Anne.

Still there? and *Wya?*

The last had come in at twenty minutes before midnight. Natalie had not responded to either of them.

Zel pointed at the screen. "Don't remember Beth Anne mentioning they were going to hang out after Natalie's babysitting job, do you?"

"No, I don't." She considered the possibilities. Natalie and Beth Anne could have hung out after midnight. They might have gone to HC, which she assumed was Hampstead College. They may have been drinking. If this were true, it would make sense that Beth Anne might hide this fact. Or they could have gotten separated. Natalie may have met someone then, someone who didn't mind taking advantage of a drunk, underage girl. All of this was plausible. But they couldn't prove any of it. "I think we're going to need to speak with Beth Anne again."

She moved on to the next few conversations. A handful of texts with classmates discussing an upcoming test, parties, and typical gossip. There was nothing there.

Callie came to another name. BG. "Do you remember any friends with those initials?"

Zel shook his head. "Nope."

She opened the conversation. The date of the first text was the Friday before Natalie's disappearance.

BG: *It's cool to talk to u without the app*

Callie glanced at Zel, goosebumps rising on her arms.

Natalie: *I know right, so much better.*

BG: *Yeah so when u wanna get together*

There was a half hour time gap before Natalie responded.

Natalie: *Maybe this weekend?*

BG responded instantly. *Tonight?*

Natalie: *Can't has to be Sunday*

BG: *What about Saturday?*

Natalie: *Babysitting*

BG: *I could come over*

Natalie: *I don't think so*

BG: *After?*

Natalie: *Maybe*

BG: *Say yes. I'll meet u anywhere u want*

Natalie had added a blushing face. Then typed: *Gotta go ttyl*

There were similar texts between them the next day. While BG seemed to have come on strong at first, he hadn't pressured her again until late

Saturday afternoon.

BG: *Hamp park whatever time u say*

behind the rocks

I got some beer and weed

sound good?

Natalie: *Idk*

BG: *I just wanna see u and talk 2 u*

Natalie: *Tomorrow ok?*

BG: *Is 12:01 too soon?*

Natalie: *Lol I'll think about it*

BG: *I think about u all the time I want to know u and talk to u about ur mom and dad and school and everything I wanna be there for u how u r for me*

Natalie: *Ur sweet my friends don't understand even my teacher doesn't understand*

BG: *Ur teacher?*

Natalie: *She caught me on the app but she's cool she won't tell anyone*

BG: *U sure?*

Natalie gave a thumbs up. There was another brief time gap in the conversation. Callie wondered if BG was having second thoughts, but his next text contradicted that idea.

BG: *The park?*

Natalie: *Gotta get to my job*

BG: *I'll be waiting*

At eight forty-eight, Natalie sent a response.

See you then

Cal and Zel reached the end at the same time. Zel pointed at the screen. "Cal, this could be it."

BG. Dating app Brian. It had to be. Her pulse raced along with her mind.

"We need to get a search team to the park." She had one arm already in her jacket, words coming out in a rush. "And track down that phone number. I'll update the captain, you fill in Hendo and Chang." This was the best lead they'd gotten, proof that Natalie had plans after her babysitting job.

For the first time in days, Callie allowed herself to hope.

Chapter Seventeen

By mid-morning, a perimeter had been set up in the park, and the designated search area roped off with yellow tape. A handful of townsfolk gathered nearby, craning their necks to see. Callie and Zel strode past the playground and the gazebo toward the large rocks that bordered the north corner of the park. Behind the rocks was a cave-like area frequented by teens and the occasional homeless resident searching for a dry bed. The beat cops did their best to keep an eye out, but no one got their kicks by hauling in kids or the homeless. Most times, they let it go unless there were complaints.

Callie trekked across the grass, bypassing the newly paved path put in by the town council the previous year. The path had been a big hit, stretching from the town to the base of the Shenandoah mountains. Business owners, shop managers, and restaurants all celebrated the addition, citing the increased number of tourists it brought. Callie liked the path, too, but she didn't want to waste a single second getting to the scene.

"What have we got?" she asked as soon as she was in shouting distance of the uniformed officer.

"No sign of anyone," the young man said as Zel caught up to her.

Callie let out a breath, and a vague feeling of relief washed over her. While she'd hoped they'd find the girl, she couldn't think of any reason for Natalie to still be in that cave after a tryst unless she was badly hurt. Or worse. But they had the thread of a trail now.

"Did you see anything unusual?"

"Nah. A couple of blankets, empty beer cans, nothing you wouldn't expect to find."

"Okay," she said as she ducked under the tape. "Is Angie here?"

"Not yet."

"Send her down when she gets here."

The detectives walked toward the cave, both nodding at a second officer serving watch. They came to a large rock that rose six feet over Zel. Faded graffiti decorated the longest edge. On the other side, the ground sloped downward. Smaller rocks jutted out of the ground, acting as ledges along the slope. Callie considered the cave's small, dark entrance. When the park had first been built, before Callie was born, there were some in town who'd wanted to board up the cave. Others wouldn't allow it. Although not deep, the cave had served as a quick hideaway or barrier during the American Revolution, and later, the Civil War. Rumor had it that George Washington himself had holed up there for a quick nap. So, the cave stayed. A gate had been erected several years earlier, but it was never locked, and while it may have deterred the smallest of children, it only served to attract the rest.

Callie and Zel picked their way down. She paused, studying the litter that lay on the ground and in the bushes that grew out of the rocks. A fast food bag, cigarette butts, empty bottles. Taking out her phone, she snapped a few pictures, then kept going. The air cooled as she stepped inside, and Callie shivered. She'd never understood the attraction of caves. Sure, they might have their beauty, but bats lived there. And spiders. And sometimes bears—although she was pretty sure the park cave had never housed a bear.

She turned on the large flashlight she'd brought and swung it in a slow circle. More trash: bottlecaps, another fast food bag, more cigarette butts, and discarded vaping cartridges. "Do we know if Natalie smoked or vaped?"

"We can find out."

She took more pictures using the flash. Angie and her team would take their own pictures, but Callie knew that often things took longer than she'd like or worse, got lost. Ignoring the sensation of spider webs catching on the brim of her hat, she stepped further into the darkness. The cave narrowed, and the rock overhead came closer. Five more steps. Ten. Her fingers brushed up against cold rock. She'd reached the end. Callie's breathing slowed. No bodies, like the officer had said. Using her flashlight, she searched the walls and the ground. A scrap of fabric caught her eye, and she bent down. Wedged under a stone, the edges dark with mud, was a piece of blue t-shirt-like fabric.

Outside the cave, she and Zel compared notes. Like her, he'd been careful not to disturb any of the bottles, vape cartridges, or empty wrappers.

"Did you see the t-shirt?" Callie asked her partner and showed him the picture she'd taken.

He sucked in his cheeks. "Could be a coincidence. Popular color of t-shirt."

Callie didn't comment. She owned a blue t-shirt. Chances are that Zel did, too. Even so, she heard her father's voice in her head. *Coincidence is a lazy detective's excuse. No such thing in my book. Everything means something, even when it isn't what you're looking for.*

Her phone buzzed in her pocket. She saw Chang's name. "What's up?"

"Gotta line on that number the girl was texting with."

Callie pressed the phone to her ear. "You got a name?"

"Nope. Burner, but I was able to trace the number to a lot of phones from a big box store over in Richmond. I've put in a request for the names."

She thought a minute. "Did you try calling the number? Do the auto warranty thing?"

"No answer. Goes right to a generic message."

"Okay. Thanks." She hung up and gave Zel the update.

"Another dead end," he said.

Callie raised a hand to the sun, watching as Angie and her team set up at the cave site. It was true they didn't have much. A text chain, a scrap of t-shirt, and a burner phone from a store that probably sold hundreds a week. But it was something. "For now," she said. "For now."

Chapter Eighteen

The man combed his hair and ran a hand over the damp skin of his face. He wondered briefly if the girl would notice he'd shaved, then shook away the thought. Stepping back, he stared at his reflection in the glass. He wasn't good-looking, although his looks had improved since he was a teenager. Time had a way of softening the rough edges, filtering out the imperfections no one wants to acknowledge. It wasn't that he thought he'd grown more attractive, more that he didn't care the way he once did. He'd learned to accept himself now, to appreciate who he was. It hadn't always been that way.

He remembered the way she'd glared at him that time he'd dropped the roasted turkey on the floor. The damn thing had slipped out of the pan, hitting the tile with a smack. Hot juice and grease had splattered across his shoes and his pants. Before he could salvage the bird, the dog had pounced, tearing into the hot flesh. The loss of the Thanksgiving dinner hadn't been the worst part, though. It was her. Always her. The way she'd looked at him as though he were lower than the piles of shit the stupid dog left all over the neighbor's yard. Even now, he remembered the disgust that had rolled off her in waves. He'd almost drowned in it.

"You know what your problem is," she'd said, her lips pursed. This had been one of her favorite pastimes, telling him what his problem was. Most times, he stopped listening, leaving the room, before she could tell him what a loser he was. But he was trapped in the kitchen on this night—stuck with her, the dog, and the gnarled turkey. If he walked out, he'd have to pass through the crowded dining room with all the aunts and uncles and other assorted family members he couldn't give a rat's ass about. He didn't know why they called it Thanksgiving. It was more like hell in his book. The only thing he'd ever been thankful for was when it was over.

"Do you?" Her hands had landed on her hips by then, mouth still puckered. "Know what your problem is?" He'd wondered briefly if those lines around her lips would be permanent soon. He hoped so.

In the silence, the dog had burped, the sound making him jump.

"Your problem…" She'd paused as though she were about to reveal a great secret. He'd stifled a yawn, knowing that would only come back to haunt him later. "Is that you lack potential."

His mouth had fallen open. "Wh-what?"

"Are you deaf, too? Christ." She'd wiped her hands on her apron. "You lack potential." She'd said it louder the second time, and it had taken all his willpower not to smack her right then and there. "I've been trying to figure out what your problem is for a while. I thought it was being boring or thinking you're smarter than you are or a bunch of other things. Then it came to me. Your real problem is you lack potential."

She'd pointed at what was left of the turkey on the floor then. "Clean that up," she'd said. Before he could get his wits about him, she'd left him there, alone with the mess and those words echoing in his head. *You lack potential.*

He turned away from his reflection now, shoving thoughts of her to the corner of his mind. She couldn't hurt him anymore. He was different now. Stronger than she was. And smarter, too.

Tucking in his shirt, he tightened his belt buckle. Wanting to make a good impression, he considered wearing a tie but changed his mind. He left his room and walked down the hall to the padlocked door. He took the key from his pocket, his fingers fumbling with the lock. He could feel the drumming in his chest, the butterflies in his stomach.

A half-hour later, the girl watched him in a way he didn't find unpleasant. There was apprehension, of course, confusion, and maybe more than a little curiosity. He liked that. She averted her gaze whenever she thought he was looking, though, eyes darting away.

"Hold still," the man said. She froze. This should have pleased him, but instead, made him sad. He didn't want her to be afraid of him. Not really. But he pushed his disappointment aside. He had other things—more pressing things—to take care of first. He held his phone up, framing her in the shot. He snapped several pictures before asking her to stand. He could see she didn't want to, but she got to her feet eventually.

He lowered the phone. "Do you like the dress?"

She looked down at the blue cotton dress with the straps that tied at the shoulder. It was short—the way girls wore them these days—ending high above her knees. The soft fabric clung to her gentle curves and emphasized her small waist.

"Well?"

"I-it's nice," she said, her lower lip quivering.

Nice. The dress was hardly more than two scraps of fabric, but he kept his opinion to himself. Besides, the dress wasn't for him. Or for her. The dress was for the pictures.

"Turn to the left." He snapped a few more. "To your right." She did as she was told, but he could see she didn't understand. "Stay there." He went closer and reached out with his hand, taking one of the spaghetti straps between his fingers. She stared down at the floor, her breathing shallow. He pulled the strap down, then pushed her hair behind one ear. He stepped back. "Better. Don't move."

He snapped a dozen more, then lowered his phone. "You can take a break."

She lowered herself to the edge of the bed, her breath still ragged. He saw the way her gaze went to the door behind him, the way her body deflated when she calculated the distance before he could grab her.

"Can I go home after this? After you get your, uh, pictures." Her voice shook now.

"Not yet. Let me see how these came out." He hadn't said no, which was cruel, but he figured she'd be more cooperative this way. He was right.

"Why do you need pictures of me?"

Her voice no longer trembled. She was still afraid, but she was curious, too. Like so many teenaged girls, having her picture taken was a daily occurrence. One selfie after another. She was no different. He knew that from her social media sites. Hadn't he caught the way she lifted her chin when he asked her to pose? She probably hadn't even known she'd done it. Instinct probably.

"Does it matter?" he asked now. The words came out gruffer than he intended, and she flinched. He made an effort this time. "Don't worry about it."

Tears threatened, but she brushed them away. "Are they okay? The pictures?"

He dragged his focus away from her in that dress and scrolled through the photos. They weren't great by most standards. He wasn't a particularly good photographer, but it wasn't that. In spite of his attempts to brush her hair and put a little color in her cheeks, she looked like what she was—a scared rabbit. *So much the better*, he thought.

"They'll do."

"Okay, good." She blew out a breath. "You said I could maybe go home if they were okay."

He'd said no such thing, but he let her beg anyway.

"So, can I go home? I won't tell anyone where I was or about you."

There was a sweetness to her, a hopefulness he admired. She amused him. He cocked his head. "And where do you think you are exactly?"

She studied the room, taking in the pink-striped walls, the dainty curtains, and the white furniture. Seeing the room through her eyes for the first time, he realized it was the room of a much younger girl, not one who was almost grown. He should have known better.

"I don't know," she said finally. "Your house?"

He didn't respond to her question. "And what is it that you won't say about me?"

She clasped her hands together and rocked back on her feet. "I-I don't know. How you took me, I guess."

"Did I? I don't remember that."

She touched a hand to her head as though struggling to remember. "In the car, and I was tied up." He waited. "I mean, I think I was."

"You think?"

Her hands fell to her sides. "I-I don't remember getting here."

"Perhaps you hit your head?" His voice took on a soothing tone. "Do you need some aspirin or water?"

"No. I don't think so."

"You don't seem to know very much, do you?"

Her mouth opened and closed, her voice a squeak.

"Well, I think it's best you rest while I send off these pictures."

Her almond-shaped eyes grew rounder. "Where? To who?"

"To whom."

She blinked. "To whom."

"You don't need to worry about that. The only thing you need to think about is getting better. We need you to be well." He paused then. "Before we can talk about your future."

Her lithe body seemed to fold in on itself, punctuated by the sound of her gasp. "M-my future? I want to go home. You got your pictures. You said."

The man waved the phone in the air. "I've got to get to work now." He backed out of the room, pulled the door shut, and threw the outside bolt in one motion. Standing motionless, he heard the sound of her feet flying across the floor, her fists pounding on the wood. He sighed, pocketing his phone.

"She'll learn," he said to the empty hallway. "She'll learn."

There would be plenty of time to teach her now. No one knew where the girl was. No one suspected. All these months and weeks of planning had paid off. Everything was perfect. It had to be.

Chapter Nineteen

Callie scratched out a list of what she knew so far on notecards, one for each scrap of information.

One: Natalie left her house at six forty-five.

Two: She texted her mother fifteen minutes later.

Three: She sent a text confirming plans to meet Dating App Brian at the cave.

She tapped her pen to her temple, shifting the data around in her head. Behind her, drawers slammed shut, and phones rang. Hendo's baritone boomed as he repeated the story of his daughter's home run in a softball game the week before. Callie drank it in, letting the sounds settle over her, calm her frayed nerves. Taking a long breath, she returned to the notecards.

Four: A scrap of blue t-shirt was found in that cave but they couldn't yet tie it to Natalie.

Five: Beth Anne thought Natalie was meeting her, but Natalie had never confirmed.

Pen poised mid-air, she sat back. Assuming Natalie ditched Beth Anne and did go to the cave, how did her car get to Charlottesville? Callie laid the cards out in a makeshift timeline, mixing and shifting. From the minute Natalie arrived at her babysitting job until late that night, she'd received thirty-two texts. Most were part of a group text about a high school party taking place at the house of another student. The teen, a sophomore, didn't appear to be a close friend, and Natalie didn't respond to any of the texts other than to give a thumbs-up about the time. During those same hours, Natalie did send a handful of texts to three people: her mother, Beth Anne, and Dating App Brian of the burner phone. Callie drew a circle around the mystery phone number she'd written. Chin in her hand, she stared down at the number.

"Cal?" She looked up to find Zel holding the phone. "Beth Anne and her mother are on the way up."

Once they'd arrived, Beth Anne couldn't sit still. She plucked at the hem of her dress and squirmed like a toddler, her foot jiggling back and forth. Her pink blush, applied in the same broad strokes as the first time they'd met, now only served to highlight the dark smudges under her eyes. Callie felt sorry for the girl. Her friend was missing. It was no wonder she'd be anxious, sleepless.

Explaining they'd been able to get a copy of Natalie's last texts, she asked the girl about them now. "It looks like you made plans to meet Natalie after her babysitting job. Is that right?"

The teen started to answer but seemed to change her mind, leaning on her mother.

"Beth Anne," Mrs. Peters said, "you need to answer the detective's question." She squeezed her daughter's hand, and the girl lifted her head a fraction. Her mother squeezed again and nodded. "It's okay."

When the girl finally spoke, her voice trembled. "Well, we did sorta make plans to go over to the college." She looked down at her mother's hand on hers. "After she finished babysitting. At least, I thought we did."

"But she didn't respond?"

"No. I waited for a while, but she never answered after that."

"Did you go over to the college anyway?"

Beth Anne shook her head. "I don't like to go by myself. And Lara had already bailed."

"Okay," Callie said. "If Natalie had answered you, where would you have gone?"

The girl didn't think about it long. "Probably the Zeta house. That's where we usually go 'cause there's a guy we know from school that goes there now."

"He's in the fraternity?"

"Yeah. He lets us in. I think..." her words drifted away.

"You think what, Beth Anne?"

She avoided her mother's gaze. "I think he has a crush on me."

"The boy from Zeta?"

"Yes. He kept texting me to see if I was coming, but when Natalie didn't answer, I couldn't. And my mom would know if I took the car."

"But you wanted to go?"

The question hung in the air. Her chin wobbled, and the tears fell then. "I did. I hate myself for that. I was so mad at Natalie for ditching me. She knows I like Ronnie even though we haven't really talked about it." She twisted her hands in her lap. "We're like sisters, you know. We can tell what the other is thinking without even saying it. Like, I always know when she stops crushing on a guy. Or if she's sad or maybe mad at someone. We're the same like that." The words poured out of her now. "We're going to apply to the same schools so we can be roommates. That way, we can move right in and have each other, you know." Her voice faltered again. "That's our plan."

Callie noticed the way Beth Anne's mother worked to keep her own emotions in check, and she knew she needed to bring the conversation back around.

"Beth Anne, Natalie texted you before she went to her babysitting job that she had something to show you. Do you know what it might have been?"

The girl's mouth dropped open, and her hands stilled. "I forgot about that."

"Any ideas?"

Beth Anne's mother watched her daughter consider.

"Something about a boy, probably."

The suggestion didn't surprise Callie, but it wasn't enough. "But she could have sent you a photo or a screenshot of whatever it was. Does she normally wait to show you something in person?"

"Sometimes. Like when she wants to see how I react. Once, she waited to show me this video of her mom freaking out 'cause she knows I snort when I laugh."

Callie's pen hovered over the page. "What do you mean freaking out?"

Beth Anne shifted on the chair. "I don't know. Like upset about some bill or something and talking to herself." Mrs. Peters pressed her lips together, but before she could reprimand her daughter, Beth Anne half-apologized. "I mean, I know it's not really funny, and we shouldn't have laughed, but we couldn't help it."

Zel picked that moment to interject. "Do you know if Natalie's mother is worried about money a lot? Is it something Natalie talked about?"

The girl shrugged again. "Some, I guess. Natalie's worried about paying for college, but she has a job for clothes and stuff. That's why she's always babysitting. And her dad gives her stuff 'cause he feels guilty."

"Beth Anne," Zel asked, the words slow as though the idea had just occurred to him, "is it possible that Natalie went to the Zeta house without you?"

Her head swung back and forth. "No way. She wouldn't do that."

"You're sure?"

She hesitated again, "Well, there was this one time, but she didn't go alone. She went with Lara 'cause I was at my grandparents' that weekend. But I know she didn't go to Zeta Saturday night because Ronnie would have told me."

Callie leaned forward, her elbows resting on the table. "Is it possible that Natalie didn't go to the Zeta house with you because she was planning to meet the boy from Hooked instead? The one you said might be Brian or Ryan?"

The girl blinked. Disbelief, and then something like hurt, made her pale lips part and her chin fall. "No. She wouldn't." Even as she said the words, she looked from one detective to the other. "Wait. Do you think she met that guy? Is that what you think happened?"

"We don't know what happened," Zel said. "That's what we're trying to find out."

"She wouldn't," Beth Anne said again, her voice firmer now. "I'm not saying she would never meet the guy, but not at night without me or someone else. Natalie's smarter than that."

Beth Anne's mother put an arm around her daughter. "Nobody's saying Natalie isn't smart, honey. They're trying to find her, that's all." She turned her attention back to Callie and Zel. "I don't know what else my daughter can help you with, Detectives. She hasn't seen or heard from Natalie since she went to that babysitting job."

"I haven't. I've sent like a hundred texts, but her phone's off." Beth Anne's lower lip quivered.

Her mother stood up, dragging her daughter with her. "Can we go now?"

"One more question," Callie said. The pair sat down heavily, and Beth Anne tensed, her legs pressed together under the table. "Do you know if Natalie vaped?"

The worry written on the girl's face cleared a little. "Not really. She tried it, but she doesn't like spending money on it. Always says she'd rather have a new crop top or jeans or something."

"Okay. Thank you for coming in," Callie said and led them to the door. Back at her desk, she wheeled over a large whiteboard. She added a copy of Natalie's picture. One by one, she taped the notecards to the board. Holding the card with *uluv2hot2handel* written across it, she stared at the name.

Who was Dating App Brian? Her only suspect, O'Neill, turned out to have a credible alibi. Had Natalie even made it to the park, or had she changed her mind? Had she ended up at the college? And how did that lead to Charlottesville? The questions kept coming, and with no answers in sight, she went back to the list of Natalie's texts. Picking up where she'd left off, Callie scrolled through the beginning and middle of the alphabet, but other than Beth Anne and Dating App Brian, there was little that appeared relevant. After someone named Olivia, she clicked over to P. Three text exchanges. One with a girl named Paulette over a test. A second with someone named Peter asking when his son's swim lesson was and a third with the name Paul R. She clicked on it, her fingers tightening over the mouse.

See u Sat night

Heart pounding, she waved Zel over. She went back to the first text as he leaned over her shoulder.

Hi, Natalie. We've just moved here and the Holts recommended we contact you for babysitting.

Callie looked back at her partner, whose eyebrows shot up. The Holts had denied recommending Natalie to anyone. The date of the text was five days before Natalie went missing. She kept reading.

Natalie: *Who is this?*

Paul: *So sorry. This is Paul Randolph. As I said, I got your number from the Holts. My wife is Diedre and we have two boys, ages five and seven. The Holts spoke so highly of you, we'd love to have you babysit sometime. Do you think you would be interested?*

Natalie: *Sure. I have a pretty full schedule tho*

Paul: *I was afraid of that. Good babysitters are in high demand. We do pay $15 an hour.*

Natalie: *When do u need me?*

Paul: *Is this Saturday night too soon? You're probably already booked, but if not, let me know.*

Natalie: *I have to check with my mom*

I'll get back to u

what time?

Paul: *7. Probably be home by 10:30. 11 at the latest. The boys go to bed at 7:30. How does that sound?*

Natalie: *Great & let u know soon*

A day later, Natalie texted Paul back.

Natalie: *I'm free Sat night*

what's ur address?

Paul: *604 Hilltop Way. Do you know where that is?*

Natalie: *The neighborhood over from the Holts?*

Paul: *That's the one. See you on Saturday. My wife and I are looking forward to our first night out since moving here. Thanks again.*

They'd arrived back at the final text, the one Callie had already read. And there it was, the address they'd been looking for. *604 Hilltop Way.*

Fifteen minutes later, Callie pulled into the Randolphs' neighborhood, the tires of her car screeching at the turn.

"Whoa, Cal," Zel said and lifted a hand toward a sign. "Speed limit."

She grunted but lifted her foot from the gas.

"Turn left up here." Callie followed Zel's directions as she took in the two-story colonials flanked by thick oaks. This neighborhood, like the Holts, had been built when the paper mill was still thriving. After it shut down, some of the houses were empty for a while, but the packing plant had changed all that. Sagging porches had been fixed, roofs repaired, and dried-out yards were green again.

"Go right."

Callie turned the car onto Hilltop Way. The houses in this neighborhood were smaller than the ones where the Holts lived, but according to Ned Holt, the owners used the same community pool, belonged to the same association. The text from Mr. Randolph stated that the Holts had shared her number. It made sense that the Holts might have met the Randolphs and recommended Natalie, but the Holts had denied it. One of them was lying, and Callie had a bad feeling she knew which one that was.

"Should be down a bit on the left," Zel said, leaning forward to read numbers on the mailboxes. "A little further."

She passed a house with a double stroller parked out front and another with an oversized flag hanging over the front door. The numbers counted down, and Callie slowed, her hands in a vise-like grip on the wheel. They'd arrived, but there was no car in the driveway. There were no children playing out front. Instead, there was a For Sale sign in the yard.

"What the hell?" Zel asked as he climbed out of the car and strode toward the sign. "Did the realtor forget to take this down? Trying to drum up more business?"

Callie looked past him to the front door. A silver lockbox hung off the knob. Was it possible the Randolphs were selling already? Slamming the door shut, she studied the house. There were no cars on the street either. No bikes. No toys. By itself, that meant nothing. It could mean the parents were at work and the kids in school or daycare. But there was that lock and an empty feel to the place. Nothing about this looked right.

The detectives approached the front door and rang the bell. Getting no answer, Callie peered through the front window, but the drapes had been drawn against the sun, making it difficult to see more than a sliver of the living room. She made her way around the house to the back, where the blinds hid any view inside the house.

"I don't like this," she said, every muscle in her body tensed. "Something's wrong."

Following her back to the front yard, he agreed. "Should I call the realty company?"

Her gaze wandered over the quiet neighborhood again. Hilltop Way was the last street in the back of the neighborhood before a thick smattering of trees. It was as close to isolated as it could be. "Yes. Call them."

Chapter Twenty

Tori Leland's bright red nails flashed ribbons of color with every word she spoke.

"I got the listing from the Simpsons. They moved up to DC for his job and had to go quick." She flashed Callie a smile, and the detective realized the toothy grin with the matching red lipstick was probably Tori's trademark in the housing business. "Hey, I really like your hat. Is that a Javits?"

"What?" Callie touched a hand to the grey hat she'd worn that day. "No." She glanced at Zel and back at Tori. "You were saying the Simpsons had to move?"

"Yep. Only had about a week to be up there, get the kids in school, stuff like that. Anyway, turns out the new company is putting them up in a house until they can find one they like, so they can afford to take their time selling. Get the best offer. Some people have all the luck, right?"

Callie mumbled her agreement, then asked, "So, this house has been empty since then?"

"Oh, absolutely. It's an exclusive listing, you know."

"I don't know what that means," Zel said.

"No one can show it but me. No other keys but the ones I have. The Simpsons are good people. Anyway, I've shown it a handful of times. Yesterday, I had a couple with a baby on the way. This house has the perfect room for a nursery." She waved a hand again. "But you don't want to hear all that. My boss said you needed to see it pronto. If you like it, I can pretty much guarantee you a good price." The mega-watt smile widened. She opened the lockbox and fished out the key.

"We're not really in the market," Callie said. "It's police business."

That halted the woman. She wasn't smiling now. "Don't you need a warrant to go in someone's house?"

"That's why you're here."

The woman's eyes widened at that. "I-I don't know."

Callie's gaze wandered over the neighborhood again as they talked. The garage faced the woods rather than the front of the house. It occurred to her that a car could be parked there without being visible to the other houses on the cul-de-sac. The same was true for the front stoop where she stood now, partially hidden from the street by a wide tree with arching limbs.

"Is this about that missing girl?" the realtor asked then, her skin suddenly pale.

Natalie Hamill's disappearance had been the talk of the small town. The press release version stated only that a teenaged girl hadn't returned home after babysitting and possibly meeting a friend at the park. Fear at the college and among the locals hadn't reached the levels of five years earlier yet, but she knew how quickly it could happen. Without a quick resolution, seeds of doubt would sprout like weeds. She couldn't let that happen. Failure came with judgments. Why didn't you protect her? Why didn't you bring her home? As though she could snap her fingers and make it so. Real life wasn't like the movies. No Liam Neeson character with a special set of skills was going to swoop in and save Natalie. Or Emma Nicholls, for that matter. Five years ago, some of the town lost faith in her father, in spite of his sacrifices, and, by association, her. She figured it wasn't fair, but that only made it life.

"We can't comment on that," Zel told the realtor, his voice dropping an octave. He spread his hands wide. "You understand."

"Yes, of course," she said, although it was clear to Callie that his words only made her more curious.

"We'd really appreciate it if you could let us inside." Zel gestured at the key in her hand, trying on a smile of his own.

The woman drew in a breath and fished her phone out of her purse. "Can you give me a minute? I'd like to let the owner know."

Phone to her ear, the realtor stepped out of earshot. Zel faced Callie who tapped her foot as she watched the woman talk.

"Assuming she was here yesterday like she says, it's not likely Natalie is here now," Zel said.

Callie agreed. "But it doesn't make sense. Someone was sending Natalie those texts asking her to babysit. We've checked the address the guy sent her. This has to be the place."

"Okay. Let's assume Natalie did drive over here for a babysitting job. If the lockbox was here, she couldn't have gotten in. She'd know something was fishy." He pointed at the For Sale sign. "And that might have been a tip-off, too."

"Someone could have been hiding in the woods."

His gaze followed hers. "Maybe. But that's still thirty or forty yards from the driveway."

Again, Callie agreed. "And she got here at seven. It would have been light out. Some of the neighbors might have seen her. There might even have been kids playing outside."

The realtor came back, her arms swinging. "He says to tell you he's happy to cooperate in any way he can."

"Great," Callie said and held her hand out for the key.

The realtor's frown returned. "He expects me to stay." There was a slight hesitation. "You know, to make sure everything is okay."

"Fine." Callie pulled a pair of plastic gloves from her pocket. She tugged the gloves over her fingers and snapped them over her wrists louder than necessary. She wasn't in the mood to babysit the realtor, but it beat waiting for a warrant. "We'll need you to stay out of the way and try not to touch anything. Are we clear?"

"Got it," the other woman said, her chin bobbing up and down.

Callie took the key and unlocked the door. "We'll go in first. Standard procedure," she explained. "Nothing to be alarmed about. Stay behind us."

Zel moved ahead, down the short hallway. Callie followed, slowing at the living room on their left. Shadows stretched across the space, crawling up the walls. She stepped into the room and swept the curtains aside, letting the sunlight in. Dust floated upward, and she scratched at her nose, fighting a sneeze. Thick carpet the color of sand covered the rectangular floor, ending at a large brick fireplace. A leather sofa faced the window, flanked by a pair of end tables. A painting featuring a pair of ducks hung centered over the sofa. She wheeled back toward the realtor.

"I thought you said the owners had moved."

"They did." She gave a short laugh and pointed at the couch. "I staged most of the rooms so the house would look more livable. You'd be surprised how many people are put off by an empty house, although if you saw some of the furniture people actually had, you'd swear none at all was better. Once, I had a seller with a house near Wintergreen. Great area. Nice sized lot. But the furnishings were crap. I mean, hideous isn't a strong enough word." She paused to take a breath. "Anyway, all this stuff is rented until the house sells."

Callie gave the room a final once-over, then headed to the back of the house, where she found the kitchen, a dining area, and a small den. Like the front of the house, the rooms were shrouded in darkness. She rolled up the blinds, blinking at the bright light. Although the rooms were furnished, there were no pictures stuck to the refrigerator or spatulas poking out of a canister on the kitchen counter. A lone magazine had been placed on the coffee table in the tiny den. Not a single TV or computer anywhere. She walked to the back door and peered outside. Weeds poked through cracks in the patio, and one of the swings on the playset hung at an angle, unused and forgotten.

"How long did you say the house has been empty?"

"A couple of months. Maybe less."

"Did you have any showings this weekend?" Callie asked.

"No. I was supposed to have one late Saturday afternoon, but the guy canceled. Annoying, really."

Callie pursed her lips but didn't comment. The realtor waved them up the stairs, where four doors stood open. The first two led to a pair of bedrooms, each with a twin bed and nightstands. The third door opened up to a bathroom with a small window that overlooked the backyard. Callie walked to the end of the hall and the master bedroom. She heard Zel and the realtor's steps behind her. There was a queen-sized bed with a tan bedspread pulled smoothly over the mattress. Light-colored drapes hung from the ceiling to the floor. Callie stared at the beige walls and the sterile furniture and the mostly empty walls. All this time, they'd been fixated on the hours after Natalie babysat. But there were no Randolphs at this address and no children to babysit. No one had lived here in weeks.

She remembered the texts then, the ones sent after seven p.m. from Natalie's phone. Several to Beth Anne, the ones to *uluv2hot2handel*, and two to her mother. Would Natalie have pretended she was babysitting? Why? Or had someone else been sending those texts? Her head hurt thinking about it, and the noise in her head grew louder, pounding against her skull. There were too many questions and not enough answers. Except one. The Randolph family didn't exist.

"Cal?" Zel reached out and touched a hand to her arm, pulling her from the thoughts.

Back downstairs, Tori's heels clicked across the floor. "Are we done? I've got another appointment."

Callie spun around in a circle. The lockbox on the front door hadn't been tampered with, nor had the back door. They had no evidence that Natalie had made it inside this house.

"Is there a basement?" she asked.

"Don't I wish? Basements always sell to families, you know. Or guys who want mancaves. I have a few clients with those at the top of their must-have lists." She gave a small chuckle. "I don't think the wives mind too much. Gets them out of their way."

Zel laughed along with her, and Callie forced a smile. She pointed at a door at the back of the kitchen. "Is that the garage?"

"Sure is. A two-car with a workbench. The washer and dryer are there, too. Big must for most buyers."

"Could we see it?"

The woman checked her phone. "Sure, but we have to be quick."

Callie and Zel followed the realtor down the two steps into the garage. A pair of oil stains on the ground marred the grey concrete, but the floor had been swept clean. To their right was the washer, dryer, and utility sink. A long, wooden table occupied most of the opposite wall. A pegboard hung over it, studded with hooks.

The realtor prattled on about the size and the double doors and Zel nodded along while Callie inspected the perimeter. She walked closer to the two doors. They were shut tight, making the air in the garage hot and stuffy. Looking up, her gaze swept past the door pulleys and came back. She stared harder, moving forward. Zel and the realtor fell silent, watching her. Callie took another step until she was under the pulley, her head tipped upward, her skin tingling. Everything inside the house had been clean, untouched. Not a wrinkle in a bedspread. No telltale drips in the kitchen sink. Nothing. The doors and windows had been locked. But the garage told a different story.

"Someone's been in here," she said, pointing up. Zel's eyes followed the direction of her finger. "This door's not locked. It's been opened manually."

"That can't be right," Tori said, her hair swinging across her shoulders.

"The owner could have left it that way," Zel suggested.

The realtor contradicted him. "No. He was adamant that I close the doors with the buttons on that wall and exit through the house. I'm sure of it."

"Someone was here," Callie said again.

Zel looked from the ceiling to her. "Okay. How would someone get in?"

She faced the door, studying the style. "There's no outside lock. Probably put a coat hanger or something like that through the top and disengaged the lock. Then it's a matter of rolling the door up from the bottom." Callie lifted a shoulder. "My dad did it a couple of times at our house when the power went out. Anyone can do it."

Zel considered the idea and nodded. "Okay. So, let's say someone was here. Nothing's disturbed. There's no sign of anything out of the ordinary."

"I think we should get forensics out here."

The realtor's hand flew to her mouth.

"To find what?" Zel asked. He jerked his chin toward Tori. "She was here with clients yesterday. Whatever might have been here is gone now."

"We don't know that."

"Cal…" He drew out her name. "It's a wild goose chase."

"I don't think so," she said, walking the perimeter of the garage a second time. At the washing machine, she slowed, started to move on, but went back, drawn by an odor. The faint scent reminded her of a hospital or the morgue, and she sniffed the air. With her right hand, she reached out toward the washer and lifted the lid. The smell, still subtle, was stronger now. She looked inside and found a single item. A wadded-up rag. There was no mistaking the scent now. Chloroform. Picking it up by the corner, she held it toward her partner.

"Call Angie."

Chapter Twenty-One

"**M**y head hurts," the girl said, her words slurry. "I feel weird."

The man stood over the bed, his hands on his hips. Was she pretending? The idea made him angry, and his nostrils flared. Her head flopped to one side then, and he relaxed. She did have a glassy look about her, and her movements were slow and clumsy. Perhaps he'd overdone it on the sedatives, but it had been necessary after the photo shoot. She'd kept banging on the door hour after hour, stopping only long enough to rest her hands before pounding again. She was making it hard for him to post those pictures, to keep everything on schedule. He'd had to sedate her.

"I'll get you some food and something to drink," he said now. Her lips moved, but he couldn't hear whatever it was she said. Damn. He had given her too much. Now, he'd have to wean her, and that was going to cause delays. As he stood there, she drifted away again. He picked up her wrist, feeling for a pulse. It was slow but strong enough. He laid her arm back down and pulled the blanket over her. He'd return when the drugs had worn off a bit.

He slid the bolt in place and descended to the large open living and kitchen area. The floor had been swept clean, and the windows sparkled and shone. Pleased with his good work, he sat down at his computer. The pictures he'd taken were acceptable enough, although no real photographer would ever feel threatened by his work. It didn't matter though. The kind of men who would be clicking on these pictures weren't the kind who cared about such things. He knew what they would see. Young and pretty. And innocent. The dress had been a wise choice. It showed enough skin without really showing anything. The color played well with her lightly tanned skin and white-blond hair. He reached out and touched the screen with his finger. The hair alone would bring in views. Whether he liked it or not didn't matter. That's the way the world worked.

He'd already selected the best of the lot. Two side poses and one frontal shot. He loaded them into the new photo editing software he'd purchased. In each, he made sure to blur the background, the girl the sole focus of each shot. Satisfied, he saved them again.

Someday, she might understand why all this was necessary. Then again, he wouldn't count on it. Teenaged girls could be so ungrateful. He knew that for a fact. Hadn't his own sister ranted and raved whenever she didn't get everything she wanted? It wasn't like she didn't already have everything she needed. God knows she used her looks the way other people used goods and cash, trading smiles and touches and who knows what else for necklaces, dresses, and booze. She'd overspent, accumulated debts she couldn't pay. Older, looks long since faded; she was a drunk hag now. Maybe she always had been. He would have chalked it up to karma if he believed in that sort of thing.

He'd wanted to save his sister once. They'd gone to a party out in a neighborhood they had no business being in, but she'd dragged him along anyway. She'd heard about it at her school, she'd said. This was a wonder to him back then. At his own school, he was worse than an outcast. He didn't exist. No one spoke to him, much less told him about parties.

"You have to protect me." Her mouth had puckered to a pout, and her voice had left little room for argument.

He'd tried to protect her. He had. But when some guy with slicked-back hair invited her to his country club for a late night, she'd ditched him faster than you could wolf down ice cream on a hot summer's day. Winking at the boy, she'd laughed at her younger brother. "Go home to mommy. I don't need you when I've got a real knight in shining armor." The guy had only lifted an eyebrow at that, but he'd gone along with it anyway. Why shouldn't he? A roll in the hay would cost him nothing more than a couple of drinks at a bar far swankier than either he or his sister had ever seen before. When she'd come home later that night with her clothes askew and her lipstick smeared, he'd figured it out. She hadn't wanted protection. She'd wanted an audience.

Natalie wasn't like his sister, though, and he would be in control this time. He stared at the pictures on the screen again. She'd need a new name. He'd been thinking about it for a long time, thinking about what name would fit a girl like her. There was Angel. But he'd decided against it even though her hair floated around her head like a halo. There were the usual names for this type of business. Amber. Ashley. Crystal. But she wasn't any of those. He ran his fingers through his hair, picturing her in that blue dress. Angel. He kept coming back to it, but something about it wasn't right. He tapped on the keys, searching for other names that meant Angel or were similar. Ariel. Angela. No. No. And then, there it was. Angelica. Yes, that would be her name.

The site wasn't easy to get to. There were passwords and firewalls that changed on a regular basis, but he knew them all. He clicked past the images of the other girls before he uploaded the pictures, then entered the name Angelica.

His hand hovered over the send button. Once he pressed it, he couldn't undo it. Her pictures would be out there. It would start in earnest then. He went to the base of the staircase and cocked his ear to listen. Silence. Back at his desk, on the screen, her face stared back at him, unsmiling. He'd tried to coax a laugh from her, telling the only jokes he knew. He would have settled for a grin or a twitch, but she'd only stared at him. When his tone became less jovial and more growl, she'd backed away, almost falling. He'd forced himself to calm then, asking nicely once more for a smile. Still, she'd held back, refusing to give him that one small thing. Remembering now, his finger settled over the send button again. He pushed. It was done.

Chapter Twenty-Two

"We've got several hair samples, the chloroform rag, some fibers we have yet to identify, and a candy wrapper," Angie told Callie. "Some of the hair samples are blond like the girl. We'll compare those against the hairbrush from the girl's dresser."

"What about the rag?"

"Generic. No brand or markings. You can buy a dozen on Amazon or any other bulk site."

"Damn." Callie had hoped the cloth had come from somewhere identifiable. "When will you know about the blond hairs?"

"Soon. I'm doing my best, Callie."

"I know." She switched tactics. "Any usable fingerprints in the garage?"

"Washing machine lid was wiped clean. Light switch, too."

"And inside the house?"

A sigh came across the line. "There are a lot of smudged prints on the doorknobs and cabinets, places where prospective buyers might have touched." There was a brief pause. "I got a handful of good prints in a couple of the bedrooms and in the den, but that's all. I'll run them against the database."

"You don't sound optimistic."

"I'm not. Based on what we got from the garage, I doubt your guy left any fingerprints."

Callie had already guessed as much and thanked the woman again.

"Sure. I'll be back in touch when I know more."

Callie hung up and filled Zel in on the report. He nodded but didn't meet her eye.

"Sorry I doubted you, Cal." The words were spoken so softly she had to lean forward to hear.

Her heart swelled. They'd been partners for two years, and no apologies had ever been necessary. Zel was a good detective, and she was glad to have him as her partner. "Please. If you hadn't kept Suzie Sunshine chatting, I might not have seen anything at all."

"She did like to talk, didn't she?"

"That she did." She gestured toward the phone in his hand, eager to put the apology behind them. "What did you get from the neighbors?"

His face cleared as he scrolled through the notes on his phone. "Most of the neighbors didn't see or hear anything out of the ordinary. The guy that lives in the house next door is eighty and wears glasses so thick, with the right light, he could use them to start a small fire. And there's no way he heard anything either. Directly across the street is a middle-aged couple. Empty nesters." He gave her a half-smile. "That was their word. Said they were away last weekend, camping. Also, haven't seen anything unusual. The last house in the cul-de-sac is a younger family with three kids. I talked to the mom, but she didn't know much either. Well, maybe something, but I don't know. She said her son might have seen something, but she wasn't sure."

"How old is the kid?"

"Fourteen. Should be getting home from school soon."

"Good. Let's get him in here."

Forty-five minutes later, Callie and Zel sat across from Jenny Templeton and her son, Frankie. "Thanks for coming in and talking to us, Mrs. Templeton," Callie said.

"Call me Jenny," she said, her voice bright and cheery. "I watch all the police shows, you know." The woman looked around at the cinderblock walls of the small room and the awkwardly placed window cut into the far wall. The blinds were drawn on this day; no one watching from the other side. Callie got the impression the woman was a little disappointed by this. "Except SVU. A little too, uh," she paused, shooting her son a quick glance, "violent for my taste. You don't have that here, do you?"

Fighting the urge to roll her eyes, Callie told her no. "As you know, Mrs. uh, Jenny, we're investigating a possible break-in at the Simpson house a few days ago. You told my partner your son might have seen something."

"Yes, well maybe. I mean, the very idea that someone might break into a house right on our street is so upsetting to me."

"We have reason to believe this was an isolated incident."

"I hope you're right," she said, shuddering.

Callie shifted her attention in the boy's direction. "About what you saw, Frankie. Could I ask you a few questions?"

"He's ready," the mother spoke for him.

Callie wondered at the mother's description. The boy didn't look ready for much of anything. Head drooping and shoulders hunched, he'd shown little interest in the conversation so far.

"Frankie," Callie said, "do you remember seeing anyone at the Simpsons' house last Saturday evening? Maybe around seven or after?"

"Yeah. A girl was there." He tossed his head in that way that teenagers did, his hair flying back from his forehead. "Seemed kinda lost."

Before Callie could ask another question, the boy's mother chimed in.

"Tell them what you told me, Frankie. How she was looking at her phone while she was driving."

"Mrs. Templeton," Callie started.

"Jenny."

"Right. Jenny. How about if Frankie tells us his story first, and then you can help us out after if there's anything he's forgotten?"

"Oh, of course." She pantomimed zipping her mouth closed. "I'll be quiet as a mouse."

"Thank you." Callie noticed the boy was definitely paying attention now. "Frankie, did you speak to her when she was lost?"

"Nah. She was going slow and looking at her phone like my mom said. That's how come I figured she was lost."

Zel's pen scratched over his notebook. "Do you know much about cars?" he asked the boy.

"A little."

"Do you know what kind of car she was driving?"

"An old lady one." He chuckled at his own joke, shutting his mouth when his words failed to earn the laughter he'd hoped for.

"What color was the vehicle?"

"Grey, maybe. I think it was kind of dented in the back."

"Okay." Callie's fingers twitched. Ms. Hamill's car—the one Natalie had been driving and was found at the bus station—had a dent in the rear bumper. The dusky blue color had faded over the years and could easily be mistaken for grey.

Zel reached into a file and pulled out a photo of the car they'd found in Charlottesville. "Is this the car?"

"I think so. It's dented the same."

Callie picked up the questioning again. "Where did she go in her old lady car?"

The boy relaxed at that. "She parked out in front of the Simpsons' house. She didn't look lost anymore."

"Could you describe her?"

"Not really. I didn't see her face. She had blond hair; I know that."

Callie decided to keep the picture of Natalie in the file.

"Did you see her go up to the door?"

"Nope. I was riding my skateboard out in my driveway. I've got a ramp. Four feet high. My dad and I built it."

"That sounds cool," Callie said, gratified to see the boy smile. "So, you didn't see her go inside?" He shook his head, his hair flopping. "Did you notice if she was alone in the car?"

Frankie frowned as though thinking about it. "Pretty sure she was."

"Good. Did you see her go back to her car?"

"Uh, I don't know what she did." He scratched at a pimple. "I saw the car go up the driveway after that, but it wasn't right away."

"Into the garage?"

He gave a small shrug. "I guess."

Zel held his pen over his notebook, silent, and Callie continued questioning the boy.

"Was the girl driving the car?" she asked.

"Who else?" Callie said nothing, waiting. "I mean, she must have been, right?"

"But you didn't see her?"

"No. I guess not." He slumped lower.

"This is very helpful, Frankie. Really," she told him. His face brightened. "Did you see the car again that night?"

"Maybe. I think so."

"When was that?"

"Later. It was dark out. I know that. Mom made me take the trash out to the curb, and that car went past."

"You're sure it was the same car."

"Pretty sure."

"Did the car ever come back?"

"Not that I saw."

"When the car left that night, was the girl driving again?"

Frankie didn't answer right away. "I don't know. I didn't see."

"Thank you, Frankie. That's a big help."

The boy frowned again. "Did that girl break into the Simpsons' house?"

"We don't know what happened yet," Zel said and closed his notebook. "That's what we're trying to find out."

"Frankie," Callie said, "Is there anything else you can think of that might help us?"

"No. Well, maybe one thing, but it might be dumb."

"Nothing you have to say is dumb." The boy perked up again.

"Well, I could be wrong, but I think someone stole the For Sale sign that was in the yard 'cause I remember it wasn't there that day, and the next day it was back. I told my mom about it." He looked over at her, and she nodded. "But she said since the sign was back, not to worry about it."

Jenny spoke up then. "I told him it could have blown over in the wind or a storm or something, and someone set it up again. I didn't think it was important."

"No one did anything wrong," Zel assured the pair. "That could be exactly why the sign was down. No harm done."

"Was anything taken?" Jenny asked. "Or vandalized?"

"Nothing that we know of."

"Oh, good," Jenny breathed, her hand over her heart. "I wouldn't want to think we had a criminal roaming our neighborhood."

Although Zel assured her for a second time there was nothing to worry about, Callie felt sure that Jenny Templeton would be telling stories of her neighborhood break-in and police interview for months. She might even plan cocktail parties around the opportunity.

She got to her feet. "Thank you both for coming in today."

After Zel returned from walking them out, he flipped a chair around and sat opposite her. "What do you think?"

She sat back, fresh exhaustion seeping into her bones. "I think Natalie Hamill went to that house Saturday night at seven o'clock. I think the sign was gone. Not from the wind or a storm. I think someone deliberately took it down." She took a breath. "Natalie Hamill went up to the door expecting to meet Paul Randolph and his wife and kids. She met someone all right, but it wasn't a dad and his family. Instead of a babysitting job, she got a mouthful of chloroform." Callie pictured the girl going to the door, being led inside, then caught unawares. "Once she was out, he moved her car to the garage. He drove her car inside and cleaned up, wiping everything down. Then he waited until it was dark to replace the sign and drive off with Natalie in the trunk."

Zel drummed his thumbs on the back of the chair. "I'll buy it. But there are a couple of things I don't get. How did he get there?"

She thought a moment. "It's a two-car garage. There would have been room. He could have come back for his car later."

"Maybe. But returning to the house and risking being seen again doesn't fit. This guy's careful."

He was right. "Okay. He could have parked on the other side of the woods. Then he comes through the woods to the side garage where he breaks in."

Zel nodded along. "Makes sense. You can't see the garage from the other houses. And the street on the other side of the woods, Exeter, has an apartment complex and a couple of rows of townhouses. It would be easy to leave a car in one of those lots and get it later."

The detectives fell silent, each lost in their own thoughts and theories. Callie understood it didn't matter how the kidnapper managed to get to the property unseen. What mattered was that he'd staged the babysitting job to lure Natalie Hamill to that house.

"Natalie wasn't a random target," she said, voicing the thought nagging at her brain. "He'd been watching her. Waiting for the right opportunity. He used a house he knew was empty. He set her up. He used her car and her phone."

Zel considered the idea. "What about the dating app guy, then? How does he fit into this?"

It was a good question. Was it possible Natalie had two predators simultaneously? What were the odds? Or was it something more terrifying, something that meant this was no ordinary kidnapper? He was smart. Cunning. He'd set up another suspect, a fictional one, *uluv2hot2handel*, to send them spinning in the wrong direction. It made sense. She raised her head, more afraid than ever for the missing girl.

"I think this guy at the house, the one who pretended to be Mr. Randolph, I think he is the dating app guy. I don't think it's two guys at all. I think it's one."

Chapter Twenty-Three

Captain Jackson rubbed his hand across his mouth. "Probably not a good idea to go public with this." He didn't expect an answer, nor did he get one. "Have you spoken to the mother yet?"

"I'm going there after we're done." Callie dreaded telling Ms. Hamill there had been no babysitting job. No doubt she would feel she should have known, should have suspected, and maybe in a perfect world, that was true. Sadly, Callie knew life didn't work that way anymore. Kids had hundreds of "friends" online and the man who'd impersonated a dad looking for a babysitter knew how to play the game better than most.

"Good. Where are we on the forensics?"

"Should have an answer on the hair samples soon."

The captain gave a short nod and got to his feet. "Good work, Detectives. I know it may not feel like it right now, but it's damn good work."

Neither responded, both knowing that, again, no response was required. Callie liked Captain Jackson. As a detective, he'd never had the instincts her father did, but he had other skills, and since he'd taken over as captain, she'd learned to appreciate those.

"Callie?" Captain Jackson was standing now.

She stopped at the door, waving Zel on ahead. "Yes?"

"Are you doing okay?"

"Fine. I'll be better when we find Natalie."

He nodded, his heavy brows furrowed. "How's your father?"

The question hit her hard. She hadn't heard a word from either of her parents, nor had she called them. It was true she was busy with the case, that it took up every waking minute, but after the things she'd said, she should have checked in at the very least.

"I'm not sure," she said finally.

"He's heard about the case, though."

"Yes."

She drew herself up, bracing herself for another warning about not making things personal or about being careful.

"Have you asked him for his thoughts?"

Callie's mouth dropped open.

"I know your father, and I might have had different ways of going about things, and what happened with the Nicholls case might have been avoided, but I never doubted his ability or his instincts." Callie couldn't breathe, floored by his words. She tried to remember anything her father had said about Jackson and couldn't come up with much.

"Jackson's not the quickest, but he's dependable. Has a level head. Other cops, like Chang, put too much faith in their guns, real and virtual, if you ask me. A gun is only as good as the man that carries it." She'd tried to get more out of him, but he'd clammed up. When she thought about it, he'd said more than usual as it was.

The captain's face softened a little as he studied her. "I see the same in you," he said. "Good instincts. That stubbornness that drives a detective to push harder. You've got all that."

"Thank you," she said. "But..."

He arched an eyebrow.

She gave an embarrassed laugh. "I thought maybe there was a but coming."

"No, but," he said with a short chuckle of his own. "This time, anyway." He paused as though considering. "Say hi to your dad for me, will you?"

"Sure."

"Good." He stood, all business again. "And Callie, keep me in the loop. No exceptions."

Chapter Twenty-Four

"She took that pretty well," Zel said as they left the Hamill house.

Callie said nothing, her heart hurting for Erin and Jeremy. She hadn't missed the way the boy had put his arm around his mother, or the way he'd asked the questions when she'd been unable to.

"Does this mean you're closer to finding her?" he'd asked, his voice small with hope.

"It means we're closer to figuring out the sequence of events on Saturday night, which puts us closer to finding her, so yes." It wasn't a lie exactly, nor was it the truth. It wouldn't matter if they knew every step of Natalie's abduction if they couldn't figure out who took her or where. The boy had nodded, accepting her words at face value. Ms. Hamill, too, seemed to take comfort in that.

"Does that mean it wasn't Natalie who texted me not to wait up for her?" she'd asked, hands trembling only a little.

"Probably not," Callie had answered. "Either he told her what to text, or he used her phone to keep anyone from suspecting anything was wrong."

Callie remembered the way the woman had visibly shivered then but found the strength to hold it together. Looking at Zel now, she gave a short nod. "Yeah, it could have been worse."

"Hey, it's getting late. Would you mind if I ducked out to have a bite with the wife? I'll be back in about an hour. We should have Angie's full report by then."

Callie didn't mind and told him so, leaving out that she had a task of her own. She pulled into the driveway of her parents' house at half past six.

In the old days, her father had called that cocktail hour. He'd make one drink, savoring it before dinner. At seven, he and her mother would sit down to dinner and talk about their days. Even as a child, she'd hung on his every word, fascinated by the stories of the department and the cases and the evidence. John Forde may not have been a superhero like Batman or Superman, but to her, he might as well have been. She knew she wasn't the only one who felt that way. Growing up, she'd often heard him described as brilliant, brave, and strong. What girl wouldn't idolize a father like that?

She sat behind the steering wheel, still and unmoving. Maybe she was angry at her father for what he hadn't done since the accident, the way he'd allowed himself to wither on the vine like an overripe tomato, but maybe she was angry at herself, too. He'd never told her he was invincible.

Taking a deep breath, she climbed out of the car. At the front door, she knocked once before walking in. The silence in the living room made her stop. She couldn't remember the last time she'd been in the house when the TV wasn't on. The tray next to her father's chair was empty. The soft sound of voices drifted down the hall, and she walked past the living room to the back of the house and the kitchen. In the doorway, she froze. Her father, in his wheelchair, had his back to her. He sat at the table, a plate in front of him. Her mother bustled at the stove, spooning mashed potatoes and gravy onto a plate.

"Catherine said to tell you hello," she was saying. "I can't tell you how delighted she was that I called her to go to lunch today."

Her mother had gone to lunch? She'd left her father? Alone?

"You went out?"

Her mother whirled around, her hand rising to her throat. "Oh, Callie," her mother said. "I didn't hear you come in. Are you okay? You look white as a ghost."

Her gaze wavered from her mother to her father. He remained facing away from her, his back ramrod straight. "I'm fine."

"Thank goodness. Are you hungry?" She waved a hand at the food on the stove.

Her stomach gurgled in response. "Uh, yeah, I guess I am."

Her mother's grateful smile made Callie want to cry. She took the plate her mother offered, the comforting smells tickling her nose.

After they were both seated, she asked, "Did I hear you say you went to lunch with Catherine, Mom?"

Her mother flushed. "I wasn't gone long, and your father insisted he'd be fine. I brought him an Italian with extra salami. You know how he loves that."

"And how is Catherine?"

"Oh, wonderful as always. It was so good to see her." Callie half-listened as her mother launched into a story about her oldest friend and her brood of grandchildren. She had no doubt that Catherine had dropped everything to have lunch with Maura. In the months following the accident, her father had kept her mother at his side night and day, and he'd vetoed visitors other than Callie soon after he'd gotten home, preferring to wallow alone. He said nothing now.

Studying his face, she couldn't help noticing the hard set of his jaw and the vein twitching at his temple. He was still angry. He'd yet to speak to her or even acknowledge her. Although disappointed, she couldn't blame him. Not really. It didn't matter that everything she'd said had been true. She didn't know how he felt, not really. But the more she thought about it, the more irritated she became. If she didn't know how he felt or how much he was hurting, maybe that's because he hadn't told her. It wasn't like she hadn't asked over the years or that she hadn't suggested counseling or any other number of things. He'd closed himself off to everyone but Maura, and even then, he was barely there.

Callie stabbed at her meatloaf, her fork pinging against the plate. After a moment, she realized her mother had stopped talking, the kitchen silent. Although her father still avoided looking at her, her mother stared openly.

"Are you sure everything is okay, Cal? You seem like something is bothering you."

So much is bothering me, she wanted to shout. My father won't speak to me. You walk around as though nothing is wrong. A girl is missing, maybe dead. She set her fork down and wiped her mouth with her napkin. "I need to talk to Dad for a few minutes."

His head came up, and his eyes landed on her. Hard. Unflinching. She knew that gaze. She'd seen it in the precinct, usually reserved for the lowest of the low. She forced her chin up.

"Alone."

Chapter Twenty-Five

"Whatever you have to say, I've heard enough," Callie's father said. His jaw clicked in barely suppressed anger. His hands found the wheels, and he started to back away from the table.

"Maybe so, but I'm going to say it anyway, and you're going to listen."

He threw up his hands, red-faced now. "Fine. Get it over with then."

She gazed at the man who was her father, the man who'd taught her to ride a bike and swim and chase after bad guys. He wasn't always this angry. It hurt her to see him push everyone out of his life, to see him quit. It hurt even more that he couldn't see the man he still was. She sat on her hands to stop them from trembling.

"When I was little," she said finally, "I made up superhero names for you. FordeMan the Super Detective and SuperForde. Everything you did—"

"I don't want to hear this." His hands returned to the wheels.

Callie ignored him. "Everything you did was for other people. It didn't matter whether it was searching for hours to find Mrs. Rackley's cat or driving Mom all day and night to visit her cousin when she got in that wreck or keeping Hampstead safe. You made it look so easy. And it isn't. I know that now. It's hard to be that amazing. It takes work and dedication and..." her voice softened. "And love. It takes so much love."

From under her lashes, she stole a glance at her father. Although he still held the wheels in his hands, the chair stayed still. His chest rose and fell.

"The other night, I said some things I'd wanted to say for a long time. Maybe I didn't have that right. I haven't been where you are now. Or where Mom is. But I have been where I am. And from where I'm sitting, the man I worshiped is giving up. And I love him too much to let that happen without a fight." She paused again, her voice shaking with emotion. "I don't expect you to save cats or be the town superhero anymore. But I do expect you to be mine. My superhero. And mom's. And all we want is for you to be here with us. Really here. Not pushing us away every chance you get." A tear rolled down her cheek. "I'm here to ask you to give us a chance to be a family again. Please."

Callie watched the face of the man she'd loved for as long as she could remember. He sat frozen in his chair, his legs unusable, his hands gripping the wheels, his expression unreadable.

"You can think about it if you want. However long—"

"I don't need to think about it."

He wheeled back to the table and picked up his glass of water, draining it in two swallows. The minutes dragged on, and she waited for him to say something, anything, holding her breath so long her chest hurt.

"What you said the other night," he started, "about your mother. That was maybe the worst. I don't care about me. I still don't, but your mother deserves better. You're right about that."

"I'm sorry, Dad. I didn't—" She stopped when he held up a hand.

"It's my turn to talk." Her mouth snapped shut. "I was angry with you the other night. I still am. No father should be talked to like he's been a naughty child." He let out a long breath. "But I've been angry for so long now, I can't remember when I wasn't. I'm not sure when the last time was that I felt anything else."

Callie wanted to reach out and take his hands in hers, but she held back, recognizing he didn't want her sympathy. Not right now.

"You were right about your mom. Did you see how happy she was tonight? It was good to see her smiling. I'd almost forgotten how beautiful she is, you know. Actually, I forgot a lot of things these last few years." He rubbed his hands over his thighs. "I forgot your mother makes a damn good meatloaf. And mashed potatoes. Sounds pathetic, doesn't it?" He half-smiled, but it was tinged with a sadness that made tears spring to her eyes. "I owe you a thank you, I guess. Dragging your mother down was never my intention."

Whatever trace of a smile he'd attempted faded. "I'm not going to make promises I don't know if I can keep, but I'll try harder." He raised his palms. "That's the best I can do."

"I'll take it." Cheeks wet now, she reached out and took his hands. To her surprise, he let her.

When he looked back at her, she could see he was fighting his own tears. "I'm not a superhero, Cal," he said, his voice a whisper now. "I never was."

"You're wrong, Dad. You're the best kind." She swallowed the lump in her throat. "The real kind."

Chapter Twenty-Six

Callie helped her mother load the dishes while her father wiped the table. No one spoke, the comfortable silence like a favorite blanket that had been lost and recently found. The clink of silverware and splash of water from the faucet were music to Callie's ears. She was home. When they'd finished, her mother gave her a warm hug and a kiss on the cheek.

"I'm going to knit a while," she said. "I'm guessing the two of you have some catching up to do."

"What do you mean?" her father asked, a gruff edge to his voice. "We did that already."

Callie almost laughed. Her father wasn't a man prone to introspection, and he'd already had enough emotional talk for one night—hell, for a month. She realized then that her mother hoped the visit was about more than a reconciliation.

Maura dried her hands with an old kitchen towel. "Callie needs your help, don't you, Cal?"

Her father's brows rose high on his head before his eyes lasered in on her. Callie felt her skin grow hot. "Uh, yes, maybe."

Her mother gave her a pat and padded out of the kitchen. In the quiet, the captain's words came back to her, forgotten temporarily in light of the family breakthrough. *What are your father's thoughts?* That question had driven her home, something she hadn't had the courage to do since she'd berated her father. She guessed she owed the captain a thanks for getting her here, even if she wasn't sure about the rest.

121

"What's this about, Callie?"

She sat down across from him, her legs suddenly weak. She'd never known a wiser man, a better detective. Maybe he couldn't chase after bad guys anymore, but she'd once believed he could outsmart them again. She'd begged him to try. But he hadn't been interested. He'd rebuffed every overture she'd made, ignored every plea. If she brought him into the investigation now, even for something as simple as his opinion, would that only be reminding him of what he couldn't do? A drop of water fell from the faucet, the splatter loud in the silence. What if she failed? What if she never found Natalie? Would he plunge deeper into depression—from despair to hopelessness? It would be her fault this time. She knew she owed him an answer, but the words she'd planned to say stuck in her throat.

"You've grown more beautiful, if that's possible," he said.

Callie felt the sting of tears again, sure that only a father could say such a thing and mean it. It wasn't true, of course. She'd never been beautiful. Pretty maybe—in the right light—and if her hair and makeup were done, but certainly not now. Not after long days and sleepless nights. Not when she couldn't remember the last time she'd washed her hair. She touched a hand to her ponytail, smoothing the flyaways that hung past her cheeks.

"Is this about the missing girl?"

The air went out of her. The other night, he'd been angry. But more than that, he'd been afraid. On this night, though, she heard something worse—dread.

"It was, but it's not important." To hell with the captain's question. This was her call, and she had no intention of dragging her father down again. The legs of the chair scraped against the floor when she stood. "I actually need to get back. We're expecting a forensics report any time."

"Angie doing it?"

She jammed her hands in her pockets. "Yep. She's still the best around."

He eyed the badge she had clipped to her waist and sighed, his breath whistling. She withdrew her hands, so her jacket fell over the badge again.

"I really should get going." She gestured toward the hall. "You want me to give you a push to the living room?"

He could get there himself, and they both knew it, but he nodded. She grabbed the handles and wheeled him to his spot in the living room, the one that faced the TV. She picked up the remote and handed it to him, then leaned over and gave him a kiss on the cheek. "I love you, Dad."

His hand caught hers. "Callie."

She froze. How many times had he said her name like that through the years? Half rebuke. Half insistence. The message always clear. Stop whatever you're doing and listen.

"Yes?"

"Sit down."

She sat, hands clasped in her lap, knees pressed together.

"Tell me about the girl."

Chapter Twenty-Seven

*Z*el picked up the pages from the printer. "I'm going to drop a copy on the captain's desk."

Callie nodded, aware that Jackson had insisted he receive a copy of Angie's report as soon as it arrived. Zel could have forwarded it, but Jackson liked paper. He was old school that way. Staring at her computer, she read through the report, zeroing in on the section regarding the hair found at the house.

Two dozen samples of hair were collected from the house located at 604 Hilltop Way. All samples were discovered in several locations throughout the house and will be identified in the following manner: HS0001 (six strands), HS0002 (four strands), HS0003 (four strands), HS0004 (four strand), HS0005 (three strands), HS0006 (two strands), and HS0007 (one strand).

The report went on to give an analysis of DNA characteristics from the hair samples as well as toxicology reports. Sample HS0003 had traces of amphetamines. HS0004 tested positive for blood pressure medicine. The others were clean.

Callie considered the seven samples. If one of the samples came from the abductor, this information could be useful, although there was no guarantee that any of them had. According to Tori the realtor, she'd shepherded a handful of potential buyers through the house in the weeks since it had gone on the market. It was also possible that in spite of the deep cleaning Tori insisted had been done before the house was put on the market, some of the hair samples might belong to the owners or their children or the cleaning company. The possibilities made her head swim.

Zel plopped down in his chair. He tipped his head toward her computer from across their desks. "Is there a match?"

"Haven't gotten that far yet." She focused on the screen again.

The sample designated HS0001 was found in the entryway, kitchen, and garage.

Callie read the locations of each sample, but her mind kept coming back to HS0001. This was the one that mattered most. Four similar strands had been found in the garage, one near the washer and dryer although there had been none on the chloroform rag.

She scrolled down, scanning the next pages. Reaching page six, she drew in a breath, then read out loud.

From sample HS0001, two strands were compared against the samples provided from Erin Hamill for Natalie Hamill, minor. These strands, referred to as HS0001-3 and HS0001-4, were located on the floor of the garage. In a comparison of HS0001-3 and HS0001-4, each of which included the follicle, to the sample provided by the family, there were consistencies in characteristics with the samples for Natalie Hamill.

A chart listing each sample and the criteria used followed. Callie skipped ahead to the summary.

In the opinion of the tester, the sample HS0001 most likely belongs to the minor identified as Natalie Hamill.

Cal sat back. Hair analysis had been lambasted in recent years, the result of questionable results and overly enthusiastic prosecutors. While testing had improved, the FBI had stopped trumpeting microscopic hair analysis after it was reported that there had been errors in dozens of cases. As a result, Callie didn't expect to use this hair analysis in a court of law, but it was compelling enough on its own. *Consistencies in characteristics. Most likely belongs to the minor identified as Natalie Hamill.* Combined with the knowledge that Natalie had gone to that address, it was enough to cement their theory that she had entered the house, been overpowered with chloroform, and abducted in her mother's car.

Zel tented his fingers over his lap. "I guess that means she was in the house."

"And the garage."

He agreed. "What about the candy wrapper?"

The torn candy wrapper had been found on the floor of the garage, wedged between the washer and dryer. She'd forgotten about it but wasn't sure it mattered much. The wrapper could have been there for weeks or months. "What was that again?"

"Black licorice."

"Licorice?" She frowned. Black licorice was an odd choice of candy, but she knew some people liked it.

"Yeah. Partial wrapper."

"Any prints?"

"Nothing usable."

"DNA?"

"Nope." He pushed away from his desk. "Grabbing coffee. Want some?"

"Sure." Going through the report a second time, she made notes, starting with the positive drug screens on samples HS0003 and HS0004. Rolling her finger over the mouse, she searched for the section on the candy wrapper. There it was.

Traces of black licorice.

She wrote the words in her notebook, tapping her pen against the paper. According to the report, the candy wrapper appeared to be dust-free. This seemed odd, considering it had been found next to a dryer where lint and dust floated around like oxygen. No matter how she looked at it, that implied the wrapper hadn't been there for long. But how long was not long?

Zel set a cup on her desk. "I added some of that nasty creamer you like."

"Thanks." She took the cup and shot him a grateful smile. "How was dinner?"

"Good. Marcie made lasagna. Damn good, too." He patted his belly. "Might've had two helpings."

Her smile widened. She was glad to have a partner who found joy in small things like lasagna and second helpings and a stolen dinner with his wife. That was sometimes necessary in a job like theirs. As the daughter of a career detective and now one herself, she'd seen the way the job could bring a person down, drown them in darkness. Zel carried the light for both of them.

After another hour of picking apart the report, Zel tapped his watch with his finger. "It's after ten, Cal. We could both use some shuteye."

After ten already. Another day gone without finding Natalie.

"You won't be any good if you're a zombie," he said.

Feeling the weight of the lost hours, she closed her eyes for a long moment. "You're right. Go home, Zel," she said finally. "There's nothing else we can do tonight."

"Only if you leave, too."

"I will. I promise."

True to her word, Callie followed him out to the lot and slid behind the wheel of her car. She pulled out after him, watching as he turned north toward his house. Without knowing why, she drove west, rolling past the diner and the post office, toward farm country. The headlights of her car cut through the darkness, finally shining on the sign for Ben's family farm, Piney Dairy Farm. She peered up the long drive, a single light visible in an upstairs room of the house. Car idling, she wondered if he was alone or if he was still seeing the woman from the city. Her chin dropped to her chest. What was wrong with her? But she knew. Natalie's disappearance and the hours with her father had brought all the old emotions and losses to the surface. What she needed wasn't Ben, his husky whisper in her ear, or his arms around her. What she needed was sleep. And to find Natalie Hamill.

Chapter Twenty-Eight

The man carried the tray up to the bedroom, careful not to spill the milk in the glass. He set it down on the floor and released the bolt. Pushing the door open, he picked up the tray again, his gaze on the girl. She sat on the edge of the bed, her hands in her lap, her hair hanging over tear-stained cheeks. He liked the way she watched his every move, tracking him when he set the tray on the table he'd placed between the bed and door.

"Eggs, fruit, and toast," he said. "And milk. Good for you."

Her head came up. "If you cared what was good for me, I wouldn't be here."

His fingers curled into a fist. How dare she question his motives? She was a child. That wasn't her place.

"I want to go home." Tears slipped from her eyes, and he knew that whatever fight he'd heard in her voice moments earlier was gone. "I miss my mom and my brother."

"That's not possible right now."

He saw the way she clung to his last words. *Right now.* He liked giving her something to hang on to. And she was wrong about him. "I do care about what's good for you," he said. "I know you can't understand that yet, but it's true."

Her light-colored brows drew together. She had questions. He expected as much, but now wasn't the time. He nodded at the plate. "You need to eat."

She didn't move.

"Now." He drew himself up to his full height. "It's not a choice." He saw

128

the way her gaze flicked over the food. He'd cut the fruit into small pieces and scrambled the eggs. Next to the plate was a single napkin and a plastic fork. She'd get real silverware later, but she'd have to earn it. He cleared his throat and pushed the table up close to her. Hand shaking, she picked up the fork and moved the eggs around the plate. He waited. After a minute, hunger took over as he'd known it would, and she began to eat. Pleased, he reminded her to drink her milk.

He watched her as she ate, sipping from a bottle of water. Her manners were acceptable but could use some work. He'd give her lessons when she was more compliant.

When she finished eating, he said, "That was very good, Leigh."

Her chin jerked upward, her mouth parted. "That's not my name."

"A name is an arbitrary thing." He knew this to be true enough. For the website, he'd chosen Angelica. It suited her. But so did Leigh. That name was for him. He gave her a smile. "Names are random, really. John or David or Michael. Mine could be any one of those and none of them tell you who I am." She frowned. "Think about it. You're assigned a name at birth before you're even a person." Pausing, he wiped the table with a cloth he pulled from his pocket. "You were given the name Natalie by your parents, right?" He didn't wait for her to answer. "Do you know what Natalie means?" The girl slowly shook her head. "It comes from the Russian name Natalia and has two meanings. The first is birthday, which isn't that special since the name is actually given on the day of your birth. The second, though, is more interesting. Natalie also means Christmas."

He liked the way she leaned forward. In spite of her fear, she was curious. It was one of the things that had drawn him to her. She had a group of friends, was popular in that way that only high school girls seemed to care about, but she kept herself apart. Maybe it was her parents' breakup. Maybe it was being a swimmer. He couldn't understand wanting to spend so much time in the water, but he did recognize the solitary aspect of it. He'd read a story once about an Olympic swimmer who'd said the water was her source of strength, her place of meditation. When she was in the water, she forgot about the rest of the world—it was just her and the water. Although he hated pools, he'd liked that. The man imagined it was something like that for Natalie, too. Swimming was an escape. Of course, she wouldn't be able to do that anymore.

"I'm not sure why you would want a name that means Christmas, though," he said now, "but like I told you, a name is arbitrary. I suppose one could stretch the meaning to something like the spirit of giving, but still…" He lifted his palms. "I mean, look at you. Nothing about you makes me think of Christmas. You're not fat. You don't have a beard. You're not an elf." She didn't laugh, but he didn't care. At least she'd stopped whining. "If I call you Leigh, it's because that's who I think you are."

He waited a moment to see how she would respond. When she did speak, he was pleased again, although not surprised. Teenaged girls were more predictable than people thought.

"Who am I?"

His lips twitched, but he held back the answer on the tip of his tongue, answering another question instead.

"The name Leigh means from the meadow, like a field full of flowers. It also means delicate." He gestured toward her with the water bottle. "You, for example—"

"I'm not delicate."

The man bristled. He didn't like to be interrupted, but he understood she hadn't been taught that yet. Manners weren't prized in today's world, not the way they used to be. He forced himself to relax, keep his voice even. "You are not delicate in the sense that one might think. Breakable or weak, but delicate as in full of grace. In your case, Leigh means full of grace."

"Oh. That's nice, I guess." Her chin lifted even as her voice quivered. "But my name is Natalie."

Her refusal to understand, to respect him could not be allowed. His fingers curled over the plastic bottle. "Your name is whatever I tell you it is."

"Not to me."

The bottle flew across the room, droplets of water spraying into the air. The girl ducked, falling backward. Shaking, she curled into a ball, her knees drawn up to her chest. The bottle missed her, landing in the middle of the bed. The water pooled on the bedspread, a dark splotch in a sea of pink.

He stared at that water, at the girl still cowering, and forced a calm into his voice. "This is your fault, Leigh."

She said nothing, didn't move.

With a sigh, he slid the table back and gathered the plate and cup. At the door, he looked over his shoulder. "You'll learn, Leigh, you'll learn."

Chapter Twenty-Nine

"Callie, I didn't expect to see you this early," her mother said as she pulled the door open wide. "We ate breakfast, but..." Her words faded as her gaze flew to the stack of papers tucked under Callie's arm. "Oh. You're here to see your father."

"Gold star, Mom," Callie said with a smile. "Is he up?"

"Oh, he's up." She wiped her hands across her apron. "Ate like a horse this morning, too," Maura said. "Asked for extra eggs." She pointed toward the living room. "He should be out in a minute." Her bird-like hands fluttered over her apron. "He's doing better, isn't he?"

Callie heard the crack in her mother's voice and was tempted to reach out, but she sensed doing so might not be wanted. Instead, Maura waved a hand in the air, her sleeve slipping back, exposing an arm that was barely more than skin and bones. The sound of Callie's sharp inhale made Maura jerk her sleeve down and back away.

"How about some coffee cake?" her mother asked, hurrying down the hall. Callie followed. "Mom."

Her back to her daughter, Maura cut a large slice and set it on a plate. "Shall I warm it up?"

"Mom. Turn around."

Maura stood a moment longer before facing her daughter. "I've lost a little weight," she said.

"A little? You're as skinny as a..." Her words fell away before she could say she'd been reminded of some of the addicts she'd seen, hardly more than walking skeletons. Why hadn't she noticed the way her mother's clothes hung off her or the way her flesh sagged? "Are you sick, Mom?" Her voice trembled with each word.

"Don't be ridiculous, Callie. I'm a little thin."

Her mother had never been overweight, but there had been a roundness to her body and a fullness to her face. Her father used to laugh when she'd threaten to go on a diet, saying he liked a woman he could hold onto. Her chest tightened as she studied her mother now. Of course, she had worried about her mother. Worried she was isolated. Worried she was depressed. Hadn't she said all of this to her father the other night? But she hadn't seen her mother. Not really.

She exhaled. "Mom. I'm so sorry." The words sounded lame even to her ears, but Callie didn't know what else to say.

Her mother lifted her chin, shaking her head. "You have nothing to be sorry for, baby. You have your own life to live. Babysitting me and your father isn't your job. Or your brother's."

If not her, Callie thought, *then who?* Her older brother had joined the service after school, moved up the ranks, and was deployed overseas. He had another year before he'd be home.

"Besides," her mother said, "things will be better now." She pointed at the papers Callie had brought with her. "Your father will be better."

Callie didn't acknowledge the hope or the fear etched into the lines of her mother's face. "I told Dad about the case last night."

Maura's lips turned up at the corners. "Oh, I know. He made notes for an hour after you left."

"He made notes?"

Her mother nodded before handing Callie the plate of coffee cake.

"Thanks," Callie said, her mind already straying to Natalie and the report.

"Go wait in the living room," her mother said. "I'll tell him you're here."

Waiting for her father, Callie stood at the front window, watching the neighborhood come to life. Outside lights were extinguished, and garage doors rolled up. Mrs. Calloway hobbled down her driveway to retrieve her paper. A man in a baseball hat walked a large, black dog of indeterminate breed. These things were normal. But there was nothing normal about life inside the Hamill house, nothing normal about a missing girl.

"Callie." She whirled around to find her father watching her. "Is something wrong?"

"No, no," she assured him and gestured at the pages she'd laid on the table. "I just wanted to run something by you."

He nodded. "What is it?"

"Forensics on the hairs and the garage."

Wheeling over to the table, he looked down at the report, but made no attempt to touch it.

She remembered their conversation from the previous evening and the way he'd looked drained when she'd finished talking.

"You're up to speed now," she'd said. He'd stayed silent, unmoving, except for a single tic near his left eye. There'd been nothing more to say then, and when she'd leaned over to kiss him good night, he'd grabbed her, his fingers closing hard over her arm.

"Don't let him get away with it, Cal. You can't let him."

She almost hadn't brought the report, but something about it nagged at her, and she couldn't rest until another set of eyes—a set she trusted—read it, too. Still, she realized bringing the report was crossing a line and he might not be ready.

"It's okay if you don't want to read it, if you're not up to it."

He reached out and fingered the edges of the pages. "I'll read it."

Callie watched him skim over the first few pages. Once or twice, he grunted but was otherwise silent; his mouth closed in a grim line. He flipped to the next page. To counter her growing anxiety, she got to her feet, her hand wrapped around her phone.

"Callie," her father said, peering over his glasses. "You're going to put holes in the carpet if you keep that up."

She started to remind him that any holes in the carpet had been made by him years earlier, but when her phone buzzed, she lifted it in the air. "Saved by the bell." Moving to the corner of the room, she answered. "Forde."

Zel's voice cracked over the line. "Frannie Carter's boss called. Says she hasn't shown up for work and isn't answering her phone. It's the second day he hasn't been able to get ahold of her."

Brian O'Neill's girlfriend. Callie straightened and grabbed her bag. "On my way."

Her father held the pages in his hand, a question in his eyes.

"Gotta go, Dad." She pointed at the report. "You can keep that." If he said something as she rushed out the door, she didn't hear.

On the way back to the station, she dialed Angie.

"Hey, Callie," Angie answered. "I don't have anything new for you yet. It's going—"

"It's not that," she said. "Do you remember the ink pen and paper I brought over, the one from the guy we interviewed at the plant? Were you able to get the prints?"

There was a moment of hesitation. "Yeah, I remember. That went on hold when you put a rush on the evidence from the house."

"I know, and I'm sorry, but I need those prints, too."

There was a second moment of silence. "I thought you said you knew who they belonged to already. This is for confirmation, right?"

It was what she'd said, but now Callie's mind churned with possibilities. Frannie was O'Neill's alibi and until she couldn't be reached, they hadn't had a reason to question her credibility. "Right, but something has come up. I need to know if those prints match anything at the Randolph house. Even a partial."

"Ah." The sound of Angie's fingers tapping on her keyboard echoed over the line. "I'll get on it as soon as possible, but I'm not making any promises. Anything else?"

Callie pulled into the lot at the station, her phone cradled between her shoulder and her ear. "Maybe. I don't know yet."

"Well, at least you know your own mind," she said with a snort before the line went dead.

At the station, Callie raced up the stairs to find Zel standing with Jackson, heads bent together, faces grim.

"What have we got?" she asked.

Zel answered. "Other than what I told you, not much."

The captain handed them a sheet. "Here's her address, but let's not overreact here. She could just be sick and turned her phone off. Could have left for a family emergency."

"We'll check it out." Zel pocketed the page.

On the ride to Frannie's apartment, Callie thought about their visit to the bookshop where she worked. A small woman with a round face and rounder figure, she wore her hair in a bun that sat low on the back of her neck. She spoke in a soft, girly voice and had a penchant for chewing the inside of her cheeks.

"Saturday night?" Frannie had asked. "I had to work late, but I went over to Brian's when I got off."

"When was that, ma'am?"

She'd had to crane her neck to look up at Zel. "Um, nine-thirty, I think."

"And you were there all night?"

Her face had flamed to match her rose-colored lipstick. "I'm old enough to spend the night out, Detective."

"No one's saying you aren't, ma'am. Just verifying where you were."

She'd looked from Zel to Callie and back, chewing at the inside of her cheek. "Brian is a nice guy. He is." When neither of the officers commented, she filled the silence. "He told me about his past after you came to see him. He's changed. He wouldn't hurt a fly."

"No one said he hurt anyone," Zel said.

More chewing. "But you think he did, don't you?" Her small hands found her waist as she rushed to assure them that he didn't. "He couldn't. We were together," she said. "All night." The door to the store had opened then, and she'd straightened. "I have to get back to work."

Zel thanked her for her time and handed her his card. She pocketed the card without a glance, her attention already on the customer who'd come into the store. Callie started to follow Zel out, but stopped, facing the woman again.

"Ms. Carter?" Frannie's head came back around. "I was wondering how you met Mr. O'Neill."

"Why does that matter?"

"It doesn't really," Callie said with a shrug. "Call me curious." She held up her left hand. "Single."

A tiny smile crossed the woman's face for the first time that afternoon, and for a brief moment, she stopped biting the inside of her cheek. "Yeah. It's hard to meet people in this town, isn't it?" She stepped closer to Callie. "I went on one of those dating sites. Matchme.com. Do you know it?"

Callie didn't, but she lied. "Sure."

"Anyway, at first, there were no matches I had any interest in, so I widened my radius, you know." When Callie shook her head, Frannie explained. "I included D.C. and Virginia Beach, the whole state. I have a friend who met a guy from Harrisonburg, and they're married now." She took a breath, her gaze cutting to the customer browsing through the cookbooks. "Anyway, after I did that, I got a hit on someone right here in Hampstead, and that turned out to be Brian."

"How lucky." Callie dipped her head. "But what made you click on him? Was it his picture?"

Frannie laughed, a high, tinkly sound. "No way. His picture was a cartoon photo of The Incredible Hulk. I figured he had a sense of humor. That's why I clicked on it." Her smile took on a rueful quality. "And now here we are."

"You must be more trusting than me. I haven't been able to make myself really get out there yet."

"Oh, you should. We have to have trust, don't we? Otherwise, it would be a very sad way to go through life."

Callie didn't comment. In her experience, that kind of trusting attitude is what got people in trouble or killed. "How long have you and Mr. O'Neill been dating?"

"Four months."

Callie gave an appreciative nod. "That's nice."

The customer held two books in her hands now and was coming toward the counter. "I've really gotta go," Frannie said, chewing again.

"Sure. One more thing."

The woman let out a long breath. "What?"

"Did Brian use his real name or something else? I never know what to think of those things when I'm on one of those sites."

"Oh, right. Yeah, a lot of guys have these funny names they use to make them stand out." She slipped behind the counter, watching as the customer stopped again, this time near the display of bestselling mysteries. "Brian had one. It was kind of cute, especially because of the picture." She leaned forward. "It was *callmeincredible*. I mean, it sounds stupid out loud, but beggars can't be choosers."

The fact that Frannie had met Brian through a dating site had bothered Callie, but he'd been out five years without incident, and she'd verified his alibi. Their inquiry into O'Neill had stalled. But that was when they'd believed Natalie hadn't gone missing until after her babysitting job, a job they now knew never existed.

Callie's mind whirred. Natalie arrived at her job at seven. If O'Neill posed as Randolph, he'd still have plenty of time to knock her out and get home to Frannie by nine-thirty. But that only presented more questions. Presuming he didn't take Natalie to his house, where did he take her?

She looked at Zel and the captain. "When was the last time anyone saw Frannie Carter?"

"That we know of?" Zel asked. His brow creased, and the worried look he flashed her made her draw in a breath. "Monday night, when we interviewed her."

Chapter Thirty

Neither detective spoke as they drove to Frannie's Chatford Apartment on Cherrywood Road. Zel pulled the car into an empty space, his hands wrapped around the steering wheel. The complex was small, housing only twenty apartments total, ten on the first floor and ten on the second. Shaped like a horseshoe, the complex faced the road, each apartment overlooking the parking lot and accessible from the outside. There was no sign of Frannie's car in the lot.

The pair climbed the stairs, passing four apartments before coming to number nine. Callie scanned the area again. A pair of cars passed by the building and half-empty lot without slowing. Other than the muted sound of a TV down at the end of the row, there were no other sounds. Zel knocked once, waited, and knocked a second time.

"What do you think? Should we find the super?" he asked. They'd agreed this would be the plan if there was no answer.

The building manager answered the door with a cigarette dangling from the corner of his mouth. "What d'ya want?"

Callie held up her badge. "A few minutes of your time is all."

The scowl he wore deepened. "Christ, what has the idiot gone and done now? It's not my fault, you know. I send my check every month, but that bitch keeps it all for herself. I know she does. He wouldna even been in that store if his mother bought him some decent clothes."

Callie's eyes narrowed. The clothing comment came from a man wearing a sweat-stained crew neck tee from another decade and low-hanging pants decorated with dust smears, paint, and a heavy keyring.

"She's always whining for more," he said, "but I told the judge you can't get blood from a turnip and—"

It was Zel who cut him off. "We're here about Frannie Carter."

The cigarette dropped lower, the ash curling. "Frannie? What's she done?"

"Nothing," Callie said. "Her boss reported she hasn't shown up for work, and she isn't answering her door or her phone."

He caught the cigarette between his bony fingers before it fell from his lips. "She missing?"

"We don't know that," Zel said. "Do you have a key to her apartment?"

He took a long drag from his cigarette before blowing the smoke over his shoulder. "You got a warrant?"

"We're making a welfare call."

"What the hell does that mean?"

"It means we don't need a warrant to enter a home if we have a reason to check on the welfare or safety of a resident," Zel said.

"Yeah? You say welfare. I say nosing around someone's place."

An edge crept into Zel's voice. "Do you have a key, or do we need to get a locksmith?"

"Shit." The super looked past the detectives to the quiet parking lot. "I gotta key." He stepped outside and closed his door. "I don't like it, mind you, but I'll do it."

They waited for him to stub out his cigarette, then followed the man back to the apartment. The man took the keyring from his beltloop, flipped through the keys, and inserted one into the lock.

Both Zel and Callie pulled on gloves. The super's dark eyes widened.

"We'll take it from here," Zel said.

Callie saw the play of emotions on the man's face. Anger. Curiosity. Fear.

"Sure," he said, running his hand through long, brown hair. "I'll be downstairs if you need me."

"Prick," Zel muttered under his breath after the guy left. It wasn't like Zel to let a guy like that get to him, but Callie recognized he was more anxious than he was letting on. "Ready?"

Callie's hand went to the butt of her gun. "Ready."

"Frannie? Ms. Carter?" Zel called out the woman's name in the dimness of the dark apartment.

Callie fumbled for the lights, feeling her way until she found a pair of lamps. She exhaled as light filled the small living room. Zel crossed to the front window and drew the heavy curtain aside. He let it drop again, then faced her before walking down the hall and peeking into the bathroom and bedroom. "All clear. Guess we can rule out home sick."

A silence fell over the apartment, interrupted only by the hum of an air conditioner. Callie sized up the apartment in a few short minutes. Shaped like a box, the front end consisted of a living, dining, and kitchen combo. If the current state of the apartment was any indication of Frannie's housekeeping skills, the woman bordered on obsessive-compulsive. The magazines on the coffee table were stacked in a neat pile. Two yellow accent pillows looked out from the navy blue sofa like a pair of eyes. Only a coffee maker, tucked under a cabinet, sat on the otherwise clear kitchen countertop.

Going into the kitchen, Callie opened the refrigerator. Examining the contents, she frowned. Where Callie's contained takeout cartons, condiment packets, and an open can of soda, Frannie's held lettuce and vegetables and milk that hadn't yet expired. With a sigh, she moved on. Inside the cabinets, she found the usual collection of plates, silverware, and glasses. The last cabinet, though, served as a pantry. Coffee. Rice. Oatmeal. She started to close the door when something plastic caught her eye. She stood on tiptoe to see around the staples. A package of licorice. Black licorice.

"Jesus," she said out loud. "The Randolph House."

"What?"

"Look." She pointed at the red and black package as Zel stepped around the tiny kitchen table. "Black licorice. The same kind we found in the garage at the Randolph house."

The lines on his forehead deepened to ruts. "What are the odds?"

Callie didn't comment. She pulled out her phone and snapped a couple of pictures before closing the cabinet again. "Find anything?"

"Nah. She likes mysteries. She's got an entire bookshelf devoted to the Sue Grafton series." Callie followed his outstretched finger, pointing to the wide bookshelf. "The rest of it is stuff I don't recognize."

The pair searched the bathroom next. A purple toothbrush sat next to a tube of toothpaste. Callie nudged Zel. One toothbrush. That could mean either O'Neill didn't keep one at Frannie's apartment, or he did, and Frannie had packed hers. Closing the door, they moved on to the single bedroom. A double bed flanked by a pair of nightstands ate up most of the space. The only other furniture, a tall chest, had been shoved into the corner next to a long closet with sliding doors. Callie opened the drawers of the chest one by one. None of the clothing appeared to have been disturbed. If Frannie had gone on a trip, she was neat about it. Zel slid open one closet door. Dresses and pants and tops hung in neat rows, arranged by color. A shoe rack on the floor held four pairs of flats, one pair of almost-new sneakers, and a well-worn pair of winter boots. No one would ever mistake Frannie Carter for Imelda Marcos, Callie thought.

Callie looked up at the three boxes sitting on the closet shelf, each labeled in black marker. Pictures. Papers. Mementos. She pulled down the first box. Inside, pictures were sorted into envelopes. She sifted through a few, but none seemed to be recent, and none were Brian. She searched the second box. Again, she found nothing. In the third, she found a cocktail napkin and a paper drink parasol. The Mint Julep. Callie recognized it as a nice restaurant in Charlottesville. She found herself wondering if these were from a date—one with O'Neill. She replaced the box, and Zel slid back the second door, revealing the other half of the closet.

"Ah," he said in a rush of air.

Under the hanging clothes was a large, navy blue suitcase with red trim. Callie reached out and touched the bag tag. There was Frannie's name and phone number, written in the same style as the lettering on the boxes. Her fingers traced the red trim. The suitcase looked new, like a promise that had yet to be fulfilled. She picked it up, but it was empty.

"She could have a smaller bag if she was only planning to be gone a couple of days," Zel said.

"Without telling anyone?"

"She could be with O'Neill."

She scanned the room a second time when another thought struck her.

"If she decided to go out of town, why would she leave her laptop?" She pointed at the computer resting on one of the nightstands. The size of the pit in her stomach doubled. "Seems odd, doesn't it?"

"Some people like to unplug, but yeah, strange."

Callie crossed the room. On top of the laptop was a photograph of Frannie and O'Neill. In the picture, the small woman gazed up at him, her face in profile, her lips parted. She wore a peach-colored dress and a sweater. The pair sat on a bench in Hampstead Park, an area Callie realized wasn't far from the cave that had been searched only the day before. Unsmiling, O'Neill's eyes were half-closed as though he'd been caught mid-blink, his head bent and obscured in shadow. Callie imagined the scene almost as though she were there. A walk in the park on a cool spring day. Frannie, newly smitten, asking someone to take their picture.

She showed it to Zel. "The happy couple."

Her partner grunted in response and pointed at the computer. "Better leave that. In case."

Zel didn't say what in case was, but she understood. If Frannie's disappearing act turned out to be something more suspicious, the computer would be evidence, the kind better accessed by LJ, their favorite tech expert, or someone from Angie's team. Replacing the photograph, Callie took another look around the tidy apartment. Frannie Carter wasn't the type of woman to leave her boss in the lurch. She wasn't the type to go on vacation on a whim. Or without a suitcase. Something was wrong. Very wrong.

Chapter Thirty-One

B rian O'Neill lived in a small bungalow less than ten minutes from Frannie's apartment. A call to his work and his cell went to their respective voicemails. Another call and the detectives met his landlord at the front door.

"Has Mr. O'Neill done something wrong?" the woman asked, her heavily veined hand pushing back thick grey bangs. "I'd hate to lose him as a tenant. He's one of the best I've had. Never a moment's problem."

Callie's phone buzzed, making her jump. She pulled it out. Her father. She hit the automatic "I can't talk" reply and switched the phone to silent.

"No, ma'am," Zel said. "We don't know that he's done anything. He hasn't shown up for work, and we're checking things out." He gave her the same welfare speech.

She harrumphed, her bangs lifting a little. "He's a good guy. Fixed my computer for me last month."

Zel shot Callie a look. Neither of them liked the sound of that. "The key, ma'am."

The woman snapped a key from her clip. "It's this one. With the star on it," she said with a sniff. "You can leave it under the mat when you're done."

Callie watched the woman climb back into her car and slam the door before she peeled away, tires squealing. "Making friends wherever we go."

"Ain't it the truth?" He put the key in the lock. "Shall we?"

Callie took two steps inside and froze, her blood running cold.

"Holy shit," Zel said before turning his head away.

Frannie Carter sat slumped against a bloodied wall, eyes unseeing, ashen skin mottled with cuts and bruises. Forcing herself to breathe, Callie walked closer, taking stock of the room. Shards of ceramic lamp littered the floor, and an upended coffee table blocked the hall. A yellow purse, its contents scattered, peeked out from under the sofa.

Next to her, Zel drew his gun from his holster and raised a finger to his lips. She nodded, falling in behind him. He pointed from himself to the hall and looking at her, jerked his thumb toward the kitchen and dining area. Pulling out her own gun, she crept through the dining room, a smallish room furnished with a card table and four chairs. Blinds covered the single window, shrouding the room in semi-darkness. Beyond the table, she came to a pair of wooden swinging doors, the kind that reminded her of her grandmother's house. Inching one open, she peered into the kitchen. She blinked in the dim light. Empty.

Backing out of the kitchen, she crossed the living room to the one-car garage. A broken lock hung from the knob. Gun raised, she pushed the door open. A fury rose in her belly. The garage wasn't a garage at all. An extra-long desk took up most of one wall; monitors, wires, and an abandoned router were scattered across the polished wood. Above the desk, pieces of tape stuck to the walls, the torn corners of whatever hung there still attached. More wires stuck out from several outlets. This was a computer center of some kind. She backtracked to find Zel in the living room.

"All clear," he said.

She nodded and called it in. "The M.E.'s on their way."

Zel pointed at the blood-stained wall over Frannie's body. "What is that? In the blood?"

Callie moved closer to inspect what he saw. The bloodstains had darkened, but bits of light-colored bone and clumps of hair stuck to the wall's surface. She crouched down next to the dead woman, swallowing before answering. "Something bad."

His inhale sounded loud in the quiet of the house, and he shook his head. "There's no way he didn't do this."

Frannie's head lolled to one side, exposing a concave piece of skull. "He slammed her head into the wall over and over."

"When? After we talked to her?"

She slipped two fingers under one of Frannie's arms. "She's still stiff." The M.E. would give them a more accurate window, but she guessed Frannie hadn't been dead long. "Maybe late last night? Or this morning?"

She stood up and crooked a finger. "You need to see something." Zel followed her down the hall. "It's a computer room of some kind." Zel circled the space. "I think Frannie started wondering. She wanted to believe in her boyfriend, but there was this locked room. Maybe it ate at her after we talked to her. Maybe she came over while he was still supposed to be at work," Callie said. "Maybe she broke the lock, and he found her."

Zel picked up where she left off. "She doesn't understand what she's found. She's upset, and they argue. It gets out of control. He grabs her. She tries to fight back, but..."

"Yeah."

Sirens wailed in the distance, and Callie walked over to the long desk, drawn to the taped corners hanging from the wall. Up close, she could see the scraps weren't paper at all, but something glossier, like photographs. The sound of sirens came closer. Cars screeched to a stop outside, and doors slammed like a drum solo. It hit her then. Pictures had been on this wall. Pictures of girls.

Chapter Thirty-Two

"That was Angie," Callie said to Zel. "They're done."

He sat back in his chair and yawned, his long legs stretched out. "Good. The sooner they process everything, the sooner we'll know what we've got."

Callie rubbed her fingers over her stinging eyes. She knew what they had. A dead woman, a missing girl, and a killer on the run. That was enough. But Zel was right. There would be prints. If they were lucky, there would be DNA. She grabbed her cup and headed to the coffee maker.

They had an APB out on O'Neill and his car. So far, there'd been no sightings. Considering he had a head start, she figured as much. He could be in another state by now. Still, the man had to eat and sleep sometime. Someone may have seen him in a diner or at a roadside motel.

Taking her cup back to her desk, she worked through the timeline in her head. They'd visited O'Neill on Monday. Two hours later, they'd spoken to Frannie. Sometime between Tuesday night and very early Wednesday morning, Frannie had gone over to O'Neill's house. They'd argued. After killing his girlfriend, O'Neill decided it was time to pull up stakes. Or he could have decided even before Frannie came over. At this stage of the investigation, it didn't really matter. He had enough of a head start that finding him wouldn't be easy.

Sinking back into her chair, she stared at the complete copy of Brian O'Neill's arrest record and opened the folder.

As a teenager, Brian O'Neill had attended a fancy private school in Northern Virginia, the kind that specialized in sending kids to Ivy League colleges. Brian wasn't like the other kids, though. He didn't come from old money or any money. O'Neill had earned himself a scholarship. This she found interesting. She thought about the story he'd told the detectives, how he'd been bullied for his size and his awkwardness. She flipped through the transcripts of his interviews with the police. One caught her attention.

Detective Palmer: You say you were bullied, Mr. O'Neill. How so?

O'Neill: I didn't play sports for one.

Detective Palmer: Was that a problem?

O'Neill: Yeah, it was a problem. Have you heard of Campbell Prep? They win everything. Even the benchwarmers thought they were hot shit. Look at me. Do I look like the image of a Campbell man?

Detective Harris: I wouldn't know what that image looks like, Mr. O'Neill. But I do know that Campbell Prep is hard to get in, isn't it?

O'Neill: Not if you've got enough money or can dunk a basketball.

Detective Harris: Which if I understand correctly, leaves you on the outside. So, how did you, a short white guy with no money, manage to get into this fancy school?

O'Neill: Technology.

Detective Palmer: Technology?

O'Neill: They need kids who can ace the SATs to balance out the ones who can't do more than sign their name at the top. My mom decided I wasn't getting enough out of the county school and took me over there. Of course, they told her they didn't have any spots, but that I could take their admissions test to have it on file—in case something opened up.

Detective Palmer: Let me guess. You did well on the test.

O'Neill: Not that they believed it. They made me take a second test with a guy watching over me the whole time. Turns out I had the highest score in the history of the test. Even then, I don't think they wanted me all that much, but they needed me.

Detective Harris: What did you mean about technology?

O'Neill: Oh, yeah. They were setting up a STEM program. I knew a lot about computers, so the teacher in charge asked to meet with me. It didn't take long for either of us to figure out I knew more than he did. He put in a word for me with

the administration. Said I would be an asset in setting up the program. Which I
was. Not that anyone other than him cared.

Detective Palmer: Let me guess. You got bullied for that, too.

O'Neill: Coders don't get the girls. At least not back then.

Detective Palmer: And now?

O'Neill: Do I look like I get a lot of girls? Look, I said I'm sorry about what
happened. I didn't plan it that way. I only wanted to talk to her.

Detective Palmer: Uh huh. And that's why you slipped something in her
lemonade?

Callie set the interview aside. O'Neill had given them a similar story about being bullied and how he'd developed an unhealthy obsession and dislike of women. From what she could tell, this dislike stretched to his mother and his sister, although he did seem to have some affection for his grandmother. In the rest of the interview, he continued to express remorse, although without viewing the tape, it was impossible to know whether or not his apologies were genuine. They were only words on a page. She did know that he didn't deny the charges and he didn't have any priors. And while the woman who'd been assaulted gave a statement, she'd been reluctant to testify unless necessary. All of these factors had led to a plea with a modest sentence, the only caveat being O'Neill would be a registered sex offender. His prison record—although not in high security—was clean. No fights. No demerits. No problems of any kind. Still, the parole board chose to crack down on sexual predators, and O'Neill got five years of probation following his release. He'd stayed out of trouble since, but he'd been hiding something in the garage, something Frannie Carter had the misfortune to find.

"Forde." Callie's head whipped around. Trina, the woman who worked the front desk, came toward her with a stack of slips. "You forgot to pick up your messages." She held them out in front of her. "Three from your dad."

Her father. Callie remembered she'd silenced her phone in the wake of finding Frannie Carter's dead body.

"Thanks," Callie said as she rifled through the small stack. The last message from her dad had come in less than five minutes before she'd returned to the station.

He picked up after the first ring. "Callie?"

"Dad, I really can't talk. I'm up to my ears in—"

"I read the report. I need to see you."

She started to tell him that wasn't possible when her chin jerked up. *The report. There was new evidence now.* A tingling crawled up her spine, and she slid back to her desk, sorting through the papers. There. The report cited hairs found in the house and in the garage. Maybe one could be matched to O'Neill. If he'd left in a hurry the way they thought, he wouldn't have had time to clean his house. She needed to call Angie.

"Dad, I really can't right now," Callie said in a rush. "I'll call you later."

"It's important. It's about the case."

She looked up to see Zel watching her. "What about it, Dad?"

"I think it's the same guy."

Callie wasn't sure she understood. Did he mean the person behind the fake dating profile and the one pretending to be Paul Randolph? Either way, she didn't have time to bat ideas around. "Dad, I've really got to go. We've got a body."

She heard his indrawn breath. "Natalie?"

"No, but the victim is connected to our suspect."

His voice shook now. "You need to be careful, Cal."

She didn't have time for this. "Dad, I—"

"I think it's the same guy. The one who took Emma."

The words took her by surprise at first, and then she sat back heavily. This was her fault. She could hear the quickness of his breath and the hope now. She understood his need to solve the five-year-old case. She did, but it was making him see things that didn't exist. Sure, there were similarities, but that's where it ended.

"I've got to get back, Dad," she said now, her voice softer than it was before.

"Cal, you're not listening. I read the report, the list of items found in the garage of that house."

The most incriminating evidence in the garage had been the chloroform-soaked rag.

"I'm sorry. I don't see the connection."

"That's because we didn't release all the information publicly. When nothing came of it, we had to drop it, and Weston left it out of the report."

Callie hesitated. She'd pored over the official files more times than she could count, knowing it wasn't healthy but unable to stop herself. Until today, she'd not known that anything had been left out. But holding evidence back from the media and the public was an old trick of the trade. She'd done it herself a few times.

"So, what's the evidence, Dad?"

"A candy wrapper. Black licorice."

She couldn't speak for a minute. "What did you say?"

"Black licorice. They found a wrapper in the garage at that house, right?"

Her pulse skittered faster. "Yes."

"There was a wrapper, the same brand, inside Emma's car and another at the scene of the shooting. Her car had other trash, so at first, no one thought anything of it. But the one later, at the meet, was one coincidence too many." He paused a moment, letting his words sink in. "I didn't find out until a couple of years later that there had been other wrappers in other cases. Such a small thing, really. Easy to miss. Anyway, what I'm telling you is that I think that whoever took Natalie left that wrapper in the garage as his calling card. Same as he did before. Do you understand now?"

She pictured the wrapper in her mind, wedged between the appliances but easy to spot. The thumping of her heart pounded in her ears. And there'd been the unopened package they'd found at Frannie's apartment. Red and black like the scrap in the garage.

"It's the same guy," her dad said again. "It has to be."

Chapter Thirty-Three

The air in the small conference room reeked of greasy takeout and burnt coffee. At one end of the table sat Henderson, sporting the heavy undereye bags and pasty skin that came with the job. If you were lucky, you had a week between cases, time enough to sleep eight hours rather than in fits and starts, time to eat something other than fried chicken sandwiches out of a paper bag, and time to see family and friends. It didn't last long, although some cases were more time-consuming than others. Hampstead didn't have the luxury of a large police department, and the one they did have was usually spread thin. This was one of those times.

Zel took the seat across from Callie, his large hands holding a thick file, but seemed more focused on the man next to her, John Forde. She couldn't blame him. Her father had wheeled his chair right up to the table as though he'd never left—a statement maybe—but she didn't miss the way her father folded his trembling hands in his lap. In front of him, on the table, was a box, the cardboard bent and battered from repeated openings. Callie wondered how many times he'd reread his notes, studying the evidence and asking himself over and over how he'd gotten it wrong. She didn't have to question him to know that it was true. She would have done the same herself.

Captain Jackson cleared his throat and got to his feet. "Thank you for all for being here." He nodded toward Hendo. "Chang called in sick this morning."

For the most part, Hendo's partner had been spending time at the Hamill's house, ready to intercept any ransom calls, keep an eye on the mother, and distract Jeremy. A uniformed officer had gone over on that day. Jackson gestured toward Callie's father.

"As you can see, I've asked retired Detective Forde to join us today." He gave a brief summary on the disappearance of Natalie, followed by the discovery of Frannie Carter at O'Neill's. "Right now, Brian O'Neill is our prime suspect in the murder of Ms. Carter and a person of interest in the disappearance of Natalie Hamill."

"How's O'Neill connected to the Hamill girl?" Hendo asked.

It was a good question, and Callie picked up the mantel. She outlined his background and his previous conviction, closing with his computer expertise.

"In the past, he used a popular internet site to lure the woman to his home. It's possible he's expanded to dating sites and apps. His background suggests high-level hacking skills." She updated them on the private group and app Natalie had used. "We think he may have also posed as a father to get Natalie to agree to babysit."

"Hate to tell you," Hendo said, arms crossed, "but almost any teenager can do what you've described—maybe not the hacking, but even some of that if you point them in the right direction."

"But most teenagers aren't listed as predators, suspected of murder, and on the run," Callie countered. The group around the table said nothing, and she kept going. "So, while we have theories, we need to pin down the evidence. We've got warrants out for information from the dating app website. We've also traced the phone used back to a supercenter in Richmond. O'Neill's name wasn't on the list of buyers, but that doesn't mean anything. He could have bought the phone from a friend. He could have an account under another name. We're going to need someone to get down to the store and show his picture around."

Hendo raised his hand. "I'll take it."

Callie nodded. "We've got a BOLO out on both O'Neill and his car."

"What else?" Jackson asked, his face creased with deep-set lines.

Zel flipped open the folder in front of him. "Whatever computers or phones O'Neill had at his house are gone, so it's impossible to know what he was doing on them, but he wasn't able to take his work computer." He held up a hand. "I know, I know. Why would he be stupid enough to do anything suspicious on his work computer when he has burner phones and hidden laptops? I can only speculate that he got a little too comfortable, figured no one was looking at him for anything, and he couldn't leave the office. That's not to say he didn't take precautions. He wiped his history, logged off the company's internet, hacked into another one. But we have our own hacker, a better one."

A couple of heads around the table bobbed up and down, including Callie's. Lewis Johnson. LJ. Technically, he belonged to the county and not the town of Hampstead, but his usefulness was legendary. Rumor had it he'd even consulted with the FBI a couple of times and been offered a job with the bureau. Lucky for local law enforcement, LJ liked small-town life, and more than that, he liked his grandmother. Maybe after she was gone, he'd reconsider, but until then, his loyalties lay with family and home.

Zel flipped to another page in his file. "O'Neill logged onto one website seven separate times in the last three months. The most recent was the day we interviewed him." The detective looked up from the page. "We can't get to the site yet. There are firewalls and passwords, but LJ is working on it."

"What kind of site are we talking about?" Hendo asked.

Zel didn't answer, his glance shifting from Hendo to Callie's father.

Jackson spoke up. "We can't be one hundred percent sure, but it has the makings of—"

"Human trafficking," John Forde said, his quiet voice cutting off the captain. "Women—no, girls—for sale to the highest bidder."

Chapter Thirty-Four

T he man ripped open the plastic wrapper and pulled out a twisty length of licorice. The scent, sharp and medicinal, appealed to him. Perhaps it was because it reminded him of loss and heartbreak. Or maybe it was simply because it set him apart. He liked to be set apart. He wasn't always that way, of course. Like all small boys, he'd craved the approval of his father. But his father's presence in his life was virtually nonexistent, leaving him with a mother who was either incapable of dispensing approval or unwilling and a sister who couldn't be bothered. Either way, he'd given up. School had been no better. He'd been a loner—not by choice, really—but by happenstance. He didn't fit in. Not in the real world, anyway. But there was another world, one that was better. On a computer, he was king. And that skill was paying off in spades now.

The last light of day faded, and the sky outside grew thick with clouds. The man sat in the darkness, listening to the quiet. He'd laced her food—only a little—but he needed her to understand, to go along. This wasn't a game he was playing. He flipped open his laptop, and the light of the screen cast looming shadows on the walls. He settled deeper into his chair, sipping whiskey from a leaded glass.

Working his way through the walls of the website didn't take him long. He scrolled through the pages until he found the one he was looking for. Even though he'd been expecting it, her image—the images he'd uploaded—jolted him. Angelica. As he'd suspected, there'd already been interest. He flipped through the inquiries. Mostly age and price. The requisite question of her virginity. This one made him grit his teeth. How dare anyone assume that

155

Angelica wasn't pure? The age question, though, was to be expected. She'd be too old for some of the site's clients and too young for others. While he found both distasteful, he was a realist. That was the nature of the business. Perhaps there would be a bidding war. The idea brought a smile to his face.

Outside, the wind whipped up, battering the trees, and some of the smaller and drier branches snapped. The dirt from the rocky drive swirled above the ground like mini tornados. He allowed a glance up the stairs, wondering if the heavy winds would wake her. Deciding it didn't matter, he turned his attention back to his computer, searching the local news. He saw the story then. *Local woman found dead in Hampstead house.* He read the article twice, then tipped his glass back and took a long drink.

"To Frannie Carter," he whispered. "May God have mercy on your soul."

Chapter Thirty-Five

"I want to go with you," Callie's father said. The conference room had emptied. Only Callie, the captain, and John Forde remained.

Jackson stepped forward. "No, John. This isn't your case anymore."

"It will always be my case," he said, his voice steely.

"You're not a detective. You don't work for this department."

Callie winced for her father. Jackson hadn't sugarcoated the message. Still, he was right.

"I'm sorry if that sounded harsh. I brought you in as a courtesy," he said. "You caught the connection with the licorice, and you could be right that it's the same perp. *Could* be," he said again with more emphasis. "My detectives will pursue that possibility, and if that includes going back to the family of Emma Nicholls, then that's what they'll do. But you will not be a part of it."

"You're pushing me out."

The captain leaned over, resting his palms on the table. "This isn't about pushing you out, John. I'll keep you in the loop when I can. You're a valuable resource. But as I said, you don't work for the department, and this is not your case. It's your daughter's."

Naked longing in his eyes, John's mouth closed in a hard line. A few days earlier, he'd been almost comatose in front of home movies, reliving the past over and over again. Now, he seemed to burn with a fever that worried Callie almost as much. The captain was right, though, that her father's mind was stuck in the past. Natalie's disappearance and, by extension, Frannie's murder, might be related to what happened to Emma Nicholls, but they didn't know that for sure. There had been no wrappers in O'Neill's house or at his office. The theory that Natalie was taken by the same group was only that—a theory. She would follow up with the Nicholls family, but she couldn't have him there. For all their sakes.

"Sorry, Dad, but I agree with the Captain. I'll update you after Zel and I talk to Sarah and Fred Nicholls. I promise."

He didn't comment, but he didn't have to. Hope seeped out of him like air out of a deflating balloon, replaced by something harder for her to witness—disappointment. She had to bite down on her lip to keep herself from taking it back.

Captain Jackson cleared his throat again. "Your wife is here to take you home, John."

The man drew himself up as much as he was able and stared up at Jackson. "Can't wait to get rid of me, Frank?"

"You know that's not true." The captain came around the table and clapped him on the back. "It's good to see you. Maybe we can have lunch later this week?"

Callie's gaze followed the wheelchair out of the room, her jaw locked with tension. She listened as the two men chatted about long-retired detectives, wives, and children. She still watched after their voices faded and the hallway was empty. Zel came up behind her.

"We need to get some rest, Cal. We'll go see the parents first thing in the morning."

She didn't comment.

"You look wiped," Zel said. "No offense."

She tried to smile, her shoulders sinking lower. She was wiped. She had two cases now, both of which seemed to point to the same man. And even if they were right, they were no closer to finding Natalie or catching O'Neill. Either way, finding Natalie and O'Neill wouldn't bring Frannie back. She thought about the way her father had connected the five-year-old unsolved case of Emma Nicholls to Natalie Hamill. Was he right?

Her head ached, and even though she'd eaten little, her stomach roiled. She knew without checking a mirror that she looked as tired and anxious as she felt, but none of that mattered. She allowed herself a few seconds more to wallow before she lifted her head, chin high, and looked at her partner.

"You get out of here, Zel. I'll go home soon."

"Promise?"

She touched two fingers to her temple in a mock salute. "Sir, yes, sir."

After the last of his steps faded, Callie reached out and opened the box her father had left.

"Okay, Dad, let's see what you got."

Chapter Thirty-Six

Callie climbed out of the car, scanning the family-friendly street. The sun, already warm, shone like a spotlight on the glossy leaves of a fat magnolia. She lifted her hat and wiped a bead of sweat from her brow. The two-story house might have been painted a cheery yellow once but now appeared bleached with strips of paint peeling from the siding. The lawn, while technically green, consisted of weeds sprinkled with the heads of dandelions. If it weren't for the car in the driveway, Callie might have thought the house had been abandoned.

Emma's mother answered the door in her bathrobe, one hand holding it closed. She didn't seem surprised to see them. "I was wondering when you'd get around to me. This is about the missing girl, isn't it?"

"Yes, ma'am," Callie said. "Are you Sarah Nicholls?"

"'Fraid so."

"We'd like to ask you a few questions."

The woman studied her now, recognition setting in. "You're his daughter, aren't you?"

"I'm Detective Forde." She indicated Zel. "And this is my partner, Detective Zeleniak."

"How is he?"

Although Sarah Nicholls didn't say his name, Callie knew who she meant. "Fine."

"Your mom?"

"She's fine, too. May we come in?"

"Why not?" the woman said with a shrug.

They followed her down a hallway decorated with photos, all of them Emma. Ms. Nicholls flicked her hand toward a kitchen table and tightened the belt of her robe. "Have a seat. Do you want coffee?"

When they declined, she poured herself a cup and took the seat across from them.

"Every time the doorbell rings, I hope it's her." She wrapped her hands around the mug but didn't drink. "Today, when I saw you, I hoped...well, I hoped, that's all. I keep thinking she'll find her way back." Her eyes filled then, and her chin quivered. "But if she could, she would have by now, wouldn't she? I have to accept that now. I wish..." her voice faded, replaced by a hollow laugh. "But maybe not. Maybe knowing would be worse."

Callie considered reminding her that Elizabeth Smart and Jaycee Dugard both made their way home but decided against it. She had a feeling Sarah Nicholls understood how unlikely that really was.

"I've seen the stories about Natalie—that's her name, right?" Callie told her it was. "But I don't know the family. I'm not really sure how I can help you."

Callie thought about how many times her father must have spoken with both parents about Emma, how many times he'd told them he'd do his best to bring her home.

"Is your husband home, Ms. Nicholls?"

"Husband?" she repeated. "No. He hasn't been here in a long time."

The detectives exchanged a look.

Sarah Nicholls looked past them, her voice trance-like. "My mother never liked him, you know. She always said I could do better, that I should have married Ronnie Johnson, but Ronnie didn't ask." Her eyes slid back to Callie's. "And so, I married Fred, and we had Emma, our beautiful Emma. She was our world." Tears threatened. "We stayed together for a few years after...you know, in case she came home, but..." She swiped at her cheeks, voice shaking. "We're divorced. Well, not technically, I guess. Next month, it will be official."

"I'm sorry," Callie said.

"Don't be." Her gaze dropped to her lap along with her hands. "Fred,

161

he…well, it doesn't matter now. I don't think either of us ever got over Emma being gone. We've both been grieving her in different ways, or that's what my therapist says."

Callie decided it didn't matter whether or not they spoke to the parents separately or together. She made a note to get the contact information for Fred Nicholls.

"Ms. Nicholls—"

"Call me Sarah."

"Okay. Sarah." Callie paused. "We're here because in cases of abduction, it's not unusual to look at other cases with commonalities."

"Commonalities," the woman said, repeating the word slowly. "You mean because they're both high school girls. Both blond hair."

"Yes. Those are two big factors. And combined with the fact that they're both from the same small town, it's a pattern. A loose one, I'll grant, but nothing can be ruled out."

"With Emma, your father said it was sex trafficking." The words were a whisper.

"Yes." The initial investigation had stalled until the FBI had received a tip about a website advertising girls for sale to the highest bidder. Emma's picture had been front and center. The FBI had descended on the town and the department, grudgingly allowing John Forde to remain as consultant. That was the generous accounting of events. In reality, the FBI kept him in the dark as much as possible until they realized the family wanted him in. They trusted him.

Eventually, they'd learned that over a five-year span, thirteen girls aged fourteen to nineteen had been abducted in the mid-Atlantic region—those were the ones they knew about. An undercover source learned enough to find out the ring operated out of D.C. but took girls from various counties and states in order to avoid suspicion. Of course, sex trafficking wasn't new to law enforcement or the FBI, but this ring was different. They didn't target runaways or girls from the street, the kind of girls no one missed. These girls had families and friends and normal lives. Some came from affluent families. Some came from large cities. Others were from small towns. There were no requests for ransom. No bodies were ever found. The crimes themselves were murky. Each of the girls left their homes to meet someone they thought they knew, someone they met online. Social media, it turned out, was their secret weapon.

Emma's disappearance fit the pattern. The FBI took action and inserted an undercover agent in a high school in Richmond. The young-looking woman posed as a shy teenager who used social media as her outlet. A few months passed before she was befriended by a "boy" who claimed he "liked" her. After several weeks of this communication, they agreed to meet in person. At the last minute, though, the boy changed the location to a half-empty strip mall. The agent tried to get word to the bureau, but for reasons that could never be explained, no one got the message. Except Detective John Forde. That day, an FBI agent lost her life, and Hampstead lost a good detective.

"In this case, we don't know for sure if Natalie was taken by one man or by something more organized, but we need to consider both possibilities."

Sarah's hand went to her throat, and she bit her lip. "I still don't know how I can help you," she said finally. "I don't know what happened to Natalie. Or my Emma."

"I know you don't. But it would be helpful if I could ask you what you recall about the days leading up to Emma's disappearance." Callie wasn't sure anything Sarah remembered would make any difference, but she had to try.

The woman sat back against the hard chair. She swallowed. "It's hard remembering sometimes," she said finally. "Not because I don't want to. I do. But that was five years ago. I didn't know I'd need to remember those days. They were like any other, you know. Everyone got up. Fred and I went to work, and Emma went to school. She stayed after if she had dance team practice or field hockey, but otherwise, she came straight home. I can't remember anything unusual. I wish I did." Her voice caught. "I really do."

Callie recalled something she'd read in the file. "Your daughter and your husband had gotten in a fight the week before?"

"Fred didn't like her to be out without us knowing where she was. He's protective that way. And Emma had driven a friend home after dance practice one day." Her forehead scrunched. "I think the friend might have been upset about something—a boy, maybe. Anyway, they sat in the car for a while outside the girl's house."

"So, she was late getting home."

"Yes, which wouldn't have been a problem, except she didn't answer her phone when we called to see where she was. Fred was really upset. I think he would have called the police that day if she hadn't shown up." Her hands twisted over and over in her lap. "They fought about her not picking up her phone. She said she didn't hear it, and that was another fight." Her voice shook as she remembered. "But that was it. Fred got over it. Emma couldn't really do any wrong."

"And did Emma get over it?"

"What?" The woman stared at Callie a moment. "Yes, I'm sure she did."

Callie's thoughts whirled. If Emma was feeling penned in at home, would that have made her more eager to meet this boy she'd met online? The texts Emma had sent to her friends in the days before she disappeared would support that theory. Still, even if Callie knew that to be fact, the knowledge wouldn't explain who had taken Emma, and chances are, saying it out loud would only add to Sarah's pain.

"Ms. Nicholls—I mean Sarah—did Emma ever eat licorice that you know of?"

"Licorice? Is this about that candy wrapper in the car?" She looked from Callie to Zel to Callie again. "Your father told me they found an empty wrapper, but there weren't any usable prints on it."

"It's not a popular candy."

Sarah lifted one hand and dropped it again. "Fred was sure she didn't, and I have to agree. I never saw her eating licorice, and we certainly didn't have it in the house. It could have belonged to one of her friends."

"You're probably right," Callie said, although she knew her father had exhausted that idea. None of Emma's friends ate licorice. She pushed her chair back and stood. Zel followed. "Thank you for seeing us today, Sarah. I'm sorry I don't have better news for you, but your daughter's case is not closed. I want you to know that." An image of Emma's picture on the bulletin board flashed through her mind.

The woman nodded, her features contorting as she fought back fresh tears. Gripping the table with both hands, she got to her feet, too.

"I'm sorry I couldn't be more help," the woman said, her gaze drifting to one of the many framed photos of Emma that hung in the hall. "Forgive me."

Callie understood the woman wasn't really talking to her anymore, but she answered anyway.

"Nothing to forgive," she said. "Nothing at all."

Chapter Thirty-Seven

"I have good news and bad news," Angie said.

Callie transferred her phone from one ear to the other, slamming the car door shut. "Okay, hit me."

"The fingerprints on the pen don't match the ones in the system for Brian O'Neill."

"Are you sure?" Callie's brows furrowed. Had she made a mistake? Given Angie the wrong pen?

"Not only that, there's not a single print in his house that matches what's on record. At least not an exact match."

Now she was really confused. "Hold on, Angie," she said. "I'm going to put you on speaker." Callie walked around the car and stood next to Zel. "Okay. Go."

Angie's clipped voice came over the speaker, all business. "As I said, the prints on the pen and the ones inside the house don't match the prints in the system for Brian O'Neill. The reason is that the new prints have been altered."

Zel stiffened beside her. "I'll be damned."

"Go on," Callie urged.

"They've been burned. Might have been a chemical or straight burn, but the ridge patterns have been damaged, and there's some evidence of scarring."

"Jesus," Zel muttered.

Callie fought not to scream out in frustration. O'Neill seemed to be one step ahead. Again. "What's the good news?"

"Well, for one thing, if you hadn't taken that pen, we wouldn't know that O'Neill has new fingerprints. But since you did, that makes any prints found on Frannie Carter easier to identify as his."

"Angie. Zel here. Are you saying that it doesn't matter that the prints are altered?"

"No, I'm not saying that. I only got one good print from the pen, and it's not perfect. Do you know how many people might have handled that pen before him?"

Callie knew the answer to this one. "I opened a new box of pens that morning. I don't think anyone else touched it but me."

"Good, but maybe not good enough."

"Why not?"

"Well, theoretically, your prints should be the only other ones on it. That would imply the altered print most likely belongs to O'Neill, but without the man himself, I can't swear to it in court. It's possible someone else with an altered print picked up that pen. Someone who packaged the pen, for example."

"But since you found those same prints at his house, it stands to reason that those are his prints."

"Sure. But any good lawyer can claim there's no proof someone else wasn't in that house."

Callie shook her head, her tone sharp. "Who just happened to handle the same pen?"

"I'm on your side, Detective."

Her irritation faded as quickly as it had flared. "I know. What's the solution?"

"Find Brian O'Neill." She paused. "I do have one more piece of good news. It takes time, but I might be able to match the altered print to the original print if I can recreate the area that's been damaged."

"How?" Zel asked.

"Well, whatever method O'Neill used, he didn't burn the whole print. Perhaps he didn't think it was necessary, or maybe it hurt too much, but it's only partially altered. Enough not to match, but also maybe enough to recreate it."

"Okay," Callie said. "What about the partial you got from Erin Hamill's rearview mirror? Could you match that to the pen?"

"Got some consistencies but inconclusive."

"Damn. Thanks anyway, Angie. You're the best."

"Tell me something I don't know."

Clicking off, Callie and Zel walked toward the building.

"The only reason to alter your fingerprints is because you don't want to be caught," Callie said.

"And now he's desperate. Which means there's something else we need to consider."

She stopped at the base of the stairs. "What?"

"If he went to the trouble of burning his fingertips once, he won't hesitate to do it again. He's killed a woman now. That's life without parole. Think about it."

She didn't have to. He was right. "Then we'd better find him fast."

Chapter Thirty-Eight

Callie hung up the phone and swiveled toward her partner. "Natalie never ate licorice that her mother knows of. No one in the family did." Although there was no evidence of the candy in the Hamill car, Callie had called Erin anyway.

Zel grunted before asking, "How's she doing?"

"Surviving. She said her church group has been rotating coming around. They've been doing lots of praying."

"Whatever works." He held up one of the files from her father's box. "Lot of work here. Your dad, he came close."

"Yeah." She punched the end of her pen, clicking it on and off. Her father had come close. He'd gone to the meet at the strip mall, all the while trying to reach his FBI contact. By the time he'd gotten through, he was on site. Click. Click. Click. The agent, not knowing she wasn't covered, had driven to the end of the lot, stopping in front of an abandoned restaurant. She'd disappeared inside. Click. Click. Click. Things had gone downhill fast after that. She threw her pen on the desk. None of this was leading her to Natalie or O'Neill. She looked around. Hendo was on the phone, and Jackson in his office. A handful of uniformed officers manned the rest of the desks. Chang was out again, his desk empty and computer dark. Her gaze landed on the stickers covering the back of his monitor, all video game characters. His gaming addiction bled into the job, the same as it had in his marriage. No one in the department would ever forget the day his former wife had shown up at the station armed with what turned out to be video game controllers.

"You promised me a new car. A bigger house," she'd screamed, even as she hurled controllers at his face. Chang sat as still as a wax figure, the controllers bouncing off him one by one. "But all you do is sit around and play your stupid games like some idiot teenager, gawking at cartoon girls. You're a pervert. Do you hear me? A disgusting pervert." After she'd stomped out, an awkward silence had settled over the detectives. It was Chang himself who'd finally spoken.

"I guess I can get that cabin I always wanted," he'd said, shrugging it off. But his open-mouthed expression looked more shell-shocked than relieved.

"Where's Chang?" she asked now.

"Called in sick."

"Again?" She didn't bother to mask her irritation. They needed all hands on deck.

"I've got a patrol over at the Hamills."

"Fine," she said with a wave of her hand. She didn't have time to worry about Chang, his illnesses, or his eccentricities. "When's O'Neill's P.O. coming in?"

"Four o'clock."

Callie swung around in her chair toward the whiteboard she'd rolled up behind her. O'Neill's name was written in a circle in the center of the board above the timeline she'd made from notecards. A line connected that circle to the name Frannie Carter. There were a handful of other names. O'Neill's mother. His sister. A cousin. Grandmother. A co-worker. None had been able to shed any light on where O'Neill might be.

"A waste," his mother had said. "What good is being that smart if all you're gonna do is sit in front of a computer all day and work at some stupid plant?" A deep cough sounded, followed by the click of a lighter. "I shoulda known it was a waste of time to send him to that fancy school. He was always a weird one, you know. Must have come from his father's side."

For half a second, she'd felt sorry for O'Neill before remembering that his mother—in spite of having the maternal instincts of a rattlesnake—did not kill Frannie Carter or drug a woman and sexually assault her. Those acts were committed by a grown man named Brian O'Neill.

Callie picked up the pen again. O'Neill didn't socialize outside of Frannie.

A man who kept to himself might be described as a loner, or as a man who had a reason to be alone, a man with something to hide.

Going back to the whiteboard, she reached out and touched Natalie's picture. "I can't keep sitting around waiting. I need to do something," she said, her other hand clenched in a fist.

Zel cocked his head toward the door. "Tell you what. We've got a little time before the P.O. gets here. Why don't I go pick up some real coffee?"

"That I could go for."

"I don't know why we don't get one of those coffee pod makers."

"Cheap as Jackson is? No way."

"True." He snapped his fingers a few seconds later. "How about if we pool our money and get it ourselves?"

Callie laughed. "Hendo wouldn't contribute to the heart association if he went into cardiac arrest. And Chang doesn't even drink coffee, which is downright weird, if you ask me. It's practically on the job application."

"Maybe he'd drink it if it was good. Or tasted like ouzo. He likes that shit." He paused, frown lines creasing his face. "Ever had ouzo?" She shook her head. "Tastes like licorice. Nasty stuff."

"Huh. I didn't know that," she said, already forgetting about Chang, her thoughts going back to O'Neill and his P.O.

"Did you know that my dad interviewed Brian O'Neill?" she asked Zel when he came back with two cups.

"What? When?"

"A couple of days after Emma went missing. Same way we found him. Predator list."

Lines appeared between his brows. "I don't remember hearing he was a suspect."

The interview with O'Neill hadn't been all that different from their own, even down to the fact that he had an alibi.

"He wasn't. He was new to the area, and the P.O. saw him regularly then. But that wasn't why he was cleared. He was in Northern Virginia the weekend Emma disappeared. His mother and his grandmother both verified it. There were bus receipts." Callie remembered the notes his father had made on those interviews. "So, they dropped him as a suspect. And then Emma's picture turned up on that private site, and the FBI got involved." The FBI's insider hadn't recognized O'Neill's name or his picture. And they already had a suspect, a bigger fish they'd been watching for years. "The FBI liked Martin Connor."

Zel blinked. "As in the Connors family?"

"One and the same."

The Connors, like the Vanderbilts, were pioneers in the railroad industry. Unlike the Vanderbilts, the Connors diversified, branched out. And subsequent generations of Connors didn't squander the money on gambling or other extravagances. They even managed to come through the stock market crash of 1929 and the depression relatively unscathed. The family continued to prosper, and they diversified again.

"Why would someone like Martin Connor be involved in human trafficking? That doesn't make sense."

Callie couldn't disagree. Even after reading the profile workups, she hadn't been convinced. The man had money, an Ivy League education, a family. Of course, it wasn't as though the FBI actually thought Connor had personally driven to central Virginia to kidnap Emma Nicholls or any of the girls. But they did believe he pulled the strings, although they were never able to get enough evidence to prove it—particularly after they lost an agent trying to do just that. Even so, what Callie really didn't understand was why they had zeroed in on Connor in the first place. Now, based on the licorice wrapper in the Randolph garage, the FBI would be coming back to Hampstead with new questions.

"So, we have that to look forward to tomorrow, I guess," Zel said, his face glum. He drained the rest of his coffee. "I bet your dad wasn't too thrilled when they kidnapped his case."

Her lips parted. It wasn't something she'd thought to ask because, as far as she could tell, he'd gone along with it. The only reason she could think of was that he believed Connor was involved, too. She'd have to ask him about that. And about O'Neill. A new thought occurred to her.

"The Connor family is from Northern Virginia, right?"

CHAPTER THIRTY-EIGHT

"Yeah. So?"

"Maybe Martin Connor met Brian O'Neill? Maybe they went to that school together, Campbell Prep?"

A slow smile split Zel's face. "You're thinking they were working together."

"I don't know. Maybe. Campbell Prep is the kind of school a guy like Martin Connor would go to, right? It's possible."

"I like the way you think, Forde." His fingers flew over his keyboard. "I'm on it."

"Damn," he said a half hour later, running his hand through his hair. "No go on the school. Connor went to some school in Georgetown."

"College?"

"Nope. O'Neill didn't make the Ivy League cut."

She frowned. Northern Virginia wasn't like Hampstead. It had more suburbs than a Dalmatian had spots. The probability the two men had met was unlikely and made even more so by the disparities in their household incomes. She asked anyway. "How about where they grew up?"

"Nope. Connor lived in Great Falls and O'Neill in a town called Purcellville. It's only about thirty miles but separated by way more than that."

Disappointment washed over her. "All right. Keep digging. Maybe something will turn up in his phone records or bank statements."

"Maybe."

A voice cut in. "Detective Forde?"

Callie swung around to find a man of medium height and medium-brown hair in a short-sleeved shirt and tie. She got to her feet. "I'm Detective Forde."

"Fred Nicholls. You've been trying to reach me?" The man extended his hand. "I hope you don't mind my stopping by, but if there's any chance you have news about Emma, I couldn't wait. I came right over after I heard your message."

"Oh," Callie said. She couldn't remember exactly what she'd said in her message, but she was sure she hadn't implied they had news—at least not the kind Mr. Nicholls wanted to hear. "Well, thank you for coming in." She waved a hand toward the war room. "Why don't we go in here?" She jerked her chin toward Zel to join them.

The man sat down and leaned forward, his body pressing into the edge of the table. "Have you found something? Has someone seen her?"

She took a deep breath. "Mr. Nicholls, I think you may have heard that another girl has gone missing. Natalie Hamill. No one has seen her since Saturday evening. That's the reason that I wanted to speak with you."

Mr. Nicholls blinked, his body and hands sliding back from the table.

"We wanted to talk to you because there are similarities between the cases."

The angular bones of his face hardened. "So, you're not searching for my daughter? This is about the other girl?"

"It's not that clear cut," she said. "Like I said, there are some similarities. Their descriptions, for one."

He snorted. "Do you know how many sixteen-year-old blond girls there are in the world, Detective? Even here in Hampstead? That's your similarity?" He shifted forward again. "According to the detectives on my daughter's case, Emma may have been taken for…" he faltered, his face flaming red, "for men who were looking to buy young women. The FBI thought so, anyway. If that's true, that means she might still be alive somewhere. I want to know what you're doing to find Emma. My daughter."

"It's still an open case, Mr. Nicholls."

"Bullshit. If it were, you'd be talking about finding both girls." He pushed away from the table, jabbing a finger in her direction. "Your father failed to find my daughter, and from where I sit, you don't seem to be doing any better with this one." He got to his feet, his hands shaking. "Do you have any idea what it's like for me, Detective? I lay awake at night wondering what I could have done to protect my daughter from those kinds of men. Our daughters need to know they can be safe." His body sagged then, and his voice, although softer, carried an urgency that clutched at Callie's heart. "Can you guarantee that? Can you?"

Chapter Thirty-Nine

Callie sat on the concrete stairs between the second and the third floor, head bent to her knees. Trembling, she forced herself to breathe, to inhale and exhale. She told herself Fred Nicholls had every right to be angry. His daughter was still missing. More than that, he had every right to be scornful and, beyond that, sad.

After Emma's disappearance, there had been a heightened awareness around town. Young girls traveled in pairs. That hyperawareness spread to the college, where new safety measures were put in place. Time passed, and no more girls disappeared. The town grew lax. But even if they hadn't, Natalie would still be missing. How could anyone have foreseen the false babysitting job? One might argue that she could have called the Holts to verify they'd recommended her, but that would imply she had a reason to be suspicious. And why would she? She felt safe in Hampstead. Callie wrapped her arms tighter around her knees. But Natalie hadn't been safe. Not any more than Emma had been. Fred Nicholls was right. There was no guarantee.

The door above her, the one to the third floor, opened.

"Cal?" Zel called her name from the top of the stairs. "O'Neill's P.O. will be here in about ten minutes."

She didn't turn around or stand. "I'll be up in five."

A brief silence followed before the door clicked shut again.

She sat one minute longer before lifting her head and stretching her legs. Standing, she shook out her limbs, clenching and unclenching her fists.

"Get it out," she said to the empty stairwell, her words echoing back to her.

"Get it out." Air in. Air out. Again and again, until she felt steadier, stronger.

Headed back to her desk, she decided Fred Nicholls was wrong about her father. He hadn't failed so much as been stopped. Her father had been close—close enough that he'd almost paid with his life. As far as anyone knew, Emma was still out there, and that meant she could still be found. They hadn't given up, no matter what Fred Nicholls thought.

She carried that resolve into the war room and their meeting with O'Neill's P.O., a small man with small hands and feet to match. His already pale face drained of color when Zel shared what they'd found at O'Neill's house.

"He's never been violent," the man said. "Well, I mean, he attacked that woman, but not since then. He's been clean. I swear."

"Uh-huh. And when was your last home visit?" Zel asked.

Pink spots appeared on his cheeks. "I was going to go by this week."

"When was the last time?"

"Well, I can't be sure exactly."

Taking a sheet of paper from a file folder, Zel slid it across the table. "I can. Twenty-three months ago."

"Now, look—" the man started.

"And before that, ten months, and before that, eight months for a total of seven home visits in the last four years. Seven." Zel tapped the paper. "It's all there in black and white. He's wanted for murder, possibly kidnapping, and may have been involved in sex trafficking."

The P.O. reared back. "That can't be right."

"How can you be so sure? Perhaps if you'd done a few more home visits, you might have known what the hell was going on." Red suffused the man's face and before he could sputter a response, Zel leaned in, his voice hard as nails. "Frannie might have liked to know, too."

The man flinched. Zel shot a quick look at Callie. It was her turn.

"That's enough, Detective," she said, her tone biting. "We're on the same side here, or did you forget that?"

"Not how I see it. If he'd—"

Callie cut him off. "Walk it off, Detective."

Zel's eyes flashed as his gaze swung from the P.O. to Callie.

"Now, Detective," she said, rising to her feet.

His chair banged against the floor as he jerked to his feet.

"Take your time," Callie said. When he'd gone, she shifted back toward the small man. "I'm sorry. I swear his name should be Hothead."

"H-he does have a quick temper."

"You don't know the half of it." She offered him a half-smile and folded her hands together. "Why don't we start over?" His nod was quick. "Great. Listen, I know Detective Zeleniak was trying to make a big deal out of the fact that you didn't make many home visits after the first year he was paroled, but to be perfectly honest, it doesn't seem all that odd to me. I'm guessing Mr. O'Neill hadn't given you any problems."

"No, none at all." His words came out in a rush. "I showed up unannounced a bunch of times, and everything was fine. I walked through his house. He offered up his phone. Always cooperative."

"That's what I figured. And after that?"

"Well, there's no real rule about how many times you have to go. I mean, we're supposed to focus on the ones giving us trouble. He didn't do anything." He paused and shook his head. "Brian was one of the good ones. He only had a month to go."

Callie thought about this. "Did you ever check out the bedrooms in the house when you were there?"

"Sure. A few times."

"What about the garage?"

He blanched. "I saw it once when he moved in. Had a bunch of boxes and cleaning stuff in there. I might have seen it another time, but that was a long time ago."

This didn't surprise Callie. O'Neill probably set up the garage later, after the P.O. stopped making unannounced visits.

"You say he was one of the good ones. What does that mean?"

"It means he didn't cause trouble. No fights. No drugs. No trouble at his job. Hell, his bosses at the plant loved him. An accountant who knew computers. Said he cleaned up their systems. Added in firewalls and all kinds of stuff I don't understand."

Firewalls. To keep people out, according to LJ.

"Look, I've got more than a dozen parolees at any one time, sometimes more. That comes with a lot of paperwork." He lifted his palms. "You know how that is, right? I do my best to stay in touch. I texted O'Neill off and on. Called him once in a while. I sent him to a psych the first few months, so he could work on his anger toward women. The doc said he showed up for every appointment. I had no reason to suspect him of doing what he did. None." His tone turned pleading. "I knew Frannie Carter. I bought books from her. If I'd thought—even for one minute—that he would hurt her, I would have said something. I would have."

Callie didn't like the way he'd done his job, but it would do no good to point fingers now.

"I only interviewed him once," she said. "And considering that a girl had gone missing and one of the first things we did was go to him, he wasn't happy to see us."

"No, he probably wasn't. Your visit wasn't the first. He'd had a few others."

This wasn't a surprise. Any case that might call for a list of known sexual predators would have included his name. "Can you tell me about it?"

"Not much. He would get upset sometimes, but he seemed to take it in stride. And it was always nothing. College girls that turned out not to be missing. Either they were shacked up with someone they didn't want their folks to know about, or they'd dropped out of school—another thing they didn't want their folks knowing about. One time, he asked me why every missing girl was automatically his fault."

Callie bit back on a retort. Drugging and attacking a woman was O'Neill's fault. No one had made him do that. If he had to pay the price when another woman was attacked or went missing, that was his fault, too.

The P.O. shrugged again. "But he went along with it. Answered all the questions." He angled his head as he looked at Callie. "Did he cooperate when you talked to him?"

"Yes." Nothing in the interview had raised red flags at the time, and he'd given them what seemed like a credible alibi. "Tell me about Brian O'Neill. How would you describe him if you were introducing him?"

The man rubbed a hand over his chin. "Quiet. Soft-spoken. Nerdy maybe. Good with computers, but you know that."

"What did you talk with him about?"

The man flushed again. "Video games mostly. He had an Xbox set up in his living room."

"And you play?"

"Once in a while."

Based on his pasty skin and twitchy fingers, Callie guessed he probably played more often than once in a while, but she let it go. "Did you ever play against Mr. O'Neill?"

He didn't answer for a moment, the muscles of his face tightening. "No, not that I know of anyway. You play under your username, which becomes your gamer name."

"Sounds interesting. What's yours?"

The P.O. blushed again. "Hotpocket15. My brother gave me that name because I ate so many when I was in high school."

"Oh, yeah? What kind?"

"Ham and cheese were my favorite."

"Those are good." She smiled at him. "So, O'Neill never told you his gamer name?"

"No, he did."

"But you said you've never played against him."

"That I know of. I might have before I was his P.O. and don't remember, although I probably would. It's kind of a unique name." At her arched eyebrows, he said, "He used the name FatFuryRisesAgain. All one word."

Callie frowned. Was O'Neill referring to himself as fat? Or was this a childhood nickname? "Seems like an angry name," she asked.

"It's actually after the superhero." At her blank stare, he explained. "Fat Fury was a superhero." His lips pursed. "Well, kind of."

"I've never heard of him," Callie said.

"I'm not surprised. He's a comic book character from back in the sixties. Kind of obscure. I mean, no one's putting him in a Marvel movie, but he has a following."

She considered the name again. "So, would it be a stretch to say that O'Neill was a fan?"

"He was."

"Is that because he identified a little with this Fat Fury?"

The man hesitated. "It's possible, but I never asked him."

Callie's foot swung under the table. "Tell me about Fat Fury."

"I-I don't know that much really."

"That's okay. Whatever you know is good."

"Uh, sure." He sat back, relaxing into his tale. "Well, his real name was Herbie Popnecker. He was chunky, short, had glasses." Callie nodded along as he spoke. The description wasn't exactly O'Neill, but close enough that she could see how he might identify with the character. "His father thought he was a loser, and he failed out of superhero school. Made himself a costume anyway and became Fat Fury."

"So, before that, Herbie didn't fit in."

"I guess not."

"Did he have superpowers?"

"Oh, yeah. He could talk to animals, travel through dimensions and time. And he had a magic lollipop."

"A what?"

His look turned apologetic. "I'm a little unsure of the details here, but he got some of his powers from magic lollipops, and he could bop people on the head with them."

"And they'd what? Do what he said?"

"Kind of."

Although she couldn't quite grasp the idea behind this superhero, she was beginning to understand O'Neill's attraction. "Any other superpowers?"

"One." The P.O. shifted, dropping his gaze. "Fat Fury was irresistible to women."

Callie's lips pressed together. She didn't like the sound of that at all. "Can you think of anything else?" He shook his head no. "Okay," she said, dragging out the word, thinking. "So, you and Mr. O'Neill both liked video games, right?"

CHAPTER THIRTY-NINE

"Yes."

"Did you ever talk about anything else? His family?"

"He talked about his grandmother mostly. His mother once, but I got the idea they weren't too close."

"Did you ask about that?"

"Nah. The psych stuff isn't my job. That's for the doc."

"Okay. He went up to visit his family on a regular basis. Is that right?"

"It was no problem as long as he didn't leave the state."

"Did he ever speak about his father?"

The man frowned. "Not much. Said his dad left when he was two. Walked out on the family. I got the idea he blamed the mom, though."

"Why would you say that?"

"Said she was a piece of work no man would want to deal with. I mean, his dad walked out, and he still idolized the guy."

Although Callie wasn't sure she was learning anything new about the family dynamics, she did believe some of the pieces were falling into place.

"Okay. One more question. Did Mr. O'Neill ever mention any high school or college friends? Anyone he might have stayed in touch with through the years?"

"Not to me. No, wait. There is one, but I don't know if it's a real friend."

"What do you mean?"

"Someone he played video games against. Not me," he said, a hand to his chest. "He sometimes talked about this guy and how long they'd been playing against each other and still, he couldn't beat this guy."

Back to the video games. Callie kept her voice light and her body still, but her pulse throbbed faster under her skin. "And who was that?"

"He goes by TopGun666. Or it could be TopGunner. I'm not sure, but I remember it had 666 in it. When I told Brian I thought that seemed like a bad luck number, he laughed. Told me I was superstitious, which maybe I am."

Callie didn't know much about video games but figured it might be time to pick Chang's brain. "Did you ever try to find that player? Online?"

"What for? If a guy like O'Neill couldn't beat him, I'd have no chance. The guy sounded like tournament league caliber."

"They have tournaments?"

"Sure. Big money in it, too."

"Was the TopGun guy a tournament player?"

"I don't know. Maybe."

Callie thanked the man before walking him back downstairs and extracting a promise to send over a copy of his written notes.

Upstairs, she found Zel at his desk.

"You heard all that?"

"Yep. A superhero named Fat Fury? Never heard of him."

"I don't think you're the only one," she said.

"The thing about this guy being irresistible to women, that's kind of creepy."

She agreed before asking, "What did you think about this TopGun guy? Do you think he might be able to tell us something? Or know where O'Neill is?"

"Maybe. But most likely, he's never met O'Neill in person. You can play strangers all over."

"How do you know so much about it?"

"Marcie's nephews play. I've joined in a couple of times."

"You don't think it means something that they've been playing against each other for years."

"It's possible, I guess, but gamers play lots of people for a long time, and they never actually meet. Gamers are all about playing. That's what they do. We need to focus on the people he knew in the real world, not the virtual one."

"Okay, sure, but I might run it by Chang or LJ anyway."

"Your call. In the meantime, we expand our BOLO. Reinterview anyone O'Neill ever talked to. He's bound to turn up soon."

Callie wanted to believe that was true, but with each passing hour, she was finding it harder and harder. Natalie Hamill had been gone for nearly a week. Her face haunted Callie's dreams, smiling and happy like the school photo, before morphing into that last image of Frannie, hair matted with blood, her skull cracked open. O'Neill was the only thing they had, and they were no closer to finding him than they had been the day before.

"What if he doesn't?" she asked, her voice suddenly choked. "What then?"

Chapter Forty

The man inventoried the groceries as he stacked them inside the cabinet. When he was finished, he picked up the pill bottle and shook it. The liquid was low, too. He'd had to go out more than he'd planned, and that meant using the sedatives. It wasn't that he was worried about her getting away. He kept the door locked, and the window had bars. Even if she managed to break the glass and yell for help, there was no one to hear. He didn't think she'd try anyway. One look out the window would be enough for her to know they were alone. A dense forest of trees bordered the small house on three sides. A rutted dirt drive, carpeted with rocks and broken branches, led to the house. He'd been lucky to find the place the first time himself.

The house sat near the end of the property, at the highest elevation on ten acres of land, entirely covered by trees. At first, he'd bought it as a place to be alone. He could shoot out here. He could fish. He had computers and a gaming system. Everything he wanted. He'd set up a satellite, a bank of monitors, and a security camera. He told himself it was to keep people out, but at some point, he'd realized he had another reason. A house like this—hidden in the low-rising mountains of central Virginia—was the right place to keep a person in.

He walked to the bottom of the stairs and angled his head to listen. Silence. Satisfied, he sat down at his desk. He pulled up the camera feed that focused on the drive first, then shifted to the one he'd put on the back of the house. No movement. Tapping the keyboard, he switched to the camera upstairs, the one he'd hidden in a tiny hole high in the bedroom wall. He pulled in a breath. She lay on top of the bed, her knees pulled up to her midsection, her hands folded close to her body. Squinting, he could make out the slow rise and fall of her chest. The sedative hadn't worn off yet. He sat back against the hard chair, watching.

He'd told her she would be Leigh to him. But she might have other names, too. That would partially depend on her. Rubbing his fingertips over the arms of the chair, he considered how she would adapt to her new life. Losing her old life would be an adjustment. But everyone suffered losses in life. He knew that better than most. Unlike others, though, he'd refused to break. When lesser men gave up, he switched gears. He didn't need a doctor to tell him how to live through pain. No. He channeled his anger and his grief in his own way. He got stronger. Not right away, but eventually. She would, too.

There would be resistance at first. That was to be expected—although he didn't like it—but he understood. She still had hopes of escaping or being rescued. Only he knew there was no chance of that. The police didn't know where she was. No one did.

On camera, she stirred, one long leg stretching out over the length of the bed. She sat up, blinking. He saw confusion, realization, then despair. That would change in time. After another minute, her gaze fell upon the toilet and basin he'd installed in the corner of the room. She scooted forward and slid off the bed. With a sigh, he switched off the camera. He wasn't a pervert, no matter what others might think.

He went back to the kitchen, where he made two peanut butter and jelly sandwiches. He placed them on a tray and added two apples, a glass of milk for the girl, and a beer for him. They would eat together tonight. Maybe he'd even bring a laptop and let her watch something, or they could play a video game. He picked up the tray, the hint of a smile stealing over his face. If she was good.

Chapter Forty-One

Callie crumpled the burger wrapper into a ball. Wiping the grease from her hand with a paper napkin, she tossed both in the trash, her attention never leaving the open file on her desk. Martin Connor. According to the report, he was forty-one years old, or four years older than O'Neill. Even if they had gone to the same school, it was unlikely that they would have met. By itself, that didn't mean anything. They could have met socially, although that, too, was highly unlikely. She ran through all the other possibilities she could think of. Through their jobs? Doubtful, considering one worked at a plant in Hampstead and the other in a high rise in D.C. Through relatives? No. Through mutual friends? Still no.

She picked up the file again. Martin Connor had graduated from the family business to politics. He'd received an appointment to study transportation and climate. Where many political appointments might be the result of having the right name or pedigree, Connor had those and something else—actual qualifications. He had a master's in engineering and a doctorate in environmental science. He and his research had been written up in science journals. The man had chops. Setting the file aside, she searched his name on her computer. Hundreds of hits came up, and she narrowed her search, pausing on an interview he'd done several years earlier with a website devoted to environmental causes. Much of what they discussed was old data now, but Connor knew his stuff. His answers were concise and assured. He also sounded bored. She clicked on a few photos, watched two more interviews, and paused on a presentation given in Europe the year before.

Connor stood alone on the stage, images of polar ice melts and rain forests behind him. She turned off the sound and leaned in close, focusing on the man. She watched as he roamed the stage, strutting in jeans and a designer jacket. His white teeth and slicked-back hair fit the image she'd already formed in her mind, but there was something else that caught her attention, made her catch her breath. His eyes, pale and unblinking, came back to the camera time and time again as though looking out beyond the audience to the world at large. That gaze, so detached and cold, made her shiver, and she rubbed her hands over her arms.

She turned the volume up and watched again, her overall impression of the man similar to the one she'd already gotten from the other videos. Although intelligent and extremely knowledgeable, Connor seemed uninterested in the very thing he was reputed to be passionate about. Was this why the FBI thought he'd begun dabbling in human trafficking? Boredom? Or was it the hint of malevolence she saw behind that smooth exterior?

Picking up her phone, she placed a call. Fifteen minutes later, she got out of her car, the box cradled in her arms. The front door swung open even before she reached the brand-new wheelchair ramp.

"Hi, Dad."

"Get in here. Your mother made apple pie. We'll talk over dessert."

Callie's mother dished up two pieces of pie topped with vanilla ice cream and set them on the table before kissing her daughter on the top of the head.

"I'll leave you to it," she said.

Callie itched to talk, but her father dug into his pie, moaning with pleasure, and she knew she would have to wait.

"I'd forgotten how much I love dessert. Especially your mother's pie," he said, patting his belly. "Probably need to take it easy, though."

"Me, too," she said. "I don't think I've had a vegetable in a week. Or a piece of fruit."

He chuckled. "Yeah. Well, this counts as fruit in my book." He took her plate then, stacking it on his. She started to say she'd get it but thought better of it. He spread his napkin over his lap and placed the dishes on top. He rolled to the sink and reached up to rinse the plates, then loaded them in the dishwasher. A lump formed in Callie's throat, and she almost laughed. Who would have thought that an act as simple as doing the dishes would be a sign of wanting to live?

Wheeling back around, his gaze fell on the box that sat in the center of the table. "Now, what did you want to know?"

"Everything."

If he was surprised by her answer, he didn't show it. "Why don't I start at the beginning?"

She nodded. "Yes, please."

John Forde cleared his throat. "I got the call about two in the morning. Dispatch telling me Fred Nicholls was down at the police station to report a missing daughter. The officer on duty was out, down at the Two Pints Tavern. Those were still your patrol days, right?" When she nodded, he continued, "Anyway, there'd been a brawl over at Two Pints, and the dispatcher told Nicholls she'd send the officer over when he was free. But Nicholls wasn't having it. He demanded she call a detective, that it couldn't wait. I didn't really know Nicholls, but I knew your mom was in a book group with his wife. So, I threw on some clothes and told dispatch I'd meet the man at his house. To tell you the truth, I thought there was a good chance his daughter would be home by the time I got there, and that would be the end of it."

He licked his lips and took a drink of water. "I got over there before two-thirty, and the house was lit up like a birthday cake, every light blazing. I remember it was hot that night. And humid. You know the kind—where the air's so thick it's hard to breathe." He set the glass down and wiped his mouth. "When I got to the front door, they were waiting. Fred and Sarah. I knew the minute I saw their faces the girl was still missing. I got a bad feeling then. A bad feeling."

Callie's father described the police finding Emma's abandoned car the next morning. There was never any question about whether or not she'd been taken. Her purse was found on the floor of the car, and the driver's side door was still open. They'd originally speculated that the car might have broken down and she'd flagged down the wrong person for help, but that theory was discounted almost immediately when there was nothing wrong with the car. After getting the password to her phone from the parents, forensics uncovered a series of messages, the last about a meeting on the night she disappeared.

"Fred Nicholls had one of those tracking apps on his daughter's phone. Presumably, she knew that because she dropped the phone in the mailbox of a friend—the place she'd told her parents she was going—and planned to pick it up again on her way home. But when she didn't show up by ten-thirty, her parents got concerned. They called the friend. At first, the girl said Emma had left. Fred didn't buy it since the phone was still in the mailbox. By eleven, he drove over there, grabbed the phone, and confronted the girl and her parents. The friend admitted she didn't know where Emma was."

In the next couple of hours, Fred and Sarah called all of Emma's friends before driving around town searching for the car. When she didn't turn up, Fred had gone to the police station.

"Emma wasn't allowed to date. I don't mention this as a judgment on the parents. Emma's father was strict, but lots of parents are. According to Emma's friends, though, she had a hard time with it. A couple even said she hated her dad, but a lot of teenagers hate their parents for a while. Because he was strict, Emma had taken to sneaking out and making plans through messaging apps she didn't think her father knew about."

"Do any fathers really know about what dangers are out there?" Callie asked with a shiver. With phones always in their hands, teenagers were never more than a click away from an untenable situation.

"Maybe not, but Fred is a little smarter than most, or at least he thought he was. He's head of security down at the plant, not quite a cop, but he thought he understood how things work better than most. Anyway, she goes to meet this young man—"

"Or someone she thought was a young man."

"Exactly. Instead, it's a trap."

Neither of them said anything for a moment, then Callie frowned. "Was chloroform used?"

"Not that we could tell."

"Any prints or fibers?"

"Nothing that amounted to anything of note or that we couldn't eliminate." He paused. "Then there were the items in the car. An empty drugstore bag, a cup from a fast food place, and the licorice wrapper."

"Which you held back from the public."

"Not for any reason at first. We thought it was trash, like a lot of people have in their cars. We shared what we found with Sarah and Fred, and it was Fred who pointed out the wrapper specifically, telling us Emma didn't eat licorice. Sarah was less adamant but didn't disagree. So, I went to her friends, anyone who might have been in the car in the weeks before she disappeared."

"And they said it wasn't theirs."

"Right."

"Okay. Then what happened?"

"Nothing for a while. We searched the hospitals, clinics, and outlying towns. We searched the woods, farms, rivers, everywhere. It was as though she'd disappeared into thin air."

"What about the guy she was meeting? Did you get anything from that?"

"It didn't take long to discover the name used was an alias. Jones. If there was a social media presence under the false name, we weren't able to find it. It had vanished along with Emma." He licked his lips. "Callie, could you get me some more water?"

After he'd drained the second glass, he resumed his story.

"She'd been missing seven days by then. It was about that time that the FBI stepped in. They'd gotten a tip that her picture had been spotted on a private site, the kind that requires a fifty thousand dollar buy-in to look."

Callie's mouth fell open. "Who gave them the tip?"

"Disgruntled customer, maybe? I wasn't on a need-to-know basis, according to the FBI. We did eventually come to an agreement to share information, but I think it's safe to say one side wasn't sharing as much as the other." He ran a hand over his thinning hair. "I never did like playing second fiddle, you know."

"That I do," she said and offered a quick smile. "Was anyone else on the case with you?"

190

"Weston. That was before he retired." He hesitated. "And Chang stuck his nose in a couple of times."

His tone made her sit forward. "Stuck his nose in? What do you mean?"

"I don't mean anything really. Don't get me wrong. I don't dislike the man, but I've never been sure his heart's in the job. Always seemed like his mind was somewhere else to me."

Callie heard what her father didn't say. Chang had never earned John Forde's respect.

"Strange guy is all."

Callie hadn't worked with Chang much, but knew he missed more time at work than the rest of the guys. He'd been moodier of late—if that was possible—but she didn't mention that now. She was more curious about what Chang had been like then and how he'd been involved.

"Did he do anything in particular?"

He seemed to think about the question. "Not really. Not that I can remember anyway."

"Okay," she said, letting it go. "How was it working with the FBI?"

He gave a half-laugh. "Like oil and water." He tipped his head back, remembering. "I tried. I insinuated myself as best I could. They brought in an agent to go undercover and allowed me on the team. As a courtesy. I was supposed to hang back, but things changed. The plan changed. The agent didn't have cover. I couldn't leave her there." His voice grew quiet. "You know the rest."

Callie nodded. She didn't want to rehash that part of the story any more than he did. "But how did Martin Connor get tagged in this?"

"I can only tell you what I heard." His fingers curled over the arms of the wheelchair. "The site where the pictures were found was for some kind of club."

"What kind of club has pictures of young girls who've been kidnapped?"

"Not the good kind." He stared off into space a moment, then said, "According to the FBI, the membership was small, and there were really only two requirements. You had to be someone in a position of power. And you needed money. Lots of it. I was told there were senators and CEOs and former athletes, mostly older, well-established. Didn't matter which political side you were on or if you were self-made or how you got to where you were. Didn't matter if you were white, brown, or black. The only real common denominators were power and means and a penchant for young girls."

Bile rose up in her throat, and Callie was reminded of other famous and wealthy men who'd recently been accused of using young girls for their own entertainment. "That still doesn't explain Connor's involvement. Was he a member?"

"No. Owner. Manager. Whatever you want to call it. He's the one holding the dirty little secrets of all these men. Or so the FBI believes."

Thinking out loud, Callie said, "Older men in their fifties and sixties buying young girls. Yeah, I guess that's a secret they wouldn't want getting out." Her father didn't comment. "How many girls are there for sale?"

"A half dozen at a time, I think, but I don't know for sure. I was focused on Emma. What makes it hard is that the girls are generally high school age, easy to set up to meet a boy, to assume they've run off with them. In some of the cases, the parents get a message from the missing daughter."

"Let me guess. She says she's fine and wants to be left alone."

"Pretty much. Always from a burner. Sarah and Fred got one about two months after Emma had gone missing. They wanted desperately to believe the message came from her, but after listening to reason, even they knew better."

"How could you be sure it wasn't?"

"The FBI uses a linguist for one thing. She studied all of Emma's previous texts. According to her, the message was unlikely to have been from Emma based on the types of words she commonly used and didn't use, her use of contractions and abbreviations, stuff like that. But really, it was something more obvious that convinced them."

"What?"

"The text was sent to Sarah's phone and was addressed to Mom and Dad. Doesn't sound strange unless you know that Emma had never once called Fred Dad. He was always Daddy."

She thought about how carefully the abductions were planned, how little evidence there was to go on. The message didn't fit. "Sounds kind of sloppy if you ask me."

"Unless that's the point. Rubbing their noses in the fact that they have your daughter."

The cruelty took her breath away. "That must have been terrible for them."

"It was. It still is, I'd imagine. Their world revolved around their daughter. I went by their house every day to give them an update, or Fred would have been in my office at all hours. They were in bad shape. Completely broken by Emma's disappearance."

Callie's voice was quiet. "They're divorced now. Getting one, I mean."

"Huh." Her father dragged his hand over his mouth. "I wish I could say I'm surprised. Fred blamed Sarah for being too lenient. Sarah blamed Fred for being too strict. Circular logic."

Sarah's comments came back to her. "Do you think he was overprotective?"

"Probably, but lots of parents are overprotective these days. I do know Sarah convinced herself that Emma wouldn't have lied and hidden her phone if her father's rules weren't so strict. Maybe that's true, and maybe not." He gave her a knowing look. "I seem to remember another teenager who snuck out once or twice, and I'm pretty sure we weren't that strict."

"You knew about that?" she asked, eyes wide. "You never said."

"I had to let you have some fun." He patted her hand, his amusement fading a moment later. "Fred Nicholls never gave up. Even after the shooting, I heard he was at the station regularly for months. Jackson tells me he still calls every so often, visits on the anniversary of her going missing."

Callie thought about the man who'd come to the station. He'd been angry and resentful, things she understood. But there'd been something else, something that clung to him like a bad odor. Sorrow and grief.

"You talked to them?" her dad asked.

"Yes, Sarah Nicholls this morning. Fred Nicholls after lunch."

"Huh. How was Fred?"

"He wanted to know what we were doing to find Emma." How could she explain to either of Emma's parents the number of times she'd stood before their daughter's picture, the one still pinned to the large board? How often she'd trolled the databases for Jane Does? How often Captain Jackson had asked if there were any new leads? "I tried to tell him we're still working it, that the case is still open."

Her father stared past her and sighed. "It doesn't matter, Cal. Open isn't solved."

Chapter Forty-Two

C allie pulled into the station, already exhausted before the day had really begun. Having forgotten to grab a hat, she raised a hand to the blinding sun. She didn't see the shadow of the man until he was standing in her path.

Her hand flew to her throat. "Ben? Jesus, you scared me half to death."

"I didn't mean to." He bent his head toward her and offered a smile. In an instant, she was reminded of other times. A summer picnic down by the creek. A long walk in the snow. His hand, warm and strong, holding hers.

"Are you okay?" he asked.

"Fine," she said. He stood close, too close, his face only inches from hers. She caught a whiff of his cologne, the woodsy scent that sent her stomach into a somersault. Callie smoothed imaginary wrinkles in her jacket, avoiding looking into his eyes. "I'm fine. What are you doing here?"

"Client."

She should have guessed. It wasn't like he was there to see her, not like the old days when he would surprise her with a cup of coffee and a Danish. And a kiss. He'd been romantic like that, romantic in all the ways she wasn't. Funny how much she'd loved it, although she supposed those gestures were saved for someone else now. She nodded and stepped around him. "Well, good luck."

"Don't you want to know who my client is?"

Callie slowed, squinting up at the station. Did she want to play the "we're still friends" game? Did she even have time for this? "Sure," she said as calmly as she could. "Who's your client?"

"Sarah Nicholls."

She whirled toward him, jaw hanging open. "You're kidding. Why? What did she do?"

"Drunk and disorderly."

Callie's heart sank, although she wasn't surprised. Sarah Nicholls wouldn't be the first or last person to use alcohol to ease her misery or soothe her soul. "I'm sorry about that. She's had it rough."

"Yeah, she has." Callie started walking again and he fell in step beside her. "You went to see her yesterday, didn't you?"

She stopped walking. "Is that some kind of accusation?"

He raised his palms. "Not at all. I just wanted to get your take on how she was yesterday."

"Okay." She started walking again. "We had some questions. There's another girl missing. I'm sure you've heard."

Ben slowed this time, facing her. "Are you thinking the cases are related?"

Although it was a reasonable question, Callie had no intention of sharing evidence or theories. "I have no idea if they're related." This was mostly true. A licorice wrapper wasn't exactly damning evidence. "But we have to consider every possibility."

His expression darkened. "So, you were on a fishing expedition at Sarah's expense."

"Right," she snorted. "You aren't making accusations."

Ben had the decency to flush. "Look, at about three o'clock this morning, Mr. Nicholls's neighbors called the police because my client was shouting and banging on the door of his house. She was angry and crying, screaming it was all his fault. Something upset her enough yesterday that she got drunk, somehow got to her ex-husband's house, and woke up the whole neighborhood." He paused long enough for her to get the mental image. She knew his tricks, knew his tactics, and she didn't like it.

"She was fine when we left."

He angled his head toward her. "And you're not the least bit curious what she was screaming about?"

The same tactic, making her picture Sarah. But she was curious. "Fine.

What?"

"She claimed that Fred drove Emma to sneak out, that he'd driven their daughter away and she'd never forgive him, that she hoped he rotted in hell for being such a loser that Emma couldn't wait to get away from him. Of course, there were a whole lot of four-letter words thrown in, but you get the gist."

She did, and it made sense with what her father had told her, although last night was clearly the more alcohol-charged version. Sarah's only solace was to point a finger and assign blame. Fred blamed his former wife in return, but he had additional targets for his anger, the police, and, more specifically, her father.

"Blaming her husband won't bring Emma back," Callie said, her voice quiet.

"No," he agreed, "but she doesn't deserve to be punished, Cal. She's already suffered enough."

Mary from the front desk walked by, her heels clicking on the pavement. The look she flashed in their direction reminded Callie this was a small town, and that gossip flew faster than a race car could turn a lap. She took a step back from her ex, widening the space between them.

"Then it's a good thing she has you for a lawyer, isn't it?"

Chapter Forty-Three

The man's mind wandered over the latest comments on the pictures he'd uploaded to the site. *Hotter than a four-alarm fire* and *Angelica, come meet the Devil.* Whoever wrote that one thought they were cute. The man thought they were stupid. The last one was downright sophomoric. One word only. *Juicy.*

It baffled him that these were supposed to be men of high intellect. Clearly, the idea of young girls reduced them to panting teens, although it wasn't as though these were single men. Most were married, many with adult children far older than the girls on the site. Their wives were educated, Botoxed, well-dressed. They say money can't buy happiness, but he thought it could buy looks. Nose jobs. Boob jobs. He had no idea if any happiness came with that, but they looked better than the women he knew. Some of the wives were famous in their own right. He wondered now if any of these powerful men couldn't get it up with a woman their own age. Could that be it? He gave a shake of his head. It wasn't like he'd ever been particularly successful with the ladies—at least not keeping them. His past was a clear indication of that. And yet, these men remained a mystery to him. Still, it didn't matter what he thought of them right now.

The sun outsized blazed, warming the cabin enough that he cranked the air conditioner higher. Leigh hadn't been friendly that morning, but she'd been cordial enough. He'd had to withhold breakfast until she responded to her name, but hunger was a great motivator. And it was only a name. He'd tried to make her understand. Maybe he'd let her choose one herself. Yes, he smiled to himself, he'd do that.

He scoured the articles online for the latest on the girl or Frannie, although he felt sure there was nothing new to learn. Frannie's death was unfortunate but perhaps inevitable. Fingers tapping, he typed in the name Callie Forde. There wasn't much. She had only one social media account but she didn't post much. Next, he pulled up her picture on the site for the Hampstead Police. He'd looked at it more times than he cared to admit. He didn't know what it was about her face that made him so angry. He wasn't sure if he actually hated her or just the idea of her.

Going back to the browser, he went back to his saved tabs. There were four in all, each named after a state. Wyoming, Montana, Washington, and Utah. They had wide-open spaces, the kind where a person could disappear if they needed to. Under each tab were places to stay, places to eat, most off the beaten path, secluded. There were campgrounds, parks, and hostels. Now that Frannie was gone, he was glad of the files. Once again, he'd proven to be prepared. He was ready.

He had a stack of stolen license plates and a box of burner phones. He would miss the cabin, but it couldn't be helped. It was always going to be temporary in the end. Staying was too risky. But before he could leave, he needed to finish the business he'd started. It was time to open the bidding.

Chapter Forty-Four

"How'd it go with the Hamills?" Zel asked when she dragged herself to the office.

"About how you'd expect." Erin swung between manic and comatose. The ladies from the church helped, and it was clear that Jeremy needed them, too. He was thirteen going on thirty whether he liked it or not. "Jeremy asked about Chang. Wants to know when he's gonna come over and play with him again."

"Good question. By the way, did you hear about the D&D with the Nicholls mom?"

"Yeah. I ran into Ben on the way in."

"Ben? As in your Ben?"

Her cheeks flamed, but she didn't comment, changing the subject instead. "What time is the FBI getting here?"

"Four. We've got Agent Corcoran."

"Great."

The day crawled into afternoon as they sifted through old files and new, read through updated forensics, and took another run at Frannie's boss, the Holts, and anyone else they could think of. It was Hendo who brought her the call.

"Forde. We might have something on the BOLO. A sheriff called in right before you got back."

"Holy shit." Zel came around his desk. "What'd he say?"

"Not much," Hendo said and handed over a piece of paper with a phone number and name scrawled across it. "Wants to talk. Sheriff Thompkins in Bath County. They got a diner waitress who says a guy who might be O'Neill came in and picked up two burgers and fries to go."

Two burgers. "When?" Callie asked.

"About a half hour ago."

The sheriff picked up after one ring.

"Sheriff Thompkins." After introductions, he launched into his story. "This guy calls in and places an order to go. Now Jeannie's been at The Burger House for twenty years, so that struck her as a little odd. We don't do a lot of takeout up here, you know. This ain't the big city where everyone's in a goddamned hurry."

At that moment, Callie wanted nothing more than for him to hurry up and get to the point, but she kept her mouth shut.

"Anyway," he said, "this guy comes in to pick it up, and he's got on a jacket and a hat and sunglasses. The hat and sunglasses she don't think much of, but the jacket…well, it's hotter'n hell up here already, so she thinks that's mighty funny. She don't get a good look at his face, but she swears he's wearing a wig under that hat. She oughtta know, too. She's gotta 'bout a dozen of her own." The sheriff paused. "Normally, a guy pays with cash ain't no big deal, but he's shifty, like he don't want to talk much. Jeannie's real friendly, so that's kinda hard to do, if you get what I'm sayin'."

"I do," she said, directing the conversation back to the reason for the call. "The guy orders takeout and might be wearing a wig." She wasn't sure it was enough to go on, and at best, there was almost no chance a positive ID could come out of this encounter.

"And a jacket," the man said. "Don't forget he was wearing a jacket."

"Right. And a jacket." She shook her head in Zel's direction. This lead, while well-intentioned, wasn't amounting to much. "Listen, I really want to thank you for following up. We'll get back to you if we need anything more. I'll make sure—"

"I'm not done, Missy." The sheriff's tone changed, suddenly sharp. "I didn't report in because Jeannie thought this guy was strange. I sent it in 'cause Jeannie watched the man go out to his car after he got his burgers. A dark blue, late model Chevy Tahoe. That's what we're looking for, right?"

"Yes, it is." Callie's foot tapped the floor. "Did she happen to get the license plate?"

"Oh, yeah, out of state. Probably stolen if I had to guess," he said, rattling off the number, and still talking. "But I gotta tell you, that Jeannie is a piece of work. She'd be a helluva detective. Like I said, she's sure this guy is up to no good. Says she's got a spidey sense, you know, like Spiderman. So, that woman grabs a handful of ketchup packets and goes running after the guy. He didn't get any further than halfway outta the lot before she ran him down. She gets him to roll down his window so she can shove those packets in his hand."

Callie's breath quickened. "Did she see something in the car?"

"Not the girl, if that's what you're thinking. Jeanne said there was a bunch of fast food bags like he'd been eatin' in the car a whole lot. She did get her eye on something good, though."

It was all Callie could do not to scream out the words. "What was that, Sheriff?"

"Well, did you know these cars got the VIN right up there under the windshield now? No doubt to make it easy on the mechanics, but Jeannie saw it. It's a long number, too, but she got the last six digits memorized."

"The last six digits? Of the VIN?"

"Yep. And wouldn't you know? They're a match."

Chapter Forty-Five

After postponing the press conference, Captain Jackson pulled the team—minus Chang—into the war room and cleared his throat. "We've got the sheriff's office riding by as many motel lots within a fifty-mile radius of the diner as they can. If the car is spotted, we'll put out surveillance. We don't want to spook him and take a chance he might hurt the girl."

Everyone around the table nodded.

Zel spoke up. "As far as we know, he doesn't know the waitress made him. He might be feeling the stolen license plate is enough."

"I disagree," Jackson said. "He didn't risk eating in the diner. He's wearing a disguise. He's not stupid enough to think a license plate will protect him."

This made sense to Callie. "Is it possible he has a place in the area? That he's not in a motel at all."

Jackson nodded at her. "Anything's possible. Might be a good idea to get a listing of local Airbnbs, vacation homes, anyplace that does short-term rentals."

Hendo raised his hand. "I can get on that."

A knock on the door made them look around. Mary poked her head in. "Captain, LJ is on the line. Said he has something for Detective Forde."

"Patch him through, Mary." The captain punched the button. "LJ, Captain Jackson here. I've got the team assembled. What have you got?"

"Well, for starters, as you already know, O'Neill isn't your garden variety accountant." Several heads bobbed up and down, each aware of his STEM expertise. "He's the real thing. Not just coding. As far as I can tell, he sidestepped the company security system from the moment he started working at the plant which can only mean he had reason to. He knew there would be times he'd have to use the system while he was at work."

"Sounds risky," Hendo said.

"Which is why he built a series of firewalls. Some I've never seen before."

Callie sensed rather than saw the collective disappointment around the table. Without the ability to follow O'Neill's virtual tracks, they couldn't prove he'd kidnapped Natalie, much less been a part of any conspiracy to kidnap and traffic young women—if that were even what this case was. Still, if they found him, they could get him for Frannie's murder.

"Can you get through them?" Jackson asked.

"Eventually. But that's not what I called about. He received an email that I thought you should know about." Every detective at the table leaned in. "It was encrypted, of course, and behind a firewall, but I was able to break this one a few minutes ago." They heard the sounds of clicking keys. "I'm sending it to you now, Detective Forde."

"What's it say?" Jackson asked.

"It's short. It says 'You've been a bad boy. The new girl is getting interest. Where is she?'"

No one spoke, the ugly truth settling over the room. The email, for better or for worse, was proof of Callie's worst-case scenario. Natalie was the new girl and had been taken for the same reason as Emma. To be bought and sold. And O'Neill was part of it.

Callie stared down at her phone, the file open now. "When was it sent?"

"Tuesday."

Callie felt sick. Two days ago, plenty of time for bidding.

Zel asked, "Who was the sender?"

"The name doesn't mean anything. Lord of the World."

"Big ego fits the profile we have on Martin Connor," Zel said.

Fitting didn't make it true, though. Callie leaned forward. "Is there any way to find out who Lord of the World is?"

"I doubt it. The IP address is a black hole. But I'm searching for more emails behind that same firewall. I'll let you know what I find."

After he'd hung up, the team returned to the subject of the BOLO.

Callie rose from her seat. "We've got to get going, Captain."

Jackson's jaw tightened. "Keep it by the book, Forde. Let's get O'Neill but take no chances. The goal is to take him alive. If things go sideways, you wait for backup. You got that? No chances."

Like a hammer reminding her of the past, his words made her stiffen. "Yes, Captain."

"That's an order, Forde. No chances."

Chapter Forty-Six

Zel steered the car onto the turnoff lane that took them off the highway. "Any word on the motels?" he asked.

"So far, no sightings, but they're still looking." She sighed, willing the miles to evaporate, but even once they reached the sheriff, they didn't know where to look. Bath County had more than five hundred square miles and a population of less than five thousand. That meant a whole lot of land to hide in and not many people to spot you. A person might think a stranger would stand out, but as long as he had a fishing rod in his hand, he had a reason to be there. Not only that, but the county was also home to one of the oldest resorts in the country. She tapped her feet, the sound a hollow thump on the floor mats.

"We don't even know where we're going," Zel said.

"We'll figure it out after we get to the sheriff's office."

"That email—the one LJ figured out—kinda says it all, doesn't it?"

Callie frowned. *You've been a bad boy. The new girl is getting interest. Where is she?* Her knees bounced along with her feet. She angled her head in Zel's direction. "Angie didn't miss anything at O'Neill's, did she?"

"When have you ever known Angie to miss anything?" Her lack of response was answer enough. "What are you thinking?"

"Nothing." She stared out the window at open fields and a smattering of cows and horses.

"Yeah, right. I know you better than that."

"Okay." She shifted all the way around to face him. "Where was he keeping Natalie? Or any of the girls? It couldn't have been at his house or Angie would have found something. DNA, a hair, something."

"I don't know. My money's on the garage. He could have moved her the next day and cleaned before Frannie got wise to him."

"Maybe," she said, less convinced than her partner. The only thing she knew for sure was that O'Neill was far more devious, clever, and dangerous than they'd realized.

"We'll get the answers after we find him."

Before she could say more, a message from the Sheriff interrupted her thoughts.

The Payless Motel on Route 728. Car in back lot. Meet me at this gas station.

She plugged the address into the GPS and texted back.

Be there in less than ten. Wait for us.

Roger that.

"Get off up here," she said to Zel, filling him in.

The road widened—not enough to accommodate another car—but enough that they passed houses and drove through a tiny town that stretched the length of two blocks.

"Keep going straight." Zel pressed harder on the gas. For Callie, the next minutes dragged. Her foot tapped harder and faster against the floor. A cold sweat coated her skin. More than once, her hand found the smooth metal of the gun in her holster.

She peered through the windshield. "Slow down now."

Zel eased his foot off the gas.

"Turn here and then go left on 728."

He made the turn, and after a half mile, they spotted the low-rise motel. It sat next to a gas station with only two working pumps.

"Go to the back of the gas station."

Zel drove around, pulling up next to the Bath County sheriff's car. Four men got out. The sheriff, the largest and roundest of the group, stepped forward.

"You the folks from Hampstead?" He had ruddy skin, the kind that cracked and crinkled when he spoke. He held out his bear-sized paw and introduced his men. "This is Deputy Carlson, Deputy Anderson, and Deputy DuPont.

Far as we can tell, his car is still back there." He gestured to one of his deputies. "Carlson here walked over to the motel to get a list of the guests and room numbers." He held up a hand. "Don't worry. He done it quiet-like. The man that answers to Jeannie's description is in room twenty-two on the back side. He ain't left in his car or on foot since we spotted it."

Zel eyed the sheriff. "Assuming he didn't abandon this location before you spotted the car."

The sheriff seemed to consider the possibility. "You're right, son. He might've. But I don't think he knew what Jeannie was up to when she ran out with those ketchups. She's a smooth one."

"Okay," Callie said. "Let's say he's in there. He left the diner at what time, Sheriff?"

"Oh, about three or so hours ago, I'd say."

"And how long is the drive over here?"

"Half hour. Tops."

She scanned the parking lot. "How many other guests in those rooms?"

"Only two. There's a couple in nineteen and a guy in twelve. Been a little slow around here lately."

"We need to get them out."

Thick white eyebrows shot up. "How're we gonna do that?"

Callie gestured toward the front office. "Let's have the manager call the rooms and ask the guests to come up front. Tell them there's a problem with their credit card or something." The man grunted. "Is there a problem, Sheriff?"

He didn't answer right away, squinting up at the sun sinking lower in the sky. "This man is wanted for murder, right?"

"He's the prime suspect, yes," Callie said. "And he's also a person of interest in a kidnapping. A teenaged girl." She reminded them that O'Neill had ordered two burgers. "She could be with him."

The sheriff grunted again, but this time, there was no mistaking the sound for anything other than disgust. "Well, we won't have anyone saying Bath County didn't help out the good folks of Hampstead."

"Thank you, Sheriff."

"Not a problem." His hand found his gun, a reflex Callie recognized and understood. "What's the plan?"

Callie eyed the long block of rooms. Half faced the road, the others looked out at the trees behind the hotel. "Anyone in the rooms on the front side?"

"Nope."

She gave a more detailed plan to extract the guests and stash them safely in the manager's office. "How thick are those trees?" she asked, gesturing at the back of the motel.

"Pretty thick, be even thicker the later it gets."

"Good. Sheriff, you and Deputy DuPont will each take one end of the row of rooms. When we're clear, Zel and I will approach O'Neill's room." She studied Carlson and Anderson and suddenly felt old. Pinkish blemishes dotted the forehead of Carlson, and Anderson didn't have enough stubble to shave. "You two take the woods." They would be safer there, away from O'Neill. "No one draws a weapon except me and Detective Zeleniak unless absolutely necessary. Understood? We surround the room and bring him in. That's all."

The pimply-faced deputy's face paled, but he didn't flinch. Nor did the other boy. "Yes, ma'am," they said in unison.

Zel leaned in close. "Can I have a word?" The two stepped out of earshot. "O'Neill is probably armed. Wouldn't it be better to wait for the FBI to get here or," he stopped and lifted a hand toward the young deputies, "at least until we get some more backup?"

She kept her eye on the motel and the late-day sun glinting off the windows. "What if Natalie is in that room?"

He shook his head. "We do the same."

"Jackson said the goal is to bring him in alive. We're here. Waiting for backup is if things go sideways."

"You're twisting what Jackson said. Maybe we should wait—"

"Jackson said to wait for backup if things go sideways." She tipped her chin toward the sheriff. "And we're on top of that already. We have backup."

"You call that backup. Those boys probably couldn't shoot at a target ten feet in front of them. They're barely out of high school."

"You're wrong." Instinct told her these young men weren't strangers to guns, although she was also sure these boys hadn't seen anything like O'Neill before. Aloud, she said. "They've probably been hunting since they were old enough to walk. That's all there is here. Hunting and fishing. They may be young, but I bet they can shoot."

He shook his head and crossed his arms. "Call in the location, Cal."

She thought about Natalie, picturing her in that room. Was she tied up? Was she drugged? Was O'Neill planning to take her to the highest bidder? She'd phone in the location. That was the right thing to do, and she told Zel that now, but she wasn't going to sit on her hands and wait for something to happen. They had to get Natalie out of that room. Now.

"We're taking him." She wouldn't back down on this. "If your daughter were in that room, would you want us to wait?" Callie knew it wasn't fair to bring in his daughter, but she didn't give him a chance to argue. "We have backup, Zel. In case."

He chewed his lower lip, looking back at the motel. When he uncrossed his arms, she let out a breath she hadn't realized she was holding.

"Okay, Cal. We'll do it your way."

Chapter Forty-Seven

"Are they all in the manager's office?" Callie asked.

"Snug as a bug," the sheriff answered.

She gave the men a final once-over. Instructions had been issued and vests donned. She looked down at herself in the maid's uniform. This part of the plan was weak and she knew it, but short of anything else, it's what they had.

"All right," she pointed a finger at the baby-faced men. "You two get behind that tree line and hold your positions."

The pair peeled away. Callie watched them slip into the woods, their khaki-colored uniforms blending well with the fat trunks and bramble. Less than five minutes later, they were no longer visible to the naked eye. It was enough to know they were there. And safe.

"Sheriff," she said, "you and Deputy Dupont are each taking one end of the row of rooms. Ready?"

He gave her a lopsided grin. "Born ready." He circled to one end of the building while Dupont circled around to the other. Each man could get to Callie and Zel in ten seconds or less if needed. The backup was in place.

Her breath echoing in her ear, Callie pushed the maid's cart forward, Zel at her heel. Over the trees, the sun dipped low, splintering into red and golden-orange stripes. A line of sweat slid down her temple. Zel spoke in low tones.

"The drapes are drawn."

She turned her ear toward the room. "The TV is on."

Grim-faced, Zel drew his weapon from his holster and pressed himself against the wall on the far side of the door, out of the sightline of the large window or peephole.

Callie looked him in the eye, her breath heavy. If this went the way she hoped, they'd have O'Neill in custody and would be taking Natalie home to her mother and her brother in a matter of minutes. She gave a single nod.

She reached out and knocked on the door. "Housekeeping."

A second later came O'Neill's voice. "Go away."

"Sorry, sir, but I've got to change out the towels."

"I said go away." The volume on the TV rose higher. A laugh track from a sitcom filled the air.

Callie slipped her hand into her pocket, extracting the manager's room key. Her other hand went to the gun she'd hidden under a towel on the cart. From the corner of her eye, she saw movement, a shift in the drapes. A half inch, no more, and the curtain fell closed again.

"Here goes," she muttered and lifted her hand to knock again, calling out, "Coming in, sir." Zel moved in behind her, gun drawn. Callie, clutching the key, bent toward the lock when the roar of screeching tires sounded from the parking lot. Both detectives whirled around in time to see Dupont emerge from the shadows straight into the line of the approaching SUV. With a squeal of tires, the vehicle barreled forward. Dupont dove sideways but not in time. Callie winced as the man's body hit the ground, rolling to a stop. Before anyone could react, the SUV accelerated, veering in their direction. The brakes screamed as the giant hunk of steel skidded to a halt only feet away from their noses.

The driver's window came down halfway to reveal dark glasses perched above a long, shiny barrel.

"Stay on the room," Callie said, her own gun now trained on the man in the SUV, key forgotten. A backseat window rolled down, and a second long barrel appeared. The Sheriff's steps pounded as he moved in behind her. Inside the room, the TV went off.

"Nobody wants any trouble here," the man behind the glasses said. He spoke in the measured tone of a man used to getting his way. "Our friend is going to come out nice and quiet, and you're going to back away. He doesn't concern you, Detective. It is Detective, isn't it? That maid outfit isn't fooling anyone, you know."

"This man is wanted for murder," she said, trying to match his calm tone. Two men visible and two guns, both aimed at what appeared to be their heads. Her breath caught in her chest. No vest could protect Zel from a shot to the head. But there were three of them, five if you counted the boys in the trees. "We're taking him in."

The sunroof slid open, and a third man showed himself, also armed. Callie didn't like the odds as much as she had a minute earlier.

"As I was saying, our friend will be joining us. You can allow him to join us willingly, or you can die trying to stop us. It's your choice, of course, although I might rather enjoy the latter."

Callie heard the Sheriff's indrawn breath behind her.

"Lower your guns, please."

"We can't do that," she said, holding firm. "This is police business."

"It appears we're at a stalemate, doesn't it, Detective?" He seemed amused, but not for long. "I think we both know it would be a mistake for you to assume we won't shoot. Your life means nothing to me. Or your partner's. I'm here for our friend, whatever means necessary."

Callie knew that if O'Neill got in that SUV, they'd never see him again. Or Natalie. "What do you want with O'Neill anyway?"

He arched a single brow. "Questions?" He half-turned toward someone in the vehicle and chuckled. "She's something, this one." Callie didn't really expect him to answer, but the man surprised her. "We have interests to protect. Same as you. The difference is, only one of us will succeed."

"Interests like selling underage girls to the highest bidder?"

"Enough," he snapped. "This has gone on long enough. Either you stand down, or you pay the price."

Scrambling, she said the first thing that popped into her head. "What's in it for us?"

This question seemed to take the man by surprise. "In it for you?"

Callie raised her face toward his. "Yes. We give you O'Neill. What do we get?"

The man's laughter echoed in the air, the sound hollow and mirthless. "What you get," he said, voice hard as stone, "is to live."

Chapter Forty-Eight

"Put your guns and phones on the ground now. Hands in the air."
The last sliver of orange sky gave way to dusk, and the sky
darkened. A breeze blew up, lifting Callie's hair and drying the
sweat on her skin. She shivered but held her gun steady.

"Put your gun on the ground," the man said and jerked his barrel in Zel's
direction, "or my friend here will kill your partner." No one moved. "Five
seconds. Four. Three."

Zel bent down, laying his gun on the pavement.

"Now your phone," the man said. "Carefully."

Callie remained motionless, her gun still trained on the driver. She saw
them then. Two shadows, emerging from the trees like specters, creeping
across the parking lot. She held herself still, silently calculating the distance.
Fifty yards. Maybe more.

Zel took his phone from his pocket and laid it next to his gun.

The man gestured toward the Sheriff. "Now you."

At forty yards, the two deputies dropped lower, guns raised. They crept
closer.

"Last but not least," the man said, eyeing Callie.

She took her time lowering her gun and laying it on the ground. "Careful,"
the man ordered when she reached into her pocket for her phone.

Before drawing it out, she asked, "What happens next?"

He ignored her. "Put it down."

Thirty yards. She set her phone next to the others.

The second man climbed from the back seat and swept the guns and

215

phones into a sack, holding them up like a prize.

"Now see, that wasn't so hard, was it?"

The man directed Callie, Zel, and the sheriff to stand against the wall. If she'd had any doubt before, she didn't then. This was a firing squad.

Desperate, she asked, "Do you work for Martin Connor?" Callie thought she saw the pulse of a vein near his eye, but it was difficult to tell behind the glasses.

"Here's how this is going to work," the man said, ignoring the question. He pointed at Zel. "You're going to knock on the door three times, wait five seconds, and then knock twice more. That will tell our friend the coast is clear for him to come out." He jerked his gun toward the door. "Do it now."

Zel looked at Callie. She saw fear, but she also saw defiance. The man saw it, too.

"Shoot him," the leader said to the man standing through the sunroof. "There are others to do the knocking."

"Wait." Callie jumped forward. She wouldn't stand there and watch her partner die. How would she live with herself? How would she face Marcie? "I'll do it."

She was breathing hard now, blood pumping faster. The man intended to kill them the minute he had O'Neill, but the sight of those boys, only twenty yards away now, gave her courage. She had to stall. Her hand found the hard edge of the cart behind her at the same time she raised her fist to knock three times. Ten yards. She counted to five and raised her fist again. Five yards.

"Stand back," the man in the SUV hissed. Callie took two steps back, her hand keeping the cart by her side. They all waited. The door creaked open an inch, then two.

The deputies huddled at the rear of the SUV. The door swung a foot wider, and there was O'Neill, a large suitcase at his side. She strained to see behind him, but the room was dark.

"Finally," O'Neill said, a note of triumph in his voice. There was no sign of the remorseful and frightened man she and Zel had interviewed. Under a bad wig, his beady eyes flashed with arrogance, and in that moment, she was reminded of Fat Fury, the superhero who liked to bop his enemies with magic lollipops. O'Neill's grin was more leer when he lifted a hand toward the man behind the wheel of the SUV. "I didn't think you'd ever get here."

Callie rolled the maid's cart a few inches forward, heart jackhammering in her chest. The deputies gripped their guns with both hands, raised them chest high.

"Let's go, O'Neill," the man behind the glasses said.

"Yeah, I'm coming." He grunted as he opened the door wide and, lugging the suitcase, stepped out of the room. At the same moment, the boys materialized from behind the SUV. The first shot rang out, echoing across the empty lot, and Callie shoved the maid's cart forward with all her strength into the man holding the bag of guns. The sheer force sent her staggering and crashing into O'Neill. Falling, he took her with him. She hit the ground hard, her head and shoulder bouncing off the pavement. Blackness descended. More shots sounded, followed by squealing tires, thundering steps, and urgent shouting, but Callie heard only the soft hum of silence, and then nothing at all.

Chapter Forty-Nine

The doctor grabbed a penlight from his pocket and gestured toward the bed with a short, stubby finger. "Lie back, Detective."

Callie's feet dangled over the side of the hospital bed.

"Is this really necessary?" she asked.

From across the room, Zel growled.

"Okay, okay," she said, lying back.

When the doctor finished his examination, he clucked his tongue. "You're lucky."

She didn't feel lucky. Every part of her body hurt, particularly the shoulder they'd popped back into place and her head, which didn't so much pound as pulsate with pain.

"So, can I go?"

The doctor threw Zel a pained look. "She'd be with you?"

"Afraid so."

He clucked again, and she wondered if his other patients found that element of his bedside manner equally annoying. "She needs to rest and avoid any strenuous activity." He typed a few notes into his computer before focusing on Callie again. "You sustained a serious concussion, Detective Forde. If you have any elongated episodes of dizziness or memory loss, I want you to come back immediately. Do you understand?"

"She will," Zel said, shooting her a warning glare.

The doctor hesitated as though he might change his mind before nodding once and leaving them.

"Do I really have to wear this sling?" she asked once they were in the car.

218

"If you don't, I'm going to separate your other shoulder."

She wasn't sorry to leave Bath County or the hospital. "Fine," she said before letting her head fall against the headrest, eyes closing. Images of O'Neill and the man with the sunglasses flooded her brain. She had memories, fractured and incomplete at best, and she sat up again, head still pounding. Doing her best to find a position that didn't hurt, she shifted toward her partner. "Okay. Give it to me. All of it."

"Well, that didn't take long," he said. "We haven't even made it out of the parking lot."

She wanted to smile, but she was afraid it would hurt. "Tell me about O'Neill."

"He's dead."

She swayed a bit, catching herself on the door handle. "Dead," she said in a whisper. It wasn't that she hadn't guessed as much, but hearing it was something else.

"They shot him. Probably the plan all along."

"What about DuPont? The deputies?" She held her breath, dread making her chest tight. She'd dragged them into the stakeout, and if anything had happened to them, she didn't know if she could forgive herself.

"Let me tell it before you start asking questions, okay?" Without a choice, she nodded. "After O'Neill came out of the room, the man in the glasses, Mr. Cheery, gave his man the order to shoot. We were all ready to be executed, but apparently, we weren't at the top of the list. That honor belonged to O'Neill. My thinking is they were more interested in making sure he didn't talk than bringing him in. They would have turned on us next if you hadn't shoved that cart when you did, and those deputies hadn't stepped in." He gave a shake of his head. "You were right about them being able to shoot, Cal. They got the one holding the bag and might have hit the guy in the sunroof." His glum expression told her what she already suspected before he told her. "The bagman didn't make it and didn't live long enough to talk."

He pulled out onto the highway toward Hampstead. "Those kids were pretty shaken up after what happened but were more worried about you than anything. O'Neill collapsed on top of you and knocked you out. It looked like you'd been the one shot, O'Neill's blood all over you."

She'd figured something like that but hadn't been sure. It had all happened so fast.

"The Sheriff called me about an hour ago. Said DuPont has some broken ribs and bruises, but he's going to recover."

Her shoulders loosened as she let the news settle over her. They were okay. All of them. They'd be changed. Altered now, but they were okay.

Holding her breath, she asked, "Natalie?"

"Not there."

She fell back against the seat again, her energy drained. O'Neill was dead, and all their leads with him. If only she hadn't insisted they take O'Neill themselves.

"I know what you're thinking," Zel said, "and you're wrong. If we'd waited for more backup, O'Neill would still be dead. And most likely, Mr. Cheery would have gotten the files, too."

Callie's head snapped forward. "What files?"

"Pictures, for one thing, and a hard drive. I'm guessing O'Neill had that as an insurance policy."

She looked over her shoulder to the backseat, her body protesting. "Where's the hard drive?"

"You don't really think the FBI let us have it, do you?"

She sank back again. "That was cruel. Why even tell me?"

"Because I was allowed a few minutes with the pictures." She gave him a sideways glance, eyebrows high. "And I might have had my phone with me." Without another word, he handed it to her.

Heart pounding, she opened the photo app and scrolled down. The pictures were torn at the corners. She knew in an instant that these were the ones from the walls of the garage at O'Neill's house. The girls were blond, brunette, redhead, and all young. But none of them were Natalie. Or Emma.

"Agent Corcoran said their focus is trying to connect O'Neill and the girls to Connor."

She was glad, but it didn't make her feel any better. "What about his car? Anything?"

CHAPTER FORTY-NINE

"Not yet."

They drove the next few miles in silence.

"There is one other thing." She groaned, not sure she could take any more bad news. "Remember how the FBI got a tip when they found Emma on that private site? After that, the site disappeared, and they could never find it again. Corcoran thinks that's because of O'Neill. He started putting up those firewalls, making sure the site couldn't be found. Every time they got close, he moved it again." He paused. "And there's something else. They got screenshots of the latest version of the site. They haven't been able to track down where they came from, and the site seems to have disappeared again, but…" Zel paused as though gathering the courage to tell her the rest.

"But what?"

"Natalie's picture was there. Like that email said."

The new girl is getting interest.

"She's wearing a blue dress, and her name on the site isn't Natalie. It's Angelica."

It all sunk in then. O'Neill, their only lead, was dead. How many more days before Natalie was sold?

"Pull over."

Stomach churning, she stumbled from the car. Everything she'd been afraid of was happening. The past was doing what it always did, haunting anyone who dared to forget, taunting them with their past failures. Her stomach heaved again, and she sank low to the ground. Overhead, a crow cawed, and she shivered, weak and tired. It was the Emma Nicholls case all over again, except she was the one who'd rushed in and put men in harm's way.

She didn't know how long she huddled on the ground before staggering back to the car.

"Feel better?" Zel asked without taking his eyes from the road.

"No," she said, squinting up at the cloudless sky. If Natalie was on that site, available for bids, that could only mean she was still alive. That also meant she could still be found. Callie rolled her head toward Zel. "But I will be."

221

Chapter Fifty

"**F**orde." Jackson waved her toward him.

Each step made the hammer in Callie's head bang harder. By the time she sat down, she wasn't sure how her skull hadn't broken in two. The dread in her gut wasn't helping. It was time to face the music.

"Glad to see you're still with us, Detective."

"Thank you."

There was nothing glad about the expression he wore. "But you know the rules. Desk duty until—"

"No, Captain. You can't take me off the case. Natalie—"

"Detective." It was his turn to cut her off. "You will be on desk duty until I say otherwise. Standard procedure. You may remain on the case from your desk, but Zeleniak will take lead."

"Captain, I'll be fine. I am fine."

"Your arm is in a sling, and you've got a concussion. After the way yesterday went down, you're lucky I don't put you on leave."

Tears threatened, and she blinked hard to keep them from betraying her. "So, I get to push paper?" Her voice shook in spite of her best effort to stay calm.

There was genuine concern etched in the lines of his face—whether for her or Natalie or both, she couldn't be sure—but it wasn't enough to change his mind.

"Desk duty. That's an order, Forde."

No one met her eye as she walked back to her desk, and her skin grew redder with each step. When she sat down, she sighed heavily. The perfectly organized mess of files and papers that decorated her desk mocked her now.

Zel's soft voice cut through the red noise in her brain. "Hey, I don't know if this is going to make matters worse, but Ben came by."

Ben? She hated herself for the way her heart tripped at the sound of his name.

"He heard about what happened at the motel."

"What? How?"

"There's a dead body. He was bound to hear."

"Oh. Yeah."

"Said to tell you he's glad you're okay." Callie avoided her partner's gaze, afraid he'd see the way her heart was beating faster. "He also wanted you to know that they dropped the charges against Sarah Nicholls."

"Great. Thanks."

Zel cleared his throat. "I'm heading over to the plant to meet with all of the department heads and anyone else who came in contact with O'Neill."

"That's good," she said, glad for the change in subject. "His boss seems like a good source."

"Yeah." He stood, hovering. "I can hang out a little longer. Reschedule."

She shook her head. "No. We keep looking. We don't give up. We do everything we can to find Natalie." She realized she meant every word. Maybe the motel stakeout had gone awry, but they weren't any worse off than they would have been if they hadn't found O'Neill. He'd still be dead, and everything he'd taken with him gone. That was something, at least. She would beat herself up another day, after they'd exhausted every possibility and turned over every rock—not a moment sooner. Right now, the Hamills deserved everything they had. Zel needed to get to the plant and not worry about her.

"You go." Callie gestured at the piles. "I've got plenty to do here."

His mouth widened into a smile, and he nodded back. "You got it, partner."

Grabbing a notepad, she began making a list of key evidence. The bogus babysitting job. The dating app. The abandoned car. The private site with Natalie's picture. The FBI's suspicions about Connor. O'Neill running after killing his girlfriend. The pictures he'd torn from his wall. The words on the page blurred, and she reached into her drawer and downed more ibuprofen.

She was almost grateful when her phone buzzed. "Forde."

"It's LJ. I've got something, but I'm not sure what to make of it."

The high-pitched excitement in his voice made her sit up straight. "Shoot."

"Remember how O'Neill got an email from some guy who called himself Lord of the World?"

"Sure. He was asking where the girl was."

"Right. O'Neill sent a response."

Her pulse quickened. "What did it say?"

"Well, that's the odd part." The sound of keys clicking sounded over the line. "It was one sentence, well, question really. It said, 'What girl do you mean?'"

Callie repeated the words. "What girl do you mean?"

"That's it. Is there more than one? Girl, I mean?" LJ asked.

Callie sat back, the phone pressed to her ear. Her father had said the site usually had a half dozen girls or so for sale at one time. Bidding was a long process, one that the site manager let drag out to build anticipation and, perhaps, to prepare the girls. "I don't know," she said now. "Maybe." She raked a hand through her hair. "Did this Lord of the World respond?"

"Still working on that."

"Okay. Let me know when you have something."

Callie texted Zel what she'd learned and sat back. Once again, she found herself staring at her whiteboard with its circles and lines and glossy photos of Natalie and Emma. She reached behind her for the pictures Zel had printed out from his phone, copies of the photos the FBI found in O'Neill's suitcase. One by one, she taped them to the bottom of the board in order of their disappearance—if the information was known. Some had names. Some they hadn't found yet. All had gone missing in the last few years. After Emma. After the private site vanished the first time.

Her brain hummed over the ache. If the FBI was right, O'Neill made the site disappear and created new ways to make it hard to find. But that was months after Emma's disappearance. She fished out the file on her desk, flipping through the pages and poring over dates. It fit. Maybe the reason

O'Neill didn't have a picture of Emma was because she was taken before he played a role. But where was Natalie's picture? Had he destroyed it, or had he not gotten a chance to hang it?

A shadow fell over her, and she looked up to find Hendo watching her.

"Mind a little company?" He stood a few feet away, one hand shoved into his pocket. His craggy face seemed to sag more than usual, and he shifted his weight from foot to foot. She realized with a start that he was waiting for permission.

"Please."

Grabbing a chair and flipping it around, he rested his arms across the high back, his legs jutting forward.

"Where's your partner?" she asked before he could make the conversation about her. Concern was one thing, but she drew the line at having him—or anyone—feel sorry for her. Beyond that, she wasn't in the mood to rehash everything that had gone wrong the day before.

"Still out. Called the asshole, but he didn't answer, so I went by. House is shut up tight, too. Must be feeling pretty bad."

"Uh-huh." Callie had bigger things to worry about than how sick Chang was or wasn't, but she kept that to herself. "The Captain said you were going to check on Fred Nicholls. Give him the latest."

"Tried, but phone went to voicemail. His office says he's on vacation. I'm not sure I blame him. All this hits a little close to home, I bet."

Callie thought about the man who'd come down to the station. He'd been angry, sad, and lonely. Maybe the man did need a vacation. Still, it seemed odd he hadn't called Hendo back. Shifting gears, she tapped her fingers across the arm of her chair.

"Can I run something by you?"

She explained the order of the pictures she'd added to the whiteboard and her reasoning that Emma's kidnapping took place before O'Neill was deeply involved.

"Makes sense. He woulda been fresh outta jail, and his P.O. would have been coming around a lot those first few months."

"Right. But they found those licorice wrappers in Emma's car and at the scene with the undercover agent. There's the wrapper in the garage at the Randolph house, the last place we know Natalie was, and the package Frannie had in her apartment."

His skin wrinkled in confusion. "I don't know what you're getting at."

She didn't answer right away. Her gut told her O'Neill was involved—heavily—but it was hard to imagine him lifting a sedated girl into or out of a trunk. This didn't mean he wouldn't be capable of kidnapping or violence. He'd proven that, but even the manner of Frannie's death struck her as more reactive than calculated.

"I don't know either, but he's a web guru, right? It's safe to assume that's his role."

"Sure, right."

"He sets up the fake profiles and babysitting messages, lays the groundwork, so to speak. We've been focused on him with good reason, but maybe he's not the one who actually takes the girls. Maybe that's someone else." Even as she posed the theory, nausea rose up in her belly. If she was right, that was another player they had no leads for.

"But then why did his girlfriend keep licorice at her apartment?" He rubbed his temple, his eyes widening. "Unless it wasn't for O'Neill. Do you think?"

His question bounced around her brain for only a few seconds. "Jesus. You're right." She grabbed her phone. After she hung up, she looked over at Hendo. "The licorice was for Frannie's mother on the rare occasion she came to visit."

"Frannie's mother's not a suspect now, is she?" Hendo asked with a lopsided grin that faded as quickly as it appeared. "Seriously, though, if it wasn't O'Neill who actually kidnapped all those girls, who did? Are you saying all we got to go on is some guy that likes black licorice?"

She got to her feet, pacing in front of the whiteboard, thinking out loud. "Yes and no. Our licorice lover is part of the whole machine. If O'Neill is the technology, this guy is the muscle. He's not important. Not like Connor or even O'Neill. Maybe that's why the FBI hasn't focused on what we're doing. They have bigger fish to fry." She halted and looked over at him. "There's something else that's bothering me."

"What's that?"

"It makes sense that O'Neill didn't have Emma's picture, but why didn't he have Natalie's? Presumably, he—or whoever set up the scam—went to a lot of trouble to engage with her on two different fronts. He knew her face, her friends, her habits."

"Maybe he hadn't gotten around to printing and hanging it yet."

She circled back to the photos lined up across the bottom of the whiteboard. "I was thinking that, too, but the O'Neill I saw at the motel had a mean streak. It feels like he would have. They meant enough to him to take them when he ran."

"Thought that was for insurance," Hendo said.

Again, she told him she didn't think so. "That's what the hard drive was for. I think the pictures were personal. O'Neill didn't like women much. He'd spent most of his life rejected by women, starting with his own mother. Helping plan these kidnappings was how he got out his rage." She resumed pacing, her thoughts moving faster. "The dating apps served two purposes. One, he could lure the girls in for the organization. But they also let him play at being his fantasy hero, Fat Fury." She explained the character's backstory and that O'Neill used Fat Fury as his gaming name. "On those dating sites, he got to be Fat Fury. He got to be irresistible."

"That's twisted."

"It is. Although they were ultimately kidnapped and sold, for a while, they were his conquests."

"You're thinking the pictures were like trophies."

"Yes. Maybe." Callie knew there were holes the size of a small planet in her theory, but it felt closer to right than anything before. O'Neill's job was at his desk, not dragging girls from their cars and hitting them with chloroform. "I'm still missing something, though," she said, flopping back down, sure she had the answer—somewhere—if only she could figure out what it was.

Hendo got up then, flipping the chair back around. "I don't know, Cal. Whatever O'Neill was doing with those pictures doesn't change that the girl was for sale on that site and that he lured her to that house." She pressed her lips together. "Sorry. I know that's not helping."

She waved a hand at him. "No, you're right. It's only a picture. He could have dropped it somewhere, for all we know."

"Sure."

She looked up at the man standing over her. He was a good man, a kind man. "Listen, thanks for hearing me out."

"Anytime." Hendo cocked his head toward her whiteboard with its mess of notecards, lines, and pictures. "Sometimes this job is like one of those word jumbles where you have to reorder the letters to find the right word. With a jumble, the answer's right in front of you if your brain can unscramble it. The letters are all there, like a case where you got a trail of evidence, fingerprints, DNA. You just gotta put it together in the right way. Not like a crossword that only gives you one clue. You gotta find your own letters *and* figure out if the word fits in the squares right. Different puzzles. That's how these cases are. Like different puzzles." He chuckled and apologized. "Didn't mean to run on about puzzles."

"It's okay," she said. "I didn't know you liked word puzzles that much."

"Sure. I like crosswords the best. Go figure. Always use pencil, though, 'cause it's like you and your theories. A whole lotta guessing."

He left her to keep running idea after idea in her head, but nothing felt right. The notecards on the board told one story. O'Neill and his superhero told another. The licorice. The pictures. She had the sensation of drowning, of being unable to keep her head above water, as though someone or something was anticipating her every move, pushing her under again. Her head jerked up, and she frantically scanned the desks around her, her pulse racing. Hendo and Miller were still working the list of names from the big box store. Jackson had left for the mayor's office. Chang's chair sat empty. The rest were at their desks working or out on the streets. Her shoulders relaxed and she shook her head, heartbeat slowing again. She told herself she was letting her imagination run away with her, but she couldn't shake the feeling entirely.

Zel came back with sandwiches and notes, and they huddled over reports for a while. The hours passed slowly, and the afternoon dragged into evening.

"I can drive myself tomorrow," Callie told Zel when he drove her home.

"You sure?"

"Yep." She put her hand on the door to open it, but hesitated. "We're right to keep pursuing the O'Neill angle, right?"

"Yeah, Cal, I think we are. We can't get him for killing Frannie now, but we can keep trying to untangle whatever he was doing. Even dead, he's still our only lead."

"Him and those licorice wrappers." Callie's dad had told her there were other cases where wrappers were found, making them the only concrete evidence tying the abductions together.

"Right." Zel yawned. "Cal, get some rest. It's after ten."

She got out then, rapping on the hood of the car. Unlocking her front door and flipping on the lights, Callie walked through her house on autopilot. She fell into her favorite chair, swinging her feet onto the ottoman. She couldn't remember the last time she'd eaten. Maybe a pack of crackers with the ibuprofen. The ache in her head and shoulder reminded her she should take another dose, but she couldn't stop her mind from going back to the school photo of Natalie on the whiteboard. In it, the girl tipped her head to the left so that her hair fell across one high-boned cheek. She wore a wide smile, and the standard blue background accentuated the color of her eyes.

Callie touched a hand to her own limp hair and sighed. Bringing her phone to life, she returned to the last file LJ had sent.

What girl do you mean?

It wasn't grammatically incorrect, but it didn't make sense. She went back to the original message from Lord of the World, this time reading it out loud. Then back to O'Neill's.

She pulled out a pen and pad and wrote out the two email messages in order, reading them out loud a second time.

Lord of the World: *You've been a bad boy. The new girl is getting interest. Where is she?*

O'Neill: *What girl do you mean?*

Callie stared down at the page, her lips moving as she read over and over until the missing piece made her sit up straight, sliding into place.

Chapter Fifty-One

The man tucked the last of his shirts into the suitcase and zipped it shut. He placed it next to the other suitcase, the one that held her new clothes. His fingers lingered over the handle and settled on the bag tag. He'd written her new name and added a fake address and phone number. She'd probably mess it up, though, but he'd be ready. He was a man who planned for contingencies. Always prepared. That was him. It was a trait that was usually attributed to Boy Scouts, but he'd never been one of those. He might have enjoyed earning the badges, he thought now, but he wouldn't have been allowed to join something like that. There wasn't any prestige in it, and if he were honest with himself, it would have been a waste of his talents. Archery. Stamp collecting. Wood carving. Did any of that really matter in the real world?

Pushing aside the curtain, he drank in the darkness that blanketed the house. He would miss this place. He'd never minded being here alone, tucked back against a forest. No. He'd relished it, savored it as his time to escape. It was like he was the only person left in the world, like in those disaster movies where everyone dies except one man. The idea appealed to him.

Squinting, he could make out the shadow of the rental car, a grey mid-sized SUV exactly like every other on the road. Indistinct. Unmemorable. He'd left his own car in the parking lot of a busy mall. They'd find it eventually, but the fake license plate and car switch would give him enough of a head start, and he couldn't wait any longer. Not with O'Neill dead and the website down— or at least the version where he'd uploaded Leigh's picture. She'd attracted

231

the highest bidders as he'd known she would, but he got no satisfaction from knowing that.

They would look for him soon. He'd missed work. Had they already been to his house? Wondered about him? Even if they did, they'd be too late. He and the girl would be long gone. The thought made him smile. How much would he give to see their faces if they knew? They treated him like he didn't matter. He'd been thrown out, misunderstood, undervalued his whole life. She'd been the worst. Cruel.

"You're a pervert, you know that. What is it with you and staring at girls on a screen? Christ, you could be their father."

She'd never recognized his value, what he could do. He was glad of that now. He had big plans ahead. If only she knew.

In the morning, he'd prepare the breakfast tray, adding the sedative to her scrambled eggs. It would be nice if she understood that she had no choice about her new life, but she had a stubborn streak. In truth, he admired it, up to a point. He'd hoped she would have accepted her fate by now, but she remained closed. Even now, remembering her crossed arms and rigid back, an anger swelled in him. He'd been too soft. That was always his way. These young girls who thought they knew better than he did. They had no idea. But she'd learn. Tomorrow was another day. The girl would be on the cusp of her new life. And then she'd know.

Chapter Fifty-Two

C allie paced the living room, absently holding up the arm housed in the sling with her free hand. She rubbed at the scratchy fabric, her forehead scrunched in concentration. "Okay. Let's go over this one more time."

"Cal, it's two o'clock in the morning," her father said. "I'm not sure how this helps."

"Please, Dad, indulge me." The skin around his eyes was dark with exhaustion, but he didn't stop her. "Here's the general timeline," she said, pacing as she talked. "Emma Nicholls was taken five years ago. You and the FBI had a lead on a sex trafficking ring and used an undercover agent to pose as another potential kidnap victim. Things went south when her cover was blown, and they got away. And Emma was never found."

"But we know Emma's picture was on the website for sale."

"Right. And according to the FBI, the website was taken down, new security put in place, and they've only had glimpses over the years since, O'Neill always a step ahead. Until Natalie." She paused to look back at him.

"So far so good."

She went on. "When Emma was taken, licorice wrappers were found in her car. They were at the scene of the shooting. No one knew that except you, Weston, the FBI, and the parents. We're sure about that?"

"And Chang, but yes. Family and cops. That's it," her father said.

"Family," she repeated. "And cops."

"It's been five years, though. It's possible word got out. And we don't know that either Nicholls didn't say anything even though we asked them not to."

"We asked Sarah about that," Callie said. "She said they didn't. And since the case was never closed, it's unlikely anyone would intentionally release that information."

John nodded his acceptance.

"Okay. That brings us to Natalie. One of her friends admits that Natalie was corresponding with someone on a private dating group who called himself Brian. At the same time, using the local sex registry, we find Brian O'Neill, but he had an alibi for the time we thought she'd been taken. Dead end. Then we got the address for the Randolph house from her texts. That's when we realized there was no babysitting job. We find evidence of chloroform and a partial licorice wrapper. We have hairs that tell us Natalie was in that garage, in that house. But no one saw a thing. Another dead end."

"Until I read the forensic report listing the licorice wrapper," her dad said. "Jackson contacts the FBI who admits the cases might be connected. They had received a tip and discovered the screenshots but no way into the site. What it does show is Natalie."

Callie cuts in. "At the same time, Frannie confronts O'Neill, and he kills her, then bolts. LJ finds enough on his office computer to link him to the same organization and website with Natalie's picture." She slows again. "It made sense to follow O'Neill. He was the most likely suspect, even though we couldn't place him at the scene of the kidnapping. It was enough that he was involved in the same sex ring where both girls were being offered for sale."

"Agreed," her father said. "It was the right move."

"But..." Callie tapped her foot on the floor. "O'Neill isn't the actual kidnapper in Connor's organization. He spins the web to trap the girls, but that's all."

John leans forward. "What I still don't understand is how O'Neill got connected to Connor."

"I have a theory about that."

"Really? Callie Forde has a theory?"

"You're funny, Dad." She sat down on the sofa across from him, her hands clasped in her lap. "O'Neill was a big gamer, according to his P.O., and had been playing for years against some guy he couldn't beat. The reason that matters is that I read a profile on Connor where he joked about his video game skills. Said he'd never been beaten. Could be a coincidence, but one I wanted to check out anyway. I knew that O'Neill had to leave his gaming system when he fled town, and his gaming friend went by the name of TopGunner666, so I asked LJ to take a look, and sure enough, he discovered messages between the two players." She paused. "This is where it gets a little muddy, but more than a few times, O'Neill's friend couldn't play because he was at a conference or dinner or something. We were able to match those dates up with Connor's public schedule. It's circumstantial, but..."

"It's something," John said. "Were there any messages that might have been about the website or girls?"

"Not that LJ saw. I think Connor would be too smart for that." She grimaced at giving the man a compliment of any kind. "I know it's thin, but I contacted Agent Corcoran anyway. Maybe they can get a warrant for Connor's gaming system or something."

Her father seemed to consider it. "His lawyers will make that difficult, but it still puts heat on him either way. Good work."

She allowed a smile. "Thanks. But none of that tells us where Natalie is."

"Which brings us back to the reason you came knocking on my door."

"Yes, and that brings us to the emails." She could recite them from memory now. "Lord of the World: *You've been a bad boy. The new girl is getting interest. Where is she?* Connor didn't know where the girl came from and must have assumed O'Neill had gone out on his own, hence calling him a bad boy. That might also explain why O'Neill was suddenly expendable. Meanwhile, O'Neill has his own problems. We're coming around and then Frannie discovers his secret office in the garage." She paused. "So, O'Neill writes Connor back. *What girl do you mean?*"

"A strange question."

"Not if you look at it from a different perspective, one where Natalie wasn't taken by anyone in Connor's organization or O'Neill. Everything was designed to make us look in O'Neill's direction, but he didn't know anything about it, which helped him when we came around to interview him. His surprise was genuine."

John's face was grim. "Are you sure someone from inside Connor's organization didn't set up O'Neill?"

"I don't think so."

"Neither do I." He rubbed his hands over his legs. "The man that took Natalie had to have known the details of Emma's case. The licorice wrapper. The website. There's no other explanation."

"Exactly. Every piece of evidence was designed to distract us, send us on a wild goose chase that led to D.C., all to keep us from looking in our own backyard." An anger stole over her, and her hands curled into fists. "He watched her, targeted her. He knew she'd fit the profile of a girl for sale in Connor's private club."

"It would appear so." He gave her a long look. "But Cal..."

Callie understood how many ways this could go sideways if she got this wrong. She didn't have one single shred of concrete evidence, but her gut told her she was on the right path. Still, she wouldn't drag Zel or anyone else down with her if she could help it. Not again.

"Dad, thank you for hearing me out."

"I don't think you're the one who should be saying thank you." The skin on his cheeks and jowls sagged, but his eyes were alert, his mind quick. He was worried for her, but that didn't mean he wasn't glad she'd come to him. Exactly the opposite. For the first time in years, he was needed.

"Dad." She felt the sting of tears threatening.

"Don't go getting sentimental on me." He said, wagging a finger at her.

"No, sir. I mean, yes, sir."

They both laughed then. "How about more coffee?"

Returning with the pot and a fresh icepack for her shoulder, she stared out at the dark street, all joking forgotten.

"I think he took Natalie out of Hampstead, somewhere isolated, where no one will bother them. But not too far, so he could get back if he needed to.

With O'Neill gone, he'll know the diversion is falling apart. There's a good chance he'll take her out of the state if we don't find him first."

"Isolated but not far. That's a lot of places, Cal."

Her father was right, but they'd come too far for her to despair. She grabbed her laptop, fingers already flying over the keys in search of recent property sales. "Maybe not."

With a shake of his head, he pulled his old case file close. "Well, it wouldn't hurt for me to take a look through here again."

"Good idea, Dad," she said without looking up.

An hour later, the sun peeked through the drapes, sending a kaleidoscope of light dancing across the carpet. Callie poured the last of the coffee, having lost track of how many they'd had during the night.

"The elixir of gods," he said.

She'd heard him say it before, but the familiar words still brought a tiny smile to her face. John Forde liked things the way he liked them. A full coffee cup was one of them. He'd always had trouble sleeping, more since the shooting. The coffee probably didn't help.

She watched him from across the room. Head bent, he peered through his reading glasses and flipped one page after the other, his lips moving silently. Gratitude for this moment warmed her. Maybe working a case wasn't usually the kind of thing father-daughter bonds were made of, but she would take it. He was talking and smiling and, best of all, working. With her.

"Callie?" She jerked out of her trance. "I've been calling your name."

"Oh, sorry. What is it?"

He held up a battered file. "I think I know where they are."

Chapter Fifty-Three

Callie's father rotated toward her as best he could. "I don't know if this is a good idea."

She kept her eye on the road. "We have to be sure. If we're right, we'll call Zel and Jackson." She knew what he wanted her to say. That she should call them right now. That she was acting rashly. But she had to be sure first. She couldn't let Frannie's life be for nothing and she wouldn't endanger her partner a second time.

"How about this?" She laid out a compromise she hoped was good enough, and he nodded with relief.

"Yes. That's a good plan." He settled back against the seat. His face had color in it again, and she knew without being told that he wanted to be in that car with her more than anything. He was in the hunt. Like the old days. She did her best to relax, too—or as much as she could, considering where they were going.

They were nearly an hour outside of Hampstead, closer to the mountains and the thick forests of the state than anything that could be called a small city or even a town. As she pulled off the main road onto a narrow dirt lane, she felt a pang of something lost. They used to come to places like this as a family before the shooting, to camp and hike, to sit around campfires. Callie missed those days.

"I don't really mind the chair," her father said now, as though reading her mind, "but I miss being out here, in nature."

She swallowed the lump in her throat and said, "Then we should plan a trip."

He grunted, noncommittal.

"Are you sure this is the place, Dad?"

"As sure as I can be."

She thought about her father's face when he'd handed her the file, telling her to read. It had been a transcript of one of the many interviews he'd conducted on the case, this one with Chang in attendance.

Nicholls: Why is he here? Where's your partner?

Forde: He's out sick. Detective Chang offered to sit in.

Nicholls: Why? Does he like to see a man suffering?

Forde: Mr. Nicholls, let's get back to the reason you're here today.

Nicholls: Why is that anyway? I've told you everything I know. Shouldn't you be out looking for my little girl instead of asking me the same questions over and over again?

Forde: Sometimes, a person will remember something later without even realizing it. Maybe the question gets asked in a new way, or a word triggers a memory.

Nicholls: If you say so. Let's get this over with.

Chang: Do you have someplace else to be, Mr. Nicholls?

Nicholls: I need to get back to work. Not that you care about that, but it's the only thing that distracts me from thinking about Emma being gone.

Chang: What do you do, Mr. Nicholls?

Nicholls: What does that have to do with anything?

Forde: Nothing. We're curious, that's all.

Nicholls: Curious, my ass.

Forde: You work at the plant, right?

Nicholls: I manage the security.

Chang: Is that a high-stress job?

Nicholls: Normally, no, but there's a virus in our computer system. I'm on the team to take care of it.

Chang: So, you're computer security? Guess you're good at computers then.

Nicholls: I didn't say I was computer security. There are systems for that, but I'm okay with them. Can we get back to talking about where my daughter is?

Forde: You said your wife and your daughter had been arguing.

Nicholls: They were always arguing. Sarah likes to say I'm the strict one, but she's the one who drives Emma crazy. She tries to be Emma's friend, I think. Sometimes, we say we're going to sneak off to this cabin we rented last year and hide away from Mom. Fish and hike. Get away from everything.

Chang: Cabin, huh? What kind of place?

Nicholls: What do you mean? It's a cabin with woods and a stream you can walk to.

Chang: Sounds nice. Where is it?

Nicholls: Off route 212. We were supposed to go again this year, but we got too busy. And Sarah said Emma didn't like it. That's not true, though. Emma did like it.

Forde: I'm sure she did. It sounds like the two of you were close.

Nicholls: Yes.

Forde: Did she confide in you?

Nicholls: What are you getting at, Detective?

Forde: Maybe she told you something that could be a clue as to where she went or who she met.

Nicholls: No. She didn't tell me those kinds of things. Not like when she was little. She told me everything then, how she wanted to be a princess and grow up to marry a prince. She told me when someone was mean to her at preschool, and it was me she came to when she scraped her knee.

Forde: And now that she's older?

Nicholls: She's a teenager, Detective. You know how they are. I know what Sarah's saying. That my rules drove Emma to meet that boy. That it's my fault because I wouldn't let her date. But she's too young. She went with that boy because her friends and Sarah put ideas in her head. I was trying to protect her. She should have come to me. If she had, she'd still be here and not God knows where. She should have...(muffled)

Forde: Can I get you anything, Mr. Nicholls?

Nicholls: You can find my daughter; that's what you can do.

Callie understood the cabin was a long shot, but she liked their odds. She liked them more after her conversation with Sarah Nicholls.

"The cabin? God, we hadn't gone there in years. Emma was barely in high school or maybe even still in middle school the last time. She hated it, but what can you expect? No phone service. No cable. Fred loved that."

"Do you know if the cabin is still there?"

"I don't really. That other detective—Chang or Wang or something—asked me about it once. Said he was looking for a vacation spot. I told him there wasn't much to do, but he wanted the realtor's number anyway." Sarah's sigh echoed across the phone line. "I don't know why I remember that. It's just that he was so adamant about wanting a place. It's funny, really. Before Emma was gone, Fred threatened to put an offer on the place and make Emma go every weekend, but he never did." Her voice dropped an octave. "Maybe he should have."

Callie took her foot off the gas now, slowing as the dirt road narrowed. They weren't far now. Inhaling, she pulled the car as far into a thicket of trees as she could and switched off the engine.

"What are you doing?"

She had her answer ready, having anticipated his question. "The car will alert him we're here. I've got to go the rest of the way on foot."

"I don't want you going inside, Callie. Remember the plan. You look for his car. That's all. If you see it, you come back here." He grabbed her hand. "Agreed?"

When she didn't answer right away, he held tight.

"Agreed," she said.

Chapter Fifty-Four

Callie crept through the trees, stepping over fallen branches and rocks, careful not to make a sound. The terrain grew rougher as the road led up the small mountain and she grabbed at the trunks to keep from tripping. Her breathing grew heavier, but she kept going, glad she'd remembered to wear her hiking boots. A door slamming made her stop in her tracks. She moved toward the tree line and peeked around a thick trunk. The house, built of pine and glass, rose up in front of her. A man in a baseball hat and black t-shirt, his back to her, strode past the porch, disappearing around the corner of the house.

"Shit," Callie muttered under her breath. She couldn't see his face. Taking out her phone, she snapped a few pictures of the house and the car, a dark grey SUV she didn't recognize. She felt a rush of disappointment at the sight of it, but she held up her phone anyway, blowing up the image of the license plate. She sent it to her father.

Using the heavy branches as cover, she studied the house. It was rustic and weathered, exactly as one would expect, and surrounded by trees on three sides. Only one way in or out, perfect for keeping someone locked in. Atop the roof, she spotted what looked like a new satellite dish. Her gaze traveled past it to the wide front porch furnished with two white rockers. The front door, painted a dark brown, was flanked by windows covered in opaque curtains. Something glinted in the sun, and her head jerked back to the roofline. Cameras, one on each end of the roof, so small she'd nearly missed them. Unable to make out what angle they captured, her breath quickened.

The front door creaked open, and the man came out. He carried a gas can in one hand and a blanket in the other, but it was the gun tucked into his waistband that set off alarm bells in her head. Setting the gas can down on the porch, he pushed back the brim of his hat and squinted up at the sun, giving her a full view of his face. Heart thudding, she snapped three quick pictures and hit send.

He walked to the car, his pace unhurried but deliberate. Unlocking the car with a key fob, he leaned into the backseat and shook out the blanket, making tucking-type motions. She couldn't make out what exactly, but something—no, someone, it had to be—lay across the back seat. The man stood up again, finished with his ministrations. The body inside the car remained motionless and unresponsive, sending shivers up Callie's spine. He went to the house, this time coming out with two large suitcases. Opening the hatch, he threw them in and locked the car again before disappearing inside once more.

Callie's breath came out in a whoosh. She would have to act fast if she wanted to stop him before he drove away. Quickly, she tapped on her phone screen, then laid it down on a bed of pine tags with her hat. Finally, she slipped off her sling, all the while scanning the yard and house for movement. Nothing. She guessed the car was thirty yards from the porch, maybe more. It wasn't much, and the car itself wouldn't provide much cover, but the first thing she needed to do was check on the car. She had to know if the body belonged to Natalie and if she was alive. It was now or never. Before she could talk herself out of it, she took off at a sprint, legs pumping. She crossed the short distance in seconds and fell to the ground on the far side of the car. Her aching body protested the short run, and she bit down hard on her lower lip to keep from screaming at the throbbing pain.

Breathing heavily, she angled her head toward the house, listening. Still nothing more threatening than birds tweeting in the trees. She crawled to the back of the car, rising high enough to look inside the window. Even through the tinted windows, she could make out the shape of a girl, wisps of blond hair, and one gold sandal. She almost whooped for joy, but her relief quickly evaporated. She looked closer, studying the blanket now and not

243

the girl. It wasn't until she saw the faint rise and fall that she could breathe again.

The front door opened then, and she dropped down, beads of perspiration dripping into her eyes. When the footsteps didn't descend past the porch, she inched back up to peer around the back end of the car. The man tipped the yellow can, dousing the railing in gasoline. He dumped more gas around the side of the house and still more along a timber-lined path that led to the woods.

She blinked, unsure for a minute what she was seeing. The gas can had surprised her when she'd spied it in his hand earlier, but now she thought she understood. He planned to burn the house down, sending any evidence he or Natalie had been there up in smoke. But he wasn't stopping at the house. From her vantage point behind the car, she could see him walk into the woods with the can, a stream of gas dripping onto the forest floor.

"Oh, my God," Callie breathed, a new fear rising from her belly to her throat. It wasn't just the house he wanted to burn. He wanted to burn the property, the woods, all of it. Secluded as this house was, no one would see the fire start. The dry brush that covered the ground and thirsty trees would take care of the rest. By the time anyone did report the blaze, it would be too late. A raging forest fire after months of dry weather would be disastrous for the state, another distraction, an even more masterful one.

She had to get Natalie out of there. Leaving the path, the man circled around to the back of the house, leaving a trail of gas droplets behind him. The minute he was out of sight, she grabbed the door handle and yanked. The sudden blare of the car alarm sent her scrambling back. Her feet moving, she was halfway to the woods before her mind caught up. She burst through the trees, limbs scratching her arms and her face. Heavy footsteps pounded in the dirt, slowing near the car. She threw herself behind the widest trunk she could, heart pounding like a jackhammer. *Stupid. Stupid. Stupid.*

"Who's there?"

She didn't move, nor did she feel the fresh pain radiating from her shoulder down her arm. He cut the car alarm, still shouting.

"Whoever's out there, show yourself. This is private property."

Pressing her body up against the tree, she maneuvered enough to get a partial view through a pile of broken branches. He circled the car, his gun swinging back and forth from one tree line to the other. Zeroing in on the faint swirl of dust that led in her direction, he aimed. She ducked back behind the tree. The bullet whistled past, a miss, but too close for her taste. A gaggle of birds rose into the air, shrieking in protest. Hooves pounded, and the gun sounded again. He hit a tree, the bark splintering and falling to the ground. Branches cracked under the fleeing animal. A third shot rang out, followed by a thud. It was over in less than five seconds.

"Goddamned deer," he yelled at the silent pines. "Serves you right." His boots slapped against the dirt as he headed back toward the house.

Callie's body sagged, adrenaline masking the worst of her pain. If she didn't stop him, he would set everything around them on fire and take off with the girl. And her father, trapped in the brush at the bottom of the drive, would be helpless to stop him or save himself. She couldn't let that happen. Her hands curled up into fists, and she drew herself up, steadying her breaths. It was now or never. Silently, she counted to three, drew her gun, and walked out of the trees.

Chapter Fifty-Five

Climbing the porch steps, he didn't hear her step out of the woods. He reached for a second gas can, his arm outstretched.

"Mr. Nicholls."

He straightened slowly, his arm back at his side. He didn't turn around, didn't speak. She waited for him to go for his gun. When he did, she raised her own weapon.

"I wouldn't do that."

His arm froze mid-air. "You shouldn't have come here, Detective. This isn't your business."

"Natalie is my business." Her heart drummed faster in her chest. "It doesn't have to be this way. You've been hurting, but this isn't the answer." He stiffened, but she kept talking. "We know more now. The FBI has new leads. We can find Emma."

"You don't know anything." There was that same anger tinged with pain, but something else, too. Disdain.

She stole a glance at the car. Natalie must still be out of it. "Mr. Nicholls—Fred—we can work out a deal. I'll talk to the D.A., but you need to let Natalie go. It's the right thing to do here. I think you know that."

"You don't know me well enough to call me Fred." He raised his hands in the air and spun around to face her. For a short moment, her breath left her body. Although the gun remained at his waist, he held a lighter in one hand, the yellow flame of it flickering brightly under his thumb.

She swallowed hard. One toss of that lighter, and she wouldn't be able to stop what came next.

"You're right. I'm sorry. I don't really know you, Mr. Nicholls. But I know pain, and I know you miss Emma with all your heart, that every day she's missing the knife goes in a little deeper."

The lighter jerked upward in his hand. "Don't talk about Emma. You don't have that right. Not unless you can bring her home, and I don't want to hear any more promises you or your father can't keep. You won't ever bring her home. No one can."

She took a step forward. "So, you took someone else's daughter. You took Natalie."

"Her name is Leigh now."

His eyes went dark, and his chin lifted in defiance, daring her to challenge him.

"Okay, you took Leigh."

He seemed to calm then. "Leigh is a good girl, but she needs a father who protects her, who takes care of her."

"She has a father, Mr. Nicholls." She kept her voice even.

The man's snort bordered on venomous. "Please. He doesn't deserve her. He let her go for that student of his. I'm Leigh's father now."

Not wanting to anger him further, she changed tactics to keep him talking. "How did you manage to put Natalie's—I mean Leigh's—picture on that website?"

His mouth puckered, as though he'd swallowed vinegar. "Brian O'Neill underestimated me. That's no surprise. It's been happening my whole life. My mother. My wife. It used to bother me until I realized that's where the real power lies. In being underestimated."

"But how did you know what he was up to at all?"

"I didn't. Not at first. But a storm a few years ago knocked the power out at the plant. The generators kicked in, and it was fine, but once the power fully returned, I went through each system with a fine-toothed comb. For security breaches. That's when I found it, although I didn't know what it was. Not then. It took me months to figure it out." His voice cracked. "They took my Emma and sold her like cattle."

"But if you knew O'Neill was part of it, why didn't you go to the police?

Turn him in?"

"Really? You, of all people, would ask me that? I pointed you in their direction. I sent the FBI screenshots." His next words landed like darts. "The FBI, your dad, they made a mess of it with Emma. I thought you might be better, but I was wrong. You botched it, just like your old man. You lost O'Neill, and now they'll go back into their caves until it's safe to crawl out again. It's no surprise, really." His lip curled. "Turns out the apple doesn't fall far from the tree."

Anger and shame coursed through her veins. Maybe she should have followed up on O'Neill again before he killed Frannie. Maybe she had botched it at the motel, but her father was blameless.

His eyes scanned the landscape behind her. "Where's your partner, Detective?" When she didn't answer, he laughed, a harsh, guttural sound. "Just like your dad, huh? Think you don't need any help."

"I have help. They're on their way."

He stared at her a minute longer. "I don't believe you, but on the off chance there's a Forde in this town whose word is good, we'll speed this along." He gestured at the glowing flame. "If you shoot me, I'll drop this lighter, and we both know what will happen next, don't we?" She shivered at the image of him laying a trail into the woods. "Lay down your gun, Detective Forde."

She looked back at the car. It was far enough from the house and the gasoline, but a falling branch or flying cinder could land on it. It wouldn't happen right away, but if the car caught fire, the gas in the tank would make it explode. Natalie, out cold or comatose, would blow up with the car.

"What's it going to be? Are you going to shoot me and risk starting the largest fire this state has seen in decades, or are you going to save the citizens?"

Again, she was reminded of her father.

"Put the gun down."

There would be no escape for a man in a wheelchair. Still, she hesitated and he dropped to his knees, extending the lighter away from his body, mere inches from the gasoline-soaked ground.

"Don't." The word stuck in her throat.

"Don't what? Burn down my own house?" The flame danced higher when he dropped it another inch, and in spite of the heat, her blood ran cold. "You know how to stop me, Detective."

Her arm fell along with her shoulders. She could shoot him, but anything other than instant death wouldn't stop the fire—and even that wasn't a guarantee. All he needed was one dying breath.

She laid her gun in the dirt.

"Now kick it." It skidded two feet from her. "Again." Satisfied this time, he drew his own gun. Only then did he extinguish the lighter.

"What now?" she asked.

"Time for me and Leigh to hit the road."

"I can't let you do that."

That guttural laugh sounded again, and she flinched. "You're brave. I'll give you that." He waved his gun at her. "You're hurt already. You think I can't see the way you're favoring one arm?"

Callie didn't bother to argue. She couldn't overpower him, but she could stall. She went back to the one thing—the one person—who'd meant everything to him. "I won't give up trying to find her, Mr. Nicholls. Your daughter is out there. Emma is out there. If you kill me, the search for her will die with me."

"Don't you get it? They don't want you to find her. You think I haven't tried?" With each word, his voice grew louder until the veins of his neck strained against his skin. "There's no record of her existence in five years. Five years." He shook his head. "No. You're trying to distract me." He pointed the gun back toward the house. "Let's go. Inside."

She didn't move. "I can't let you take her, Mr. Nicholls."

"You don't have control here, Detective. I do." He spit on the ground. "I don't want to shoot you, but you're the one giving me no choice." He lifted the gun higher, his finger tightening over the trigger.

"You don't want to shoot a cop. You'll be on the run for the rest of your life."

"I'll already be on the run."

"It's not the same. Killing a cop will put you at the top of every most wanted list in every county across the country. The manhunt won't ever stop. Every single father with a teenaged daughter will be put under a microscope. Leigh won't be able to go to school. She won't have friends. She'll have no life." His brows drew together. She had his attention now. "You know how girls like to go to the mall and shop. They like to hang out and get their nails done. It won't matter that you take care of her and keep her safe. She'll blame you. She'll hate you. Maybe not at first, but soon. And then—"

"Enough." Anger radiated off him in waves, and she instinctively took a step back. "Don't move."

She froze. Had she pushed him too far?

He waved his gun toward the house a second time. "Get inside, or I burn everything down." To prove he wasn't kidding, the lighter's flame danced in front of his face, spotlighting the feverish glow of his eyes. Her stomach sank. Nicholls wasn't the same man who'd lost his daughter five years earlier. He was possessed beyond reason. "We both know it will take less than ten minutes for this whole place to light up like the Fourth of July."

From under her lashes, she calculated the distance back to the woods. She'd be a sitting duck if she ran, but she was a sitting duck either way. Before she could take off, though, he leaped down the steps, grabbed her arm, and yanked on her shoulder. The shot of pain almost made her legs give way, but Nicholls had the strength of a man on a mission. He held her upright, dragging her all the way up the porch. Shoving her through the doorway, he pressed the revolver's barrel into her spine. She stumbled once, inhaling the sharp odor of gasoline he'd splattered around the cabin.

"Upstairs."

She tilted her head back to see over the railing. There were three doors, each closed tight, but the one at the far end of the hall had something the others didn't—a shiny bolt lock.

"Move." He nudged her forward with the gun. "I could shoot you right now and let your body burn if you'd prefer, but I'd rather give you a chance."

"A chance? In a locked room?"

"A chance for your help to arrive. I'm not without some compassion."

"I don't think you're a killer, Mr. Nicholls," she said.

CHAPTER FIFTY-FIVE

"That's because you don't know me."

Her eyes swept over the cabin. To one side was a sofa and ottoman, and beyond that, a small kitchen with a table and chairs. She reasoned that the back door was off the kitchen but she couldn't see it from this side of the room. Ahead of her was the staircase and before that, a long wooden credenza crowded with an assortment of pottery and stone sculptures. Her gaze lit on the largest piece. Constructed of rock and metal, it stood at nearly two feet tall, had a narrow base, and widened to an oval.

Callie's mind raced. Fred Nicholls had diverted them to O'Neill and to fake profiles, but he wasn't the only one who knew how to distract. Feet no longer moving, she let her arms swing forward a few inches.

"She'll never love you or listen to you, you know," she said, her tone pointed. "She'll leave the first chance she gets." The hard metal of the gun's barrel dug into her spine.

"Shut up."

"You wait. She doesn't care about you. She'll spit on you before she loves you,"

He growled, the sound strangled. "I said to shut up."

The shove, when it came, propelled her straight into the credenza. "Leigh isn't like that, like any of them."

Callie's outstretched hand closed around the base of the largest sculpture as he closed half the distance between them. He was still close enough that with each word, his spit sprayed the back of her neck.

"She isn't like you, Detective. She isn't—"

The stone sculpture hit his ribcage with a crack, the sickening sound followed by a loud oomph. He staggered, and Callie swung again, missing him by inches. She tripped over her own feet, hitting her head on the corner of the credenza.

A gunshot reverberated across the small cabin, the loud blast deafening. The bullet whizzed past Callie's head, splintering the wall, and she jerked back. Scrambling, she didn't feel the second shot rip through her flesh until something hot burned her insides. One leg crumpled, then the other, as the floor rose up to meet her. Disoriented, she saw spots, blurring and receding and reappearing again. The room spun around her and she tried to get to her knees, but her body wouldn't obey, couldn't obey. Woozy, she forgot why she wanted to get up at all. She was so, so tired. The shadowy spots behind her eyes grew larger, crowding her vision until there was only darkness and then nothing at all.

Chapter Fifty-Six

Coming to, Callie groaned, the sound sticking in her throat. Where was she? How did she get here? Aching head rolling to one side, she tried hard to remember, but nothing seemed to work. Not her eyes. Not her mind. She couldn't focus, and when she tried, the effort only made her head pound harder. She wanted nothing more than to sink back into oblivion, but a burning sensation in her leg wouldn't let her. She remembered then. There'd been gunshots. She'd hit Fred Nicholls with a rock sculpture. She'd slowed him, but she hadn't stopped him, and she hadn't gotten the gun. Worse, he had Natalie. She couldn't let him get away. Attempting to sit up then, Callie rolled to one side. Fresh agony tore through her, but she gritted her teeth, managing to prop herself up with the elbow of her good arm.

Behind her, something crackled and hissed. She twisted her neck to find the source and gasped. Flames leaped from the floor to the curtains, climbing higher toward the ceiling. A corner of the couch burned bright, the cushions already disintegrating in the heat of the blaze. She scrambled backward, away from the fire, but she knew it wouldn't matter what part of the house she was in if she couldn't get out of there fast.

Callie tried to push aside the pain so she could think. She didn't know how long she'd been out or how long ago Nicholls had lit the match. She didn't know if he was gone or if Natalie was with him. She looked around. The closest way out was the front door. Relieved to find the fire still several feet from the door, she tried to get to her knees, but one of her legs wouldn't work. That's when she saw the pool of blood on the floor. Her blood. Hot and sticky, it stuck to her clothes and her hands, still spurted from her leg. Suddenly lightheaded, she caught herself before she could hit the floor again. She told herself to breathe, but the air was already too warm, a reminder that with each minute, the fire would steal whatever oxygen was left in the cabin.

Somehow, she wriggled out of her blazer and rolling the bodice tight, she placed it a few inches above the wound. Wrapping the arms of the blazer around her leg, she pulled and tied them into a knot, yanking as tightly as she could. It wouldn't stop the bleeding, but it might stem the flow long enough for her to reach the door before she could pass out again. Walking was out of the question. Her leg didn't work, and the room was already thick with smoke. She'd have to crawl on her stomach, Army style.

Callie slid forward, gulping air, her chest heaving and tight. Smoke and ash choked the air, and she pulled her shirt up over her nose. She scooted forward another inch and then another. Her vision blurred, and her head felt heavy. The crash of a window exploding jerked her back to consciousness.

Little by little, she slithered closer to the door. More than once, she glanced over at the encroaching fire, her breath catching in her throat. The red and orange flames that had danced across the sofa roared upward now, licking the ceiling. The house was a tinderbox, made more flammable by the gasoline Nicholls had splattered around the place. She watched as the fire spread to the next window, the one flanking the front door. Her mind shouted at her to move, move, move, but she kept losing track of the thought. When it did come, she inched forward. It became harder to breathe, and beads of sweat poured down her face. Her shoulder screamed with every new movement, and hot tears mixed with sweat. Memories of elementary school chants to stop, drop, and roll echoed in her head. She kept going, staying low to the floor, dragging her injured leg behind her. Closer. Closer. Fifteen feet.

The large screen TV shattered. Barely hearing it over the roar of the fire or the mantra in her head, Callie kept going. Slide. Move. Slide. Ten feet now. Each inch sapped another bit of whatever adrenaline kept her from passing out, but she crawled on. When the smoke obscured her view, she visualized the door and crawled again, nearly sobbing when her hand touched solid wood. Callie reached up with her hand, but the doorknob was too high. She struggled to her knees, woozy, and fell backward, further from the door. Even through her clothes, she could feel the heat of the fire prickling her skin. Nausea rose up from her belly. Smoke swirled all around her, and she lost her bearings again, slipping in and out. She dreamed she heard her name, softer at first and then louder.

The door banged open, swinging an inch in front of her. Hands reached under her arms and lifted her off the floor. Sirens wailed in the distance, and there were cars. Three, four, five, but she couldn't be sure if they were real or still part of the dream. Fading in and out, she searched for Nicholls's SUV but didn't see it. A sense of hopelessness washed over her. He was gone. He'd gotten away.

A voice cut through the fog, a voice she'd known her whole life. She opened her eyes, squinting in the light. There. The glint of his wheelchair. Her head lolled, and he was gone.

"Is she going to be alright?" the voice asked.

"She needs an ambulance."

Her mind drifted again. The sirens came closer. There was a flash of red. Men rushed by. She felt herself being lifted, heard the slam of doors. There were more voices, ones she didn't know, and then he was back, her superhero.

"You're going to be okay, Cal. I promise."

His hands were wrapped around hers, squeezing tight, and tears leaked from the corners of her eyes. Cold stole over, and she didn't care about the motion of the ambulance or the fire behind her. She only wanted to sleep, but he shook her awake when she tried. He leaned in close, his mouth near her ear, and talked. He told her about Zel and Jackson and meeting him a quarter mile past the turnout onto the dirt road. He told her how before they could get to the house, Nicholls came down the drive. With nowhere to go but back to the burning house, he was trapped. The standoff didn't last long. Backup arrived even before he could get out of his car. Nicholls, for all he'd done, was not a foolish man.

Callie struggled to open her eyes and roll her face toward the voice, to say something.

"He didn't want a shootout. There was nothing left for him to do but give up. Fred Nicholls never wanted to hurt Natalie. I believe that. Whatever he did, even his surrender, was for the girl, for Natalie." Did his voice crack, or did she imagine that? "He wanted to protect her to the very end. The way he couldn't protect Emma."

She'd figured the same, but that didn't change what he'd done. He'd kidnapped a girl, set off events that led to Frannie's murder, an innocent woman. He'd left her to die.

"Natalie?" she asked, but only a hoarse croak came out. Still, he understood.

"She's safe. She's going to be okay." He touched her cheek with the soft palm of his hand. All the pain seemed to lift, and she smiled dreamily, her eyes drifting closed again. "You did it, Cal. You found her."

Epilogue

allie shifted her weight under the crutches and swung her leg over the walkway and ramp. She couldn't say she had the hang of crutches, but it didn't matter. She wouldn't have them for much longer.

Maura, wearing a yellow blouse and a broad smile, waited at the front door. Both made her look five years younger than she had a few weeks earlier.

"We would have picked you up," her mother said. "I could have brought the van."

"That's okay. Captain Jackson insisted on dropping me off. Said he wanted to make sure I ate a home-cooked meal for a change. Keeps talking about how I need to get stronger so I can get off desk duty."

A shadow crossed her mother's face. She'd made no secret that there had been too many close calls in her book. She'd almost lost her husband and then her daughter. "What's wrong with desk duty? Maybe then I wouldn't be so grey."

"Mom..." Callie said, but her voice was soft. It would be a long time before she forgot the fire or the bullet, either of which could have taken her life.

"Fine," Maura said with a sigh and beckoned Callie inside.

Following, she maneuvered herself down the hall to the kitchen, where the smell of roasted chicken wafted in the air. Her father, in his wheelchair, was already in his place at the table.

"There's my girl," he said, beaming. "Now we can eat."

It took her a few minutes to get situated, prop her injured leg, and balance the crutches against the wall. Maura placed the platters on the table.

"How soon before you can use your leg?" her father asked, helping himself to a large scoop of mashed potatoes.

"Not long."

"There's no need to rush it," Maura said.

Callie disagreed. Tired of pushing papers, she wanted to be back on the job yesterday.

"I agree with your mother," her father said. She looked over at him in surprise. She'd thought surely he would understand. "The job will still be there," he said. "You won't be any good if you don't heal first."

Callie swallowed a bite of chicken. "The physical therapy is helping. Cynthia is tough. I thought nothing could be worse than the boot camp they put you through in training, but I was wrong."

"And the department counselor?" her father asked. "You're seeing one?"

"Yes, Dad." Between the department counselor, the physical therapy, and the family sessions they'd begun, Callie wondered how she had time to do desk work. She wasn't complaining about the counseling, though. They'd had only two family sessions so far, and they'd shown promise, even if her father had said little. What mattered to Callie was that he listened. The rest would come later.

"Good. A detective that doesn't have their head straight is in for a tough time."

His words found their mark, and she lowered her eyes to her lap. She'd done her best to cover the dark circles and add color to her hollowed-out cheeks, but he wasn't fooled any more than her mother was. She didn't know what was wrong with her. It had been weeks since the fire at the cabin. Containing the fire had been sheer luck. When she'd dropped the pin that told Zel where she was, she'd texted him to send in the cavalry. Not knowing exactly what she meant, he'd called them all. The fire trucks had arrived right behind Zel and Jackson. An hour later and the fire might have raged for days. She knew all this, but that didn't stop her from waking in the night, shaking, sweat coating her skin. In the darkness, she couldn't shake visions of the encroaching fire or silence the booming echo of bullets.

"There's a balance to it," her father said now, the heat of his gaze making her look up again. "The trick is not to forget. Don't block it out as though it didn't happen. Focus instead on the outcome. Focus on what you can learn."

Callie looked at him in wonder. *The trick is not to forget.* It was all she'd been trying to do.

"Fear is healthy, Cal. It can keep you safe." He reached out and gave her hand a pat before returning his attention to his plate. "Really, Maura, you've outdone yourself."

Her parents talked quietly for a few minutes before John brought the conversation back to the case. "So, Jackson tells me the Feds were able to use your tip about the video games to tie Connor to O'Neill. Turns out there was something to that after all."

He'd told Callie the same. Nicholls's cooperation and LJ's investigative work behind the firewalls had been enough for them to get a warrant for Connor's video game system, in spite of his high-powered legal team. It wasn't an indictment yet, but it was more than they had before.

"Apparently, Agent Corcoran thinks you have good instincts."

"Really?" she asked, eyebrows raised. "He didn't sound that way when he reamed me out for what happened at the motel."

Her father's lips turned up. "Yeah? Well, he did also say you could stand to think before you act if you wanted to be FBI material."

Callie rolled her eyes. "What about Emma? They can't stop looking for her, Dad. I promised Sarah. And Fred."

"I know. They won't. Corcoran gave me his word."

She didn't put as much faith in the agent's word as her father—particularly not after the way the FBI had disappeared after the shooting—but she hoped it was true. She made another silent vow of her own not to give up.

"I saw Natalie yesterday."

Maura's fork froze mid-air.

"How is she?" her mother asked.

"Physically? Fine, but I think it's going to be a while before she can trust again, before things can be more normal. I got the impression she hasn't gone out much and doesn't want to be alone."

"I can imagine," Maura said. "And no doubt her mother doesn't want to let her out of her sight."

"True. If there's anything good to come out of all this, it's that Natalie and her mom are better. Or both trying, I should say. She realizes how much her mother loves her." Callie chewed and swallowed. "And the parents are trying, too. To be better around each other, more respectful."

Maura gave an approving nod. "Yes, that is something."

The three went back to their food, finishing the meal in silence, each thinking about damaged families and pain and grief. Callie wished with all her heart that things could have been different, that she could turn back the clock for the Hamill family and the Nicholls family and her own. Yet, no amount of wanting could make it so.

Maybe that was the point of life, learning to play the hand you were dealt. Life wasn't always fair. She'd seen that firsthand. Loss was inevitable, but she thought maybe loss—real loss—couldn't exist without love first. Love and loss, the great bookends of life.

Callie made a silent wish then. She hoped that somehow, from the suffering and loss, the families could build something new and find—if not peace exactly—gratitude for what was and hope for what could be. She looked from her father to her mother, her eyes brimming. Her father was there, at the table and not lost in home movies. As for Maura, she might not be laughing out loud like the old days, but she was smiling again. And best of all, Natalie was home with Erin and Jeremy, back where she belonged. It was all she could ask.

She raised her glass high in the air, her heart full. "To family."

Acknowledgements

Like all stories, this one started as a "what if" moment. When one of my daughters took a babysitting job with a new family, I asked the usual questions: Where do they live? Who referred you? How many children? She had answers, but that didn't stop me from worrying—particularly when I woke up during the night not having heard her come in. That's a panic moment for sure. I raced to the window that overlooks the driveway to find she was, in fact, home. It's not an exaggeration to say my body sagged with relief. And yet, as I stood there, I thought, "What if?" It's true that initial seed of an idea (and true life mom moment) bears little resemblance to the final story, but that's where it started. Now my daughter Meredith calls it the book about her! I'm fine with that since—thank goodness—it isn't.

Once I had the idea for the book, it was time to put fingers to the keyboard. Every author will tell you that the act of writing is a solitary endeavor and this is mostly true, however, getting to that final draft and publication is not. The early pages of this book were read and critiqued by some of the fabulous authors who are fellow members of the Central Virginia Chapter of Sisters in Crime. I owe a huge thank you to Heather Weidner, Sandie Warwick, Susan Campbell, Amy Lilly, Cat Brennan, Marjorie Bagby, Lenette Howard, and May Kennedy. As both writers and readers, their comments and advice were invaluable as this story took shape. Thank you!

One of the amazing things about *Last Girl Missing* was how quickly I was able to get it down. I fell into the story easily and the words flowed, but I still had tough critics ahead: my daughter Cameron Murphy, my sister Donna McGrath, and my late husband David. I'm pretty sure my husband's comments were the funniest as well as being insightful, but I couldn't have finished this book without any of them. My love for all of them is infinite.

I also cannot thank my agent, Rebecca Scherer, enough for all her support, not only with this book and the Callie Forde books still to come, but in all my works. Her analysis is always honest and spot on. May we keep it going for a long, long time!

Thank you to all of the wonderful folks at Level Best Books, particularly Shawn Reilly Simmons who helps to make a book shine and is a champion for mysteries of all kinds. Thank you to Verena Rose and Harriette Sackler for bringing me into Level Best and to Deb Well for the marketing support and keeping me on track. It's a joy to be a part of this community.

Thank you so much to my son Thomas Murphy for designing a cover that was exactly what I envisioned—eye-catching and dramatic—a bit like Callie herself! Thank you also for putting up with me asking for a shade more of this and a little bigger of that. You got it just right!

Thank you to all of my newsletter subscribers who have supported me by reading ARCs, visiting me at conferences and festivals, or sending me kind and supportive emails. It makes my day every time.

Book bloggers, book podcasters, and book reviewers help authors not only to find readers but to become better writers. You inspire simply by showing interest and sharing what you love. Thank you so much.

Thank you to my amazing friends who have thrown launch parties, hosted book clubs, bought books, and spread the word. I'm afraid to list names here as I'm sure to leave someone out, but I'm so incredibly lucky to know each and every one of you. You are all the best.

And finally, I am so grateful to my family, both extended and immediate. Again, I know how truly lucky I am. You never fail to be there with love and kindness. Thank you so much to my amazing children, Cameron, Thomas, Luke, and Meredith for everything and to David, who I miss each and every day.

About the Author

The first thing K.L. Murphy wrote was a modified screenplay of a 1970s TV show. She and her siblings performed that show for their own built-in audience (mom and dad) to rave reviews (mom and dad again!). Later, she moved on to high school journalism before graduating from the College of William and Mary and taking a detour into banking and finance. Once she began writing again and focusing on fiction, the process felt like coming home.

In addition to the Detective Callie Forde Mysteries, K.L. is the award-nominated author of *Her Sister's Death*, a 2023 Silver Falchion Finalist for Best Mystery and the January 2023 Once Upon a Book Club Pick as well as the Detective Cancini Mystery Series which features *A Guilty Mind*, *Stay of Execution*, and *The Last Sin*. Her short stories are featured in several anthologies and she can be found at www.kellielarsenmurphy.com.

A member of Mystery Writers of America, International Thriller Writers, Historical Writers of America, Sisters in Crime, and James River Writer, K.L. makes her home in Richmond, VA, where she loves spending time with her family, friends, and amazing dogs.

SOCIAL MEDIA HANDLES:

Instagram @k.l._murphy
Twitter/X @klmurphyauthor
Facebook facebook.com/klmurphyauthor/

AUTHOR WEBSITE:
www.kellielarsenmurphy.com

Also by K.L. Murphy

Her Sister's Death (CamCat Books)

The Last Sin (HarperCollins/Witness Impulse)

Stay of Execution (HarperCollins/Witness Impulse)

A Guilty Mind (HarperCollins/Witness Impulse)

Short Stories in *Deadly Southern Charm* and *Murder by the Glass*

Printed in the USA
CPSIA information can be obtained
at www.ICGtesting.com
JSHW080230030824
67318JS00001B/6